MORNING LIGHT

MORNING LIGHT

THE ISLANDERS IN THE
DAYS OF OAK AND HEMP

H. M. TOMLINSON

" That which has been, is now ;
And that which is to be, has already been ;
And God requires that which is past."
ECCLESIASTES

London : HODDER & STOUGHTON Limited

FIRST PRINTED   OCTOBER 1946

PR
6039
.035
M6
1946

MADE AND PRINTED IN GREAT BRITAIN FOR
HODDER AND STOUGHTON LTD., LONDON, BY
HAZELL, WATSON AND VINEY, LTD., LONDON AND AYLESBURY

TO
SUSAN AND JANE DICKINSON
THIS TALE OF THEIR FORBEARS

Contents

CONTENTS

I

A Shipowner's Window

THE shipowner's small daughter raced upstairs, but her
eager run stopped at her father's study door. That was
shut. She did not pause to remember that his room was
forbidden to everybody, or to knock politely, but opened it
and went in. Papa was not there. Why was he not there?
He had told her at breakfast that she should have for her
own room the little model of his new ship, the *Lucy
Darton,* because it was named after her. Here she was for it.

Where was it? A number of dusty little models were
placed about as usual, some on shelves between blue ginger
jars, too high for her to reach, and some on the mantelpiece,
but she dared not touch them, for then she might upset
the samples and bottles crowded in between. Others were
on the table, with a litter of papers, and white goose-quill
pens sticking up from a pewter ink-pot, like jib sails, and
copper nuts and bolts, and short lengths of cordage, and
things she didn't know the names of. The models were
very much alike, and some were unnamed. She could wait,
if she did not have to wait very long. She disliked waiting
for anything she wanted. She examined a square of timber
riddled by sea worms, and dropped it. She moved about,
peering curiously but abruptly at whatever might be of interest, though little was in the only untidy room in Crantock
House. Mr. Darton never allowed a servant to enter it
without permission, and nobody else ever had occasion to
be there, unless invited, but Miss Lucy had the right to do
almost as she pleased. She was an only child, whose mother

was dead, and was entitled to the earth, if her father had
it to give away.

Where could Papa be? Still talking of ships to Uncle
Tom, she supposed, who must be tired of it, and to that
man from London. What was his name? Oh, Mr. Denny,
with his silly stories of what ships moved by steam would
do, some day. Papa thought it was so comical, and told him
not to put off his next visit till steam-ships had done it, but
to come again long before that. Oh, where was Papa? She
wanted to go down to the quay, if she could leave the house
without being seen, and she thought she could do it, as
there were visitors. Nobody should go to the quay from
that house on the Sabbath, of course, but she was going, just
this once. Old Killick would be down there, looking at the
ship he had built. He was sure to be doing that. He never
went to church. People called Killick the lord of the bunt
and gasket, though she did not quite know what that
meant, but Papa said that man could not only build the
best ships on the West Coast, and rig them, but sail them
anywhere, and moor them alongside home again without
losing a spar. If he could do all that then he ought to take
out the ship named after her and bring her back safely; but
Papa said no, Killick was more valuable in the shipyard,
though she thought that was most unfair to the ship. She
wanted to see its figure-head again, and get as near to it as
possible. It was her own likeness, and it was lovely. All
Papa's men said it was a lovely piece of work.

There was not much in that shipowner's office and
sanctuary to hold a young and impatient interest, so she
idled over to the window. The window was the chief
feature of the room, and drew people to it. When first they
entered the room the window was all they saw. It reached
from the floor almost to the ceiling, and because Crantock
House stood on a terrace just under the ridge of the steep

hill rising over the harbour and town of Branton, unless you went close to that window nothing was to be seen through it but the glare of the sky and the far horizon. Lucy did not bother about the horizon, but with her nose against the glass looked down past the dark layers of a cedar, and the white pigeons on the slope of the lawn, to grey roofs and chimneys below blurred in a haze of smoke. She looked past it all straight to the quay, and the ships alongside. Beyond the ships was a granite jetty curving an immense arm, on which gulls had settled, round the lower scene. It was holding off the western ocean, with a lantern in its fist. She could see her own ship down there, and no mistake about it, for though every ship had black topsides, the right one was plain because of its running gear of new manilla. There happily it was. Certainly she could have been sure of it without looking, for she had launched that vessel, but when an object is new, important and personal, it cannot be gazed at too often.

She was motionless while she stared at that, and turned only when her father and his two guests came in. It startled Mr. Darton to see her frail figure at the edge of that immense and splendid vacancy, as if she might be taken by it. He spoke sharply. "Lucy, why are you here?"

"You said you would give me the model, Papa, and I came for it, but you were not here."

"I don't like you to be so close to that window when I'm not here. It might not be fast. Now, that model? Where did I see it last? Killick left it here about the time he laid the keel, and I haven't handled it since—no, that isn't it, that's the old *Ebenezer*. She's gone, but she never did much good. And it seems to me you ought to know the difference now between a brig and a barque. Ah, here you are, here's the one for you."

Mr. Darton held up a model, and turned it in slow

admiration. "Look at it, Tom, have you ever seen sweeter lines? But I'm sure you have not. She'll fly, that ship, and never get wet."

He thrust the model at his daughter. "Put it on your table, put it in the centre, and sing a nice little song to it, every night, before you get into bed."

Uncle Tom laughed. He was a rude man, sometimes, and laughed to himself when nobody else knew there was a joke. Lucy glanced up at him sharply, but he was not looking at her, nor her ship, as she went out, but at the sea.

2

Visitor from London

MR. DARTON went to his window, picking up a spy-glass from his table as he moved across, though he did not point it; it was to give his restless hands something to do while he was talking. He looked to the horizon, but without scanning it. He noticed, but did not remark, the majesty of a line-of-battle ship, under all canvas, standing to the westward. He saw such ships every day or so, but did not ponder them; he understood what they implied for his general benefit, and for his present information this one advised him of the force and direction of the wind, and that was all he wanted to know. Stately three-deckers, seen from that window, were like the sun, the sea, the merchantmen below, and the headlands of home; they were features of an outlook with its assurance of the abiding nature of his time and place, in which he knew what he ought to do next.

"No, I won't have it," he was saying to Mr. Denny, his guest from London. "It's against all I know of ships and the sea."

He was still looking to the horizon without seeing it, and the light of morning was on the profile of his handsome head. The long face was sharp and ruddy, the nose masterly, and the thin underlip was thrust out and petulant with the good humour of conscious ownership, which could be allowed some fun with friends, and even with common men, now and then, when business was moving pleasantly. And because he disliked change, for that interferes with the smooth running of affairs, his dress was not in the latest mode, but was that of a superior man who keeps to the old proprieties, and well it suited him. His white stock and ruffle, and his coat, knee-breeches, and stockings, all plum-coloured, and black shoes with silver buckles, charmed with a reminder of a recent past that had leisure and elegance because it was sure of a good way of living and working. His presence and his speech were as if one of an ancient line, wise with the experience of history, rebuked the claims of youth to usurpation.

"I don't like your notion," he said to the London ship-builder. "I won't try steam in one ship of mine; not one. Why ask for trouble when the wind is fair? It's against nature to build a fire down below in a ship. That is just where it isn't wanted."

Uncle Tom, who felt incompetent to intervene when two owners and builders of ships were disputing the first principles of commerce, which to him did not seem like principles, was watching his brother-in-law with respect and admiration; but he also had a doubt that for once Miles Darton might be wrong. Mr. Denny, this visitor from London, where the latest news was heard from as far as China, was smiling and easy. It was not the young man's fashionable air that disturbed, nor his cleverness, but something apart, something in the air. Uncle Tom himself thought he felt that prevalence of change, which tradition rejects, but young people welcome.

So he spoke. "Only a few years ago," he pointed out, "the railroad and the locomotive were against Nature, against beautiful horses and coaches and the pleasant hills. But here they are. Dear, yes, I know they haven't got to this place yet, but they will be here before long. The locomotive whistle will be heard from your house, Miles, it wouldn't surprise me."

The mere thought of that appeared to surprise Mr. Darton, for he glanced severely at his brother-in-law, as if the bad news were already there, and till that moment had been kept from him. "You think that good?" he asked, with a touch of asperity.

"I don't know whether it is good or bad," said Uncle Tom, "nor does anyone else, really, but I know it is what busy men are trying to do, and they'll do it. I can't help that."

"I don't like it," Mr. Darton repeated stubbornly. "And fire in a ship's belly! That's the last place for it. Good can't come of it. Look at my little fleet. It does what ships have always done. My craft get their power from Heaven, and get it for nothing. There's no cost except that of canvas to catch the wind, and a few of the best of them make eight knots with it. And Denny, that is where I have you. Your new-fangled steam-ship, you can't deny it, has to carry so much coal to get her along that she has no space left for cargo, no room for profit. With her it is all cost. You tell me your ship burns up about forty tons of coal a day to raise eight knots. Ten days at sea makes four hundred tons. That's a fair load, but it isn't freight. Up it goes in smoke. And what is she to look at? She is all heavy beams and ugliness to bear the weight of engine, paddle-wheels, boiler, and fuel, and with the ruinous cost of it she can do no more than give a few passengers a ride. I tell you the dear old ships and brigs will always be wanted for long voyages, and, mark me, for making money. You be off, and talk to Noah about it."

Mr. Darton chuckled, and pointed his spy-glass at the Londoner. "What if the Ark had been a steam-ship. Try to make out Admiral Noah's command with a funnel and paddle-wheels. What would have happened when the flood floated her away? No room for the menagerie, not even a

stall for the donkeys. All left ashore to drown. And the
Noah family would have gone later, cast to the sharks.
The Ark's seams would have opened with the strain of it,
A steam-ship wouldn't have lasted forty days of such
weather as that, no, nor ten."

"Better not mention Noah," his visitor advised respectfully. "Better keep that ancient mariner a secret. His bony
hand might be building our own arks. I think our ship-
yards go on laying down keels on advice out of the Bible.
But not American yards."

"Which yards? I don't want to hear of the Yankees."

"So I've been told. My father has the same objection.
But it would do no harm to listen. Better still to make the
western passage yourself. Go over, and watch what they are
about. It would pay you. Over there they forgot Noah when
they wanted craft fast enough to slip through our blockade
against Napoleon. You'd find in Boston news about ships
to surprise you. You should remember that while they were
doing flyers to give us the slip, we were launching square-
ended wagons for convoy work. You know why. Ships in a
convoy only have to keep up with a funeral procession. Sir,
I see you've guessed what I'm at. Napoleon finished his
capers about the year I was born. Yet look at London river!
Anyone would suppose our ships still sailed in convoys.
They're all as near square as baulks. The Yankees told me
it takes about twenty years to get a new idea into our
heads . . . I'm sorry, sir, I ought not to have reported that
bit. But it is true the Americans are not building for a
leeward drift to Ararat, so they've got most of the
world's traffic with better craft. And how do we like
that?"

Mr. Darton made a sound of impatience, but he did not
speak. What his visitor had said reminded him that when
at Falmouth his attention was always drawn to the Yankees

in Carrick Roads. He had noticed that they took the shine out of the clever English packet-ships, for his eye was quick to the signs of good breeding in a ship. Moreover, he regretted the number of them. Too many! He said nothing of this to Mr. Denny. He never pointed to facts which did not support his opinions. He was not easily budged.

"Paddle-wheels!" he exclaimed bitterly, as if a malediction had burst at the remembrance of an annoyance. "I can see Killick's face if I ordered boilers instead of flax. My men would think I was off to Bedlam. I should start some mischief."

"That you would," mused Uncle Tom, as if talking to himself. "There is no doubt of that. Our new ways of doing things have excitement in them. We move more quickly, but tempers are fretful. Not long ago that docile set of people, the agricultural labourers, they were rioting. They do not prefer machines to men. They scared the Prime Minister, or so he pretended. Certainly they frightened the magistrates, who turned cruel and senseless. It is very unpleasant, this unrest. But what can we do? Can we put back the clock? The fire for a new reign has been lighted, but who can put it out?"

"Put it out? I like that!" Mr. Denny was prompt, and his confident voice was not as if he mused. "We don't want it put out, sir. It wasn't lit for that. If ignorant men grow noisy over it we shall teach them their place. Our wars at least have shown us what to do with ugly customers. But this friction is only what you'd expect to come of increased speed. You notice it when no more than a ship has to be turned round at once and sent to sea again without being overhauled. I've known sailors break discipline then; yes, sir, and forget the needs of their families. After all, when men forget the law, and what wages are paid for, they can be brought to the recollection of it. I was present only last week when a ship's crew walked ashore. Walked ashore! Desertion in daylight, if you please, and a crowd looking on, and the ship about to cast off! A lot of shouting, plenty of grievances. She leaked too much, she was pumped along, she was undermanned, she was overloaded . . . your pardon, sir, you said . . .? Why, to be sure, a ship does look dangerous when she is burdened and low in the water, but if drunken tarpaulins are to be judges of what will float many ships would never sail. Look fairly at it, and there's no doubt that if working men are to stop to consider the danger in what they are paid to do, then industry would come to a standstill."

"And what are underwriters for?" murmured Mr. Darton.

The Londoner smiled sadly. "Yes. One of that ship's crew had the brass to ask me how much she was insured for. He bawled his interest from the dock-side. At that moment the police arrived. Off the whole bunch went, safely handcuffed. They've had time to think over their danger since, in prison. Perhaps by now they've found out where danger lies. You needn't worry, sir," he said, turning to Uncle Tom, "the trouble you fear is one of the few for which we are always prepared. We know what to do with unprincipled men who object to their work and wage."

Mr. Darton nodded. The conversation had come to a point where agreement was natural. He roused from a reflection. He was gentle. "Don't mistake brother Tom," he confided to Mr. Denny. "As he lives he wonders, so he is never free from doubt, and then he goes on to worry, where you and I know there is nothing to cause concern. His family is inclined to be fearful. They fancy trouble where good sense sees only stout and hearty life. His sister was like him, and even worse. Yes, she wondered even more. People who don't understand are always afraid of what will happen next. You know," he continued, examining his spy-glass, and shaking his head as if he deplored the look of it, "Mrs. Darton's fears about things she thought she under-stood were the death of her. I've know her condemn a ship of mine and have no word with me for a week after it had sailed. It did not help to laugh at her. And when the cholera came to these parts, and you'll remember how it emptied many houses, she would have it that it was not mischance, such as happens everywhere. She declared it was dirt that did it. Nothing but dirt and poverty. She said it was what we ought to have expected, from the way we lived. She went out, into the worst of it, against all I could say, to alter that way, which is as old as our rocks . . . there are such people, but they harm only themselves. Tom means well, but he suffers from a constitutional tender heart, like the chickens . . . what were we talking about? Yes, yes, tell me about that ship of iron you say you are building on the Thames."

They bent over the table, and Mr. Denny unrolled his drawings. Uncle Tom strolled to the window, which had been opened. The morning was warm and still. The ship of battle had receded to a faint ghost, a questionable fault of the horizon. She seemed caught on the frail sky-line, as a fly wing on gossamer. The air which drifted in from sea-ward was too gentle to stir the curtains. The ocean was bur-nished, but near the coast it was scored by the dark parallel lines of a ground swell from the west. Miles had remarked that he guessed a break in the weather was coming soon.

Yet the hour in which they talked seemed poised in eternity, to rest there, to outlast a century without change. Not a movement could be seen in the town below. The smoke from the chimney of a house hidden by lower foliage was a vertical bluish column. That haven below, with its old jetty, as long ago as the year America was discovered must have looked as it did then from his outlook. There had been no change in it since he first saw it, not a stone, and no fresh names except for the newborn, and they were all given old names. Killick was said to use tools in the shipyard which his family had used for three generations. The tranquil harbour and its ships, and the ageless ocean beyond, would give even a chance wayfarer the idea that he had seen it all before, somewhere, because it was the same in all ages, and all lives.

But behind him they were talking of a ship of iron. Change was in that room. What did it mean? Coal and iron and steam. Most of the energetic new talk went that way. Tiny children, so some angry men were saying, were crawling half-naked in the mines to win that coal, and other babies, no luckier than chained slaves, were spinning the cotton in Lancashire for Miles's West African voyages. English slaves were making cheap shirts for negroes. Armies of toddlers were caught in the new machinery; they were at work before sunrise in the mills, kept it up till well into the night, and had no schools, and no hope. Yet Miles hardly glanced, except contemptuously, towards the gatherings of rebellious Chartists. He only smiled, though they had burned the bishop's palace at Bristol. The rebels also, like the projects for ships driven by engines, were against the laws of Nature, and must fail. Miles could not see that general obedience to the established way of life was getting tottery.

And then again, those two men behind him, the experienced merchant and the young one, differed from each other hardly at all. They were only Whig and Tory. They disputed only the relative values of profitable dodges. They discussed, however warmly, only the better way to get what they wanted. Both had the same aim. And they always knew the measure of their success. They need never have a doubt about that. All they had to do was to look at the figures in their account books, and there it was, much more easily read than the writing on the wall; for in fact that writing was never on the wall to be seen, except in an old tale.

3

Thoughts of a Boy

ACROSS the valley from Crantock, young Dave Gay listened for a sound in a smaller house. Was Aunt Ruth moving about below? He was tired of being left in this old room. He stood as if a mouse were at his feet and he was afraid of alarming it. No. Not a whisper. The house was playing his own game. It was as artful as the pictures on the wall, those portraits of sailors, with their stern eyes watching him from their frames. And nothing moved, except slow motes in a slat of sunshine falling from between the window curtains. The beam touched the edge of the mahogany table, and made it red-hot.

The top of the parlour table was as shiny as glass. If you looked into it you could see, very clear and very deep but upside down, a double of the white lamp hanging from the ceiling. Was that lamp ever used? Was it meant for lighting? He had never seen it alight, but perhaps he hadn't been there long enough yet, and now it was summer. He did know that Aunt never used this best room, except to get him out of her way: he was out of her way now. A seagull was crying over the house.

He stood at the table and watched the drift of a speck across the sunbeam. It was very slow. Nothing but that seabird could be heard, and now it was a long way off. He sighed. That bird could go where it wanted to, over the land, and over the sea. He could not hear his aunt downstairs, but that did not mean she was not there. She always was there, most surprisingly, if you were sure she wasn't.

He considered the door. No, leave it alone. Perhaps he had better not try. That handle was a sneak, and squeaked sometimes.

He wetted his finger, and turned over another leaf of the book. It was the only book in the room, and he had no hope of much good coming from it, but there was nothing else to do. Besides, this was the Sabbath. He had been all round the room again, but that did not take long. He had looked at everything—everything worth looking at. It did not take ten minutes, not if you wasted more time at the prickly cushion of white coral than it was worth, not if you listened again at the lips of each of the shells in the fender to hear the sea inside. That left the portraits of the sailors. You could stand and look at them, for each had whiskers that were different and marvellous, and the eyes of each followed you about—just look back over your shoulder, and there he was, still watching you. Then there were the four pictures of ships, all of them going like fury in dreadful seas.

But not a steam-ship among them! What a pity. No steam-ship. He had never seen that new sort of ship. It could cross the Atlantic, it could go anywhere, so people were saying. Aunt told him she had seen one, and didn't want to see another, the ugly stinking things, buckets of fire and chimney pots, not ships at all. But she would not tell him about those ships on the wall, though they had names. There was one, the brig *Ebenezer*. Aunt said, best keep quiet about a ship, when she's departed and out of sight. She knew a lot about ships, more than anybody he'd ever met. There were no ships in his part of London. Aunt said that all the Londoners she knew, and she knew all she wanted to know, were about as easy with ships as they were with honesty.

As he turned over that leaf of the book it moved the

23

smell of the room. What did that smell remind him of?
When he had to go into this room again, and stay there,
and keep quiet, the smell of it was strong, and he always
thought he had smelled it before somewhere. But he couldn't
remember where. Sometimes he nearly got it, could nearly
say what it was, but not quite. You might think the scent
of the dried seaweed hanging up by the window had something to do with it, only the weed was in a glass case.
Aunt said the weed was there to bring good luck to the
fishing. A silly idea! Didn't he catch it when he laughed!
Don't laugh, she said, in your ignorance of what lies round
the corner for each one of us. How he would like to go out
in one of those fishing luggers! Other boys did. Did the
smell remind him of the day of Mother's funeral? No, that
wasn't it either, though it was something like it. But there
was no frightful smell of black crêpe here. He supposed it
was the scent of the pot of musk on Aunt's window-sill
which gave him the fancy; that, and the oldness of everything. All was here before he was born. Perhaps that made
it so quiet. Though most of the things in the room were
bright and shiny, it smelled of long ago.

He turned another leaf of the book, indolently and without expectation. A Bible with pictures lasts a long time
when there is nothing to do but to spin things out. It might
be wicked to say so, as this was the Sabbath, Dave thought,
but if Elisha was like that it was awful to let bears eat the
children because they thought the prophet was funny. You
couldn't blame them for such a man as that. How could
they tell he was a prophet of God? He was sure he would
have laughed like anything. He turned more leaves with
care and respect, always damping his finger, for a leaf
crackled unless it was pushed up carefully; then he let it
drop softly the other side. Aunt had such ears. She said she
could hear people talking about her in the village. He had

to turn over many leaves to find the coloured pictures, and it was impossible to tell you had one till you came to it.

If his aunt heard him at it she would be after him. She was always after people, especially him. She could even guess what it was you didn't want to say, and she would tell you, and too quick for you to think of something else. That made your face turn red. She said she hated liars. If she heard him now she would be there before he could shove the book back to the centre of the table, to say nothing of clicking its brass clasp in time. Why should a book have a brass clasp? So you had to turn these leaves slowly. The house was too quiet. You could hear the soot if a pinch of it rustled down the chimney, and walking across the room on tiptoe would do that, the boards were very wobbly. You stay here, she said, till I want you, and that won't be till you see me, and don't forget today's Sunday, and don't you touch that book—you hear me?—don't you touch it—ten years and more I've had it, and not a mark on it yet.

Lots of "don'ts." What an awful picture that was! Most of it black and red, and tiny people rushing away for their lives. The Destruction of Sodom and Gomorrah. He could find nothing about it in the print. That ought to be worth reading about. What had those people been up to? It would be worse than bears, to have the world on fire and tumbling down. They had been doing evil in the sight of God, those people; that was it. They were always doing it. From the stories Aunt read to him, the people in the Bible were unlucky most of the time. They seemed to be getting into a mess with God without knowing it, and God was as sharp as Aunt herself. He was watching them day and night, and when you are always being watched you want to do something wicked. Then God dropped on them and they caught it. That crowd was catching it proper, catching it hot, wide cracks opening in the ground before them as they ran. Look at that man! Just tumbling into a hole with flames pouring from it. Perhaps Aunt was right. Nothing could be hidden from God, not even your thoughts when you didn't think anything was wrong with them, but there was.

He heard a movement below, gently closed the book, and made ready to muffle the snap of the clasp. It never did close properly at the first go, that clasp. He examined the brass more closely, and forgot the chance of trouble. What a stupid lock! Whoever made it was blind. The boy could see, working it about, how a more secure and easy catch could have been done, and with less brass. Why hadn't the man who made it seen that? Should he tell his aunt?

No, better not tell her. That would only show he had been at the book again. And when you told her something because you could not help talking, it started lots of questions that had nothing to do with what you said. He had often noticed that. If ever you begin to see a thing which is better than the one people know, don't say so. They never see what you see, not even when you point it out to them.

He must have been mistaken. He thought she was on her way upstairs then. He heard a creak. But sometimes the floorboards made you jump, especially at night; they moved as if they were growing again. They woke up. Even if Aunt was outside the house, and up the garden at the back, how was he to know? This place wasn't like London. There a street door is shut by day and bolted at night. Aunt's door was always open by day, and never bolted because it had no bolts. She said Branton wasn't a den of thieves and a sink of iniquity like that city of the plains he'd come from. That door was always open because somebody might want to come in. So if she left the house, how was he to know, when upstairs? And it was never safe to go and see, because then she was indoors; and if you pretended too often you were only going to the back, that meant physic. It wasn't worth it, not with a taste like that.

He could hear sounds, of course, but they were real, and far away. All the sounds in that place were far away. London was all noise, but here the sounds were separate. There was the tapping from the shipyard on weekdays. He liked those outside sounds, because he had to guess what made them. The sounds from the ships were the best, and they were of all kinds. That shipyard was the place he wanted to see most of all.

Not if I know it, said Aunt Ruth at once, not while you don't know enough to stand clear of the sheer-legs and a gang of riggers. What were such things? He didn't know.

No, there isn't much you do know that's useful in Branton, she said, and she wasn't going to trust a young innocent from London running loose there, not yet. What did he know of the tides? No more than he did of Holy Writ. The tides were dangerous to fools who never know they are in the wrong place at the wrong time.

She wouldn't let him go about the quays, either, with the other boys, not with all those hawsers and moorings about, the devils they were, those boys about the waterside, and a long drop it was, high or low water. They weren't too particular with strangers, either, to say nothing of the heathen language they threw about. That alone was enough to trip anyone up. He wasn't born to it, like a Branton baby, which could swim before it could walk, and might be playing indoors or sitting astride a boom, it was all one. But not a London child, that never knew more water than would wet its behind. She had to look after him, though she hadn't asked for it, but she would do it. She knew her sister's wish. Trials had to be suffered, she said, so make hers as light as possible, my dear, and don't worrit her more than you can help.

27

He was fiddling with a leaf of the book while remembering, and was not blaming her. She was only fussy, and didn't know. He wasn't really afraid of Aunt Ruth, though she was sharp, but he hated being dropped on when he thought he was safe, trying to sneak off.

He crept to the door and opened it without a creak. Not a sound below! He peered over the banisters. All seemed clear. Down he went boldly to chance it, and saw only Carlo the black retriever, who never barked at him now, but only wagged his tail. Carlo wouldn't follow anyone but Aunt. That dog had sense.

4

Outlook to the Deep

H<small>IS</small> aunt was then amid her patch of kitchen herbs, at
the height of the rise of her garden path. She had
filled her basket with what she wanted, and became aware,
at ease, of the kind of day it was. It was a good one. She
stood in the sun gazing seaward, taking it in. Lovely
weather. Two tiles had slipped above the boy's bedroom
window; she had better see to that before it was a dozen.
From the top of her garden path her eyes were level with
the ridge of her house. Would this weather last? She
thought not. Branton was below, and almost hidden, but its
roofs and chimneys half-filled the vase of a steep valley. A
thicket of topmasts was close behind them. She noticed those
chimneys were filmy in a bluish haze. The town smoke didn't
know which way to go. In that slaty vacancy beyond, the
sea, the figures of the Five Maids, a line of high rocks two
miles offshore, were sharp and hard.

She looked up. The clouds were mares' tails and curly
feathers. The wind was shifting. Weather was coming from
westward. About evening it would come, perhaps whistling
at night; and wasn't today the second after full moon?
Then the wind would rise with the highest spring flood this
evening. They had better look to their moorings below.

Her eyes were on the sea, and her expression changed as
an old dread and suspense came over her. Not a ship was in
sight but a stranger. How empty were the waters! Empty.
What was the good of staring into the offing, like a dummy,
whenever she came to the end of this path? Never watch

for the ship you want. Nothing will be in sight but strangers, and those sharp dark rocks off the land. Five Maids. Maids! Who called them that? Tarrying out there to catch men coming home after dark. She knew of a better name. Well, well. Keep it to yourself. Keep quiet about what you think of the deep, when you've a man away on it. They that go down to the sea in ships, these see the works of the Lord, and His wonders in the deep. Wonders enough! But there's nothing in the psalm about those ashore who keep watch, and wait for what is late in coming, is late, late.

She chided herself. That's enough of that. But a boy pulls at the heart worse than a girl. She went briskly down the path, light of step, plump as she was. She slapped her basket on the kitchen table, and rather too noisily; glanced sharply at the clock, resolutely tightened her apron strings, straightened her hair, for stooping had loosened it. Whether or no, there's always work to be done. She inclined an ear to the stairs.

How quiet that boy was up above! Rather too quiet. Up to some mischief, she'd be bound. After all, he was really a likely lad, but curious in his fancies. He had his mother's breed in him. She was glad of that. His mother had given him her eyes, nose, and mouth, and the look of a proper man to come. He only wanted to be filled out. She supposed she was rather hard on him, or he thought she was. But he was green. She must keep an eye on him. Boys are strayers. What a responsibility, at her time of life, when she had enough to think about! How could she watch another lad's foolish capers, when her thoughts were turned backwards? Pity he wasn't a girl. A girl would be something for company. Girls stay home. If they do go away, you know where to find them. But a boy, over the sky-line he sails one morning, and after that, where is he? Here, that imp upstairs was too quiet for anyone's good. She went to the foot of the stairs and called up. "You Dave! Come down at once!"

She narrowed her eyes. This house sounded hollow. She bustled up to her parlour. Her Bible was square in the centre of her table. That was all.

Gone! The little scamp. Now where should she look for him? It was useless going out after him, on those slopes, with the tracks wandering the way the sheep go. Carlo ought to have had the sense to follow him. Don't stand there wagging your tail, you black fool! Clear out! Must she wait there, and not seek him? Wait, of course, you stupid woman. But she was always waiting, and in a quiet house it isn't easy, with the door open, but nobody coming up the path. She went to that doorway, and called. "Dave!"

She listened. She heard only the sea-mews over the cliffs.

5

Threshold to Adventure

DAVE slipped behind a lower boulder. It was sitting on the turf between him and the house rather like a huge sheep, for it was grey granite, rounded and smooth. He stood there to think it out. Was that Aunt calling? He supposed he must be mistaken, very likely. He hoped he was too far down the slope to hear her. He really thought he heard a voice just now, but sea-birds often cry out very like people you can't see, if you forget they are flying about. There they were, too, a few of them, floating overhead. Of course, if he should happen to hear her calling he would have to go back, because she might want him. So he had better wait and listen, and not answer at once. He might be wrong.

He waited for the voice to call again, and kept as still as the rock behind which he was hiding, except to amuse himself by moving his head slightly. This movement made a spark flash and go in the boulder under his nose. There was fire in the rock. Down here, so they said, this rock was granite. It was real granite, in its own place. That showed how little you know, if you know only your own street. He had never seen granite before, except polished, outside a public-house round the corner in London. The only rocks in London are in the story-books, but you can't believe a word of it, because all you see there is mud and dust and bricks. The ground in London is pappy. You'd never learn there that the earth is heavy with rocks, and that they stick out of it like the enormous bones of a giant.

He did not quite see it happen, but it seemed to him the rock twitched, or cracked silently across. There was a streak of black over it; but, when he looked, there wasn't. Then under his eyes, out of a crinkle in the boulder, another lizard raised its head. They watched each other. Dave forgot he was listening for a voice he didn't want to hear. The lizard's eager glance fixed on his but saw no danger. It went over the smooth rock like a shadow and no heavier, for it was upside down. Dave turned in his interest, and at once the rock was plain. Nothing had been on it. He was sorry he had moved. You ought not to move, when you are watching. He had learned that rule already, to keep still, or else the tiny things of the earth never show their noses. And this granite was not as easy as it appeared, now his face was close to it. It was a mixture. There were white grains in it like china, black specks, and crumbs of glass. Perhaps each had a name. He would have to find out what they were. Why is it you see more when all you have to do is to be quiet, and watch what is going on?

It was a sea-bird he heard just now. There, he could hear it again! He could hear only the birds, and the sea; and he would not have known the sea could keep talking and grumbling all day long if Aunt had not told him it was always there, always complaining, and generally up to mischief, the same as sin. That beat of the waters on the shore, a long way off, was only as if the hot sunshine were being joggled a little, when you listened. Aunt said you don't have to listen for the sea when you don't want to hear it. There were some nights, she said, when it made you listen to it, calling for its own. What was its own?

He liked to hear the sea. It was drums, far away. He turned and stepped down the slope with care. The sea ought to be near, but there was nothing but a ship hanging flat above, like a tiny picture, alone and high up on a great wall. How queer, to have to guess where the sea is, when you can hear it! This land had no edge. He saw in front of him only a row of scraggy weeds, a straight line of weeds, tall and dry, not far ahead, every stick as black and plain against the light beyond it as if inked on silver paper. This land was raised up. It was near the sky. Aunt said she must find time presently to show him the way about, but she hadn't found it yet. They had no streets there, she said, so make no mistake about it, only careless tracks round about sheer falls to the shore, but good enough for the brandykegs, when they happen to come. As for the village, no streets there either, just stone ladders up and down; ladders you might call them, she said, not streets, and he was not going there unless she was with him, not till she had time to trot down some day soon. Strangers in Branton, she said, were Gentiles to be stoned, but that did nosy persons no favour.

Anyway, he could see a ship out there, so the shore must be somewhere about. He had always supposed you could never make a mistake between land and water, but you could here. . . .

He stopped instantly. He was alarmed because a gull before him sheered sideways and fast down the sky past the far side of the line of weeds, and vanished. What was before him? Was it open space without end?

This had never happened to him in London. There you don't have to stop because you're afraid the pavement is tricky and waiting to drop you. He shuffled forward warily till between the weeds his sight fell to part of the shore so much below him that he shrank back from a void, lest his weight should cause the verge to topple. What was right under him he never saw. The weeds grew on a shelf jutting into the air.

That was as near as he could get. He paused. But he knew that if you are playing the wag it is not easy to turn back, though you are afraid. It is better to go on, for that is the only way to get something out of it. He backed away from the edge of the cliff, still fearing that his weight would burst thin ground. He found signs of a track, and followed it. It often faded out. It had to be searched for in dry herbage. Not many people, he could see, ever came this way. Soon the tracing of a path took a sharp turn seawards towards the sky, as if it had given up pretending. It widened to a bald patch on a downward slope, and then went slap off the earth. He recoiled from the end of it. The track took a dive into nothing.

Yet, he thought, feet must have made that path. Other people must have been here before him, and that way they went. He tried the slope on hands and knees, to be sure of his balance, till the track turned sharply under the cliff. It traversed the sheer fall of it in narrow steps. The steps below diminished to notches, and canted the wrong way. Half-way to the bottom they turned a corner, and that was all. He considered it. Perhaps he might make his way to that point; and he could climb back, couldn't he, if round the corner it was more than he liked?

When he was safe below amid the clutter of rocks on the shore he felt as if he had been let off. One hand was bleeding, but he did not know how that happened, and his knees wouldn't keep still. With his head thrown back he admired his precipice. It was so much the real thing that it seemed to bulge over him. The top of it was out of sight. How had he managed it? He could not remember, except that his eyes went loose when he tried to see how much more he had to do. He felt then the wall was swinging over while mid-air was at his other elbow. And when a stone leaped down he had to wait a long time for a small sound to come up. Sometimes the cliff slithered in grit and stones under his hand, as if he had upset the balance of the land

and it had begun to turn round. It was a surprise to find fleshy plants holding on to dry places he could not grip. And who was it had left those rusty iron rings fastened here and there to the face of the cliff? As for climbing back, he wasn't going to think about it; not yet. Here he was below, and nobody could find him. Nobody would look for him in that place, because it seemed to be telling him that he was the first to come down to it.

He was glad he was there, but hoped there was another way out. This was the very bottom of high land. It was a small beach, imprisoned by threatening heights. The walls grew higher and worse when a drifting gull, midway the cold gloom of a steep, floated across like a scrap of white paper. Out of the sands a crag towered, and about the green shelves of it were dotted ghostly birds. Their sad cries echoed around. The walls cried back at them. The base of the tower, Dave thought, said too plainly that now and then it was a tall island. A pool was at the back of it. Then did the sea reach it sometimes? He was a little reassured by the sea itself, which was nothing but white lines dissolving distantly in bright daylight.

There ought to be another way out of this, he supposed, for he did not want to stay there very long. He could not see that either side of the beach promised escape. Of one side there was no doubt. There the deep prison was kept by the black profile of a promontory. That such a toppling mass could stand up to the clouds for five minutes longer was surprising. The shadows under the cliffs were hiding he did not know what. The cliffs threatened, and the melancholy voices of the birds, and the eddies of wind in a shivering light, made him feel the strangeness and uncertainty of the earth, and that feeling was new to him. He was alone.

The other end of the beach was more distant, and so more

attractive. The heights over it were interrupted by recesses as dark as night, which Dave hoped might be passes through them. Whatever was not plain to Dave drew him towards it, to see how it was made. The nearer he came to that barrier, the more of a ruin it was, as if a city once stood there, but storms had upset it. He paused, while on his way, and forgot his misgivings by the side of a rocky pool. The water was bright and smooth. It was hard to believe it was water, yet he kept himself from proving it. He wanted to do it, but dared not throw a stone into that transparency to smash it. It was like the good things which ought not to be touched. The pool was secret and perfect. Its clean colours were those of precious stones. Round the margin of the pool were ribbons of brown and green seaweed, and fixed, so it seemed, in solid glass.

"Hullo, you boy."

Dave was startled. A mermaid could not have surprised him more than a girl beside that pool. Where had she come from? She was looking at him across the water with an interest calmer than his own. He did not answer her, though she had called him a boy.

"Why did you come down the Cellar Steps? That was a fat-headed thing to do. I saw you do it."

He was not used to girls. He knew his face was red. She stood there as though she had a right to call anybody fat-headed, if she wanted to. He had wanted to, sometimes, but had never done it. Proud and well-dressed people always made him feel both shabby and foolish.

"I expected to see you break your neck. I know who you are. You're the London boy, and you live with Mrs. Penfold. Won't she give you something when she knows what you did!"

Dave remained silent.

"Can't you talk? You're not deaf and dumb, are you?

Why didn't you come through the village? That's the proper way."

"Then what are the steps for?"

"For those who use them."

"Who are they?"

"Don't you wish you knew! But if you did I expect you'd be dropped over them. We don't like foreigners who want to know too much. Do you like old Mrs. Penfold?"

"She's my aunt."

"I know that. I didn't ask you that. She still looks out for the *Ebenezer* to arrive, doesn't she? She must be silly. That brig has been a year missing. She won't see her son any more. I know. That ship belonged to my father."

Dave was troubled. He remembered. It was the name of a ship in a picture on the parlour wall, and Aunt Ruth must know about it. So a ship with men in her could be lost, and nobody know where? And to have a father rich enough to own a ship! He spoke humbly. "Aunt never told me."

"No, she's close. She's a hard woman, Father says. Besides, you're only from London, and it was no good telling you. You'd better go back through the town. I'll show you the way, but my father would be very cross if he saw me talking to you."

Dave had heard too much of that town. "I'm not going back that way."

"Aren't you? Then how are you going back?"

"The way I came."

"You can't."

"I can."

"But the men say it's worse going up than coming down."

"I don't care what they say."

The girl eyed him in surprise, and as if her opinion of him had improved. "All right, then I shall have to watch you do it. You will break your neck next time for certain, and nobody will know if I don't see you fall, because the tide's rising."

"I'm going up. I shan't go through the village."

"Not with me?"

"No."

He had found his voice, and answering back was easy, he discovered, because her smile was too faint to be pleasant.

"Why not with me?"

"I don't want to."

Her mocking smile went. She had never heard that from anyone before. Yet this boy was a shaving to those about the ships and in her father's shipyard. His face had no colour, except for its freckles; his hair was rough and the colour of his freckles; and he was so thin she did not believe he could hoist the sail of a boat, but he was staring at her as if she was nobody. She began to walk round to his side of the pool.

He knew why. She had good clothes, and his were old, and she had noticed it. She was clever. He could not guess that to her he was a curiosity, worth some astonishment. Everybody in Branton could name all her father's ships, one of which was called after her. It was alongside the quay then. He could not guess he was a novelty because he did not appear to respect her as much as he should. She stood beside him, eyeing a rent in his jacket.

"All right," she said indifferently, "you climb back if you want to. Don't go through the town. I hope you'll like it, half-way up. That's where the steps are crumbling away. I shall wait here to see you climb round the bend."

She hesitated, and pointed. "Do you see that corner, with daylight showing under a rock? That's the way I came. It's the right way. No, not there . . . there, close to the temple."

"The temple? What's that?"

"Only a cave."

"Is that it, that big black mark?"

"Yes, that's one way in, but there are others, if you know where to find them. I do. Nobody knows how far that cave goes back, some say right under the church, and the Devil listens to the vicar on a Sunday. The men say you can hear him laughing, but Father says that's only the tide rumbling in the tunnels. Nobody knows how far that cave goes, nobody."

"Couldn't they find out?"

"How could they? Why, high water floods it most times. Nobody would dare. You wouldn't."

"I don't know. I'm going to see it."

"The tide is flowing now."

Dave glanced seaward. Breaking water was still inconspicuous. He could see no difference. She was only daring him because he came from London. She wanted to be important; that was why she made things worse than they were. He set off for that shadowy recess under the height. She walked with him, though he did not want her. He saw how neat her feet were. They were small and tidy. His own boots squeezed large pale patches in the polished sand at every step. That drew attention to them, and he was sure nothing was larger and plainer on that part of the beach. She was keeping her eyes down.

6

The Importance of Chance

DAVE stood before the big black opening in the cliff, and hesitated. It was an awful and peculiar sight. He had a suspicion that it was unnatural, without proper right to exist. That interior darkness invited him to explore the wonderful, but he did not go to it at once. To his companion he appeared to be giving a local curiosity the respect it deserved, but in fact he was afraid of it. It was as if an earthquake had hurled down Westminster Abbey, and there it was, towers, buttresses, roof, and pinnacles, fallen, scattered, and pitched over as far as where he stood. The front wall had quite gone, and he could see inside, but only a little way. The lofty interior was there, but full of night. All that was certain was that it would never hear any hymns. It was a vast black mouth wide open. Only the empty dark was inside the cave, yet for a cause he could not see that hollow darkness supported the high and solid precipice above. For how long? And was the tide rising behind them?

Some of his daring had been knocked out of him before he reached it, because in the scramble over its threshold he had come several croppers. It was those boots again, as well as the smooth rocks plastered a bright green with weed. She laughed each time, and called it laver, and said it was good to eat. Perhaps it was, but his elbow was bleeding, though he would not look at it. He had never seen so many mussels before, enough to feed all London, and each set up so that its edge was a knife. And if this girl really knew, and the tide was nearing them, the sea would soon be here. No retreat then. He noticed with nervousness that the boulders up to the entrance, and within it, were worn into smooth rounds. What had he better do? Here he was, and she was waiting.

"Are you going in?"

"Yes."

"Then go on. You'd better hurry. I'm coming, and there isn't all day for it. This place boils over when the sea is up. Don't be afraid. I know another way out." She was going to add that the other way would bring them through the town, but did not. "Be quick. You are going to climb back home the way you came, aren't you?"

He wasn't afraid. He'd show her. And yet, soon after they were within the jaws of that open mouth, he liked it less than before. He felt this dark lonesomeness was against him. Those steps down to the beach were bad, but they were only open and risky. This chilled darkness hiding the devil when he laughed was different. Dave fancied he could smell ancient burials, and it was as quiet. Water dripped at intervals from a height. Where was the roof? And what a sneaking sound it was, the movement of unseen water, trying to creep away in the silence!

"Wait," said a voice at his elbow. "You'll see better in a minute."

He did not know she had come so close to him. "Don't let us lose each other," she whispered.

Her whisper was tiny, but as clear as a light. No, he had better not lose her there. She was right about one thing; he could see better already. There behind him, when he turned, was a vivid picture of the beach, set far back in the world outside, and the more vivid because it was in a thick black frame. The floor of the cave showed faintly towards the entrance, and it was a puzzle, for it had been quite invisible

42

when he made his way over it. The wet sand and the polished rounds of rock reflected the light, which was thin and pale, as at night under a small moon. Vague shapes overhead hung down into the light, and why they did not drop, and why they had not bumped his head on his way in, he did not know.

He noticed the girl's face near his shoulder. The faint light had touched that, too. It had changed her. She looked like a ghost, as if she belonged to the cave. The glow touched first her chin and nose. Her nose was up-tipped, and he hadn't noticed that before. And what was it she could see at the entrance that was so funny? A recollection came to him, though that was not the place for it, of his London home, where there used to be a coloured picture of a pretty girl with a smile, which was nonsense, because the picture was called "Mischief."

She turned away, and so did he. They were wasting time when they had none to lose. In another minute he thought he could make out, deep in dark ahead, a spot of daylight. That was the wrong place for it, and he asked the girl whether she could see it.

"Of course I can. Anybody could. That's where the other way out is. You climb up to it, and then climb down outside to another part of the beach. It is quite easy."

Easy! She talked too much. It was not easy. Fumbling forward, leading the way, his face flinched from unseen obstructions. They were wet and cold, so perhaps he could smell them before he bumped them. She was still chattering behind him, and he was not sorry to hear her. It told him where she was. But he didn't answer; he couldn't hear what she was saying. The cluttering stones roused grumbles and echoes. He wanted to get out of this. The right thing to do was to come here alone, some day, with a lantern. He did not want to have a girl with him.

"Here it is!" she shouted, and caught his arm.

He stopped. What was she talking about now? There came a roaring, and its echoes rioted about them. His alarm flung him round in time to see a crest of foam in lively withdrawal from the rocks at the entrance.

The sudden tumult squeezed Dave's throat. Gone, the way out! Was there another? He was ready to be angry with something or somebody. Off he went. Did she know of another way? In danger, could a girl be trusted? With the sullen booming behind him hunting his fear, he fancied the air of the cave had become warm and close. It was harder to breathe. Either that, or he was in too much of a hurry.

"Don't go so fast," she ordered. "I can't keep up with you."

The light ahead had spread. He checked his haste. Stumbling round a bend, he thought, from the hollowness of the sounds, they must have entered a hall both wide and high. How far it went into the earth he could not see. At one place in it, at a good height above their heads, the vault was perforated by strong daylight. A dazzling jagged notch was up there, and blinded the wall below it. There was only that one small hole in the dark, but it did expose some of the corrugated floor—black ridges and hummocks of rock about him trying to hide themselves, but their long polishing by the sea gave them away. Their glossiness made it certain; the tide did enter this hall. It swept in heavily.

It was coming now. He could hear it moving along, spreading within, snarling round the walls, making sudden bursting noises in its haste, flying into a temper when it found too much in its way. For a minute it would be quiet, and it might have given up, and gone. Then it rushed forward hissing, and bellowed at another awkward corner gained. How far could it reach? Could it rise to the roof?

He stared upwards, towards that bright hole, their only way out.

"Don't be a fool. Don't stare up there," cried the girl impatiently. "How can you see the way if you stare at the light? Look down here. It's easy, if you look down. There's plenty of time."

He obeyed meekly. She was right. She had been here before, and he knew nothing of it. The thick darkness, especially the depth of it below the light, was thinning already. Shapes formed in it. Right before him, and he had not known it was there, was a tangled heap of boards and wreckage, an ugly mess of rubbish, hurled into a corner, piled up above his head. Dave tried to make sense of those quiet shadows, but they neither began nor ended.

"There," said the girl, "there, look, what's that?" She was pointing forward.

She went a few steps and stooped. He could see what it was, only a barrel. But she picked up an object beside it, and turned to him.

"There you are," she said, "that's what the Five Maids do. It's because there isn't a light on them. The vicar says it is time we had one, but lots of people don't want a lamp there."

"Why?" asked Dave.

She was scornful of his ignorance. "Why? What a stupid you are. If a ship could see a light ahead she wouldn't carry on till she struck, would she? Of course not. And then the pickings wouldn't wash ashore. My, you should have seen what we got when the East Indiaman broke up here last year. I got a lovely shawl."

She held up, by her finger tips, a trifling proof of what happened when a ship falls apart. It was a soddened uniform cap, with a gilt cord about it. "What did I tell you? That's

45

a Frenchman, I expect. It hasn't been here long." She dropped it, and rubbed her hands on her frock.

It was no good now. Dave would have rescued it. Once it belonged to a man. Who was he? No, it was no good now. Where was the man? Could he be there with his cap? A ship's boards and her men would float away together. He glanced round. There was another fear now in this wet vault below the grass and trees. The smell of it was bad. Ships that struck rocks and went to pieces came here to be buried, what was left of them, tangled up in seaweed; and ships had people in them. How far did these tunnels go into the hills? Under the church, the girl said, and that meant a long journey.

It wouldn't bear thinking of, a black hollow like this beneath a church, old wreckage rotting in it, under the feet of people singing; and they knew nothing about it. The vault was chilly as well as dark, and he shivered. It was as bad as a frightful lie which nobody had found out. No, he didn't want to know what was there. He wouldn't touch a thing. Let its secrets stay where they were. He would never come here again.

Yet that heap of relics of the work of men was before him, and nobody would bother about it any more, nobody. It was lonesome, and he was always curious to know the names of things and what they mean; the names of the ships from which came these boards, what were they? Where did they belong? Were people still waiting for them to sail home?

A fragment of a boat was nearest to him. The girl said it was a broken rudder. There was also that barrel, and a coil of pale canvas. And something else was over there. That was pale, too, and the wrong shape. What was that? It was just coming through the dark. It could not be a bare arm, not a white arm, lifted out of the rubbish? You could almost believe there were fingers stretched out for the light overhead.

The girl clapped a hand to her mouth and wailed. She pointed to the object. Neither spoke, nor attended to another plunge of the waters in the passage behind them, for the vault now was continuously murmuring and rumbling. She refused to move, and tried to keep him back when he made to go to it. Somebody would have to go. Dave undid her clutch on his arm, and climbed over the slippery and awkward mass. And it was an arm, alarming in its truth.

If this had been outside in the sun he would have laughed, but not there. It was a wooden arm, and he could see the body. A woman's white face was staring up at the bright opening in the wall. A ship had lost its figure-head. There were even rings still in her ea. s. She was watching the light up there in dignity, and was reaching for it. Dave forgot the waters. He hesitated a little. The bare limb was too much like life, but he seized its rigid coldness firmly and tried to release the figure. It was as firm as if still keeping a look out over the sea for a ship, and his eagerness threw him from a slippery foothold. Down he sprawled on the figure.

The girl was a nuisance, squalling like that at him. He tried again to move the image, but it wouldn't give an inch, and that baby kept up her cries of fright. The thing was only wood. He bent to see better the lumber which held the figure down, for he meant to have it clear. He was active on it, wrenching boards away, when the explosion came which drenched him in sharp spray. He was too surprised to find his feet in one movement.

When he could stand the girl had gone. She had been waiting by that barrel, and now water was dancing round it. The dim vault in a moment was very desolate. Quiet came as the tide sucked back, and he heard her cry out.

There she was, half-way to the light. The din was hardly noticed as the sea burst again through the tunnel, smothered him in cold suds, and filled the hollow with rocketing alarms. He was quickly beside her.

"I told you not to come," she scolded. "You knew the tide was rising. But you would do it. I told you not to. I told you . . ."

Dave was too subdued to answer. She was stumbling and crying, and was going too fast. It was a simple climb, but she was not watching it in her excitement. She was scared. But he had no fear, not to notice it, for he had to be careful and attentive, helping her up. They reached the opening in the wall, and clambered out into the day.

They emerged onto a broad shelf of the cliff. The height of it, the blustery light, and the surging waters below, were very unpleasant. A strong wind was blowing into a cove beneath. There was no beach. That had gone; the combers were already vaulting the reefs. The sun was low, and dun scud was driving in express. Below them in the cave the gun exploded again, and its vapour flew past in a blast and carried away like smoke. Dave held his companion, not because she might fall, for they had room enough, but because he did not know what she might do. She was not talking now. She was shivering, but so was he.

7

Time and Tide

M RS. PENFOLD frowned at the clock: surely it was not telling her the right time. Soon she studied it again. She wanted to regain confidence in it. But another ten minutes had gone. It still ticked the day out, in steady indifference to her thoughts. Time's unconcern drove Mrs. Penfold to spend more energy on her kitchen, where it was not wanted. In that room a stain or a thing misplaced was always put right decisively as soon as blot or error was seen; but she must keep busy. Where could that young pickle be?

She paused in her work, to recall, somewhat heatedly, the pitfalls the country about kept in hiding for strangers and innocents. They were many. They were various. Whenever she stopped to think of it she could see another ugly corner she had overlooked till that moment. It was a death-trap, that coast; steeps, and the deep, and no lights. And all this time the tide was rising. It was rising with the wind. She heard them, louder than ever, when she paused. There they were, wind and sea together, the old sounds to which she often listened when she would have shut them out. She went to her door and peered out, but the fact had not altered; she was alone.

Pride kept her from taking the path down to the village. Suppose she went to the quay, and asked, what could they tell her that she did not know? Nothing, of course. How the day was greying! Those shrubs were beginning to whip about in the flurries. A faint whistling was already sounding in the tiles. Yes, and by the time it was dark!

Dark? Night at hand? That settled it. To the quay she must go. She thought she ought to shut this door, with the wind blowing right in. She secured it back against the wall instead, scotching it with a rough block of green glass, kept in the passage for that purpose. She put on her pattens. She fastened the strings of her bonnet while hurrying down the slope towards her neighbours, energetically repelling the wind, which tried to hinder her. She was telling herself that she ought to have done this before.

The ancient quay showed no more concern for her anxiety than her eight-day clock. It was as she had always known it. Its cobble stones extended as silvery rounds in a level light from the west, for they had been polished by a preliminary shower. Water interlaced them, bright as gutters of evening sky that had fallen with the rain. The glimmer of the amphibious stones of the quay, and the shine of the sky cleared by rain, made more drab the town clustered above the harbour. The running gear of the ships moored alongside was bowed to leeward, the hurrying tide was slapping the landing steps, and a few dim figures were securing ropes to old cannon that served as bollards.

In an exposed outlook, as she viewed it, considering on whom she should call, one warm patch appeared, where the lamp of the Binnacle Light Inn, which stood where men could find it as soon as they were ashore, formed a square of glowing orange. This place was aware of nothing unknown to her, she could see. It was only nearing the hour for lighting-up, and the tavern was first with comfort. It was its familiar self, this town, in a bleak ending to another day. You could like it, or you could leave it, it did not care which.

Then she saw coming towards her a man whose brisk gait told her that he had done in the town for that day all he intended to do, and was going. It was Killick. She was glad it was he, the master shipwright of Mr. Darton's yard. He was a sober man, and what was better, no fool, though no friend of hers. For that matter, nobody was, at Darton's. It was as much as she could manage it to tell him of her fear as if she were not afraid. The shipwright fingered his chin leisurely in silence, as though it was difficult to find interest in a lost boy he did not know. He eyed her meditatively.

"That's a queer one, Mrs. Penfold," he admitted at last.

"Queer? What's queer in it? You've heard of a lad missing before this day?"

"Yes, yes, I have that, and more than once. You see, I'm about your own age, and that isn't too bad, so we'll hear of it again before we've done, let us hope."

She could not trust herself to answer him, for she needed advice, and she might not get it if her quick temper said a word.

"The queer thing is," he continued, "down here the men are out searching for Lucy. She's gone, and we cannot find her. And now it's your lad."

"What, is Mr. Darton's little maid lost, and the weather coming in late, like this?"

That meant, she knew, there would be no help for her, unless the searchers happened upon Dave. It was certain the two would not be together, not if she knew that spoilt Darton child, and she thought she did.

"Yes, that's the way of it. She's gone since noon. I've just left it. The tide's along the cliff face now, and daylight nearly done. Not much left of it. Boats are out, but it's no good pulling about in this, not for long. You can see for yourself. I must find Mr. Darton."

"Where is he?"

"Don't know. Anywhere. Out and about, searching for

his little maid. You'd best come along too, unless you don't want to."

No, she didn't want to. Humble pie wasn't to her taste. Killick knew that well enough. She needn't tell him. He knew what she knew, and he could make of it what suited him. But she wasn't going home, to stay there. What, sit and wait for morning? She'd go on to Satan himself rather than turn back. She stumbled over a rope. Drat the plaguey rope! You don't know where your feet are when the wits are pestered. She must keep going. She must keep beside Killick upalong, wherever he went. Was it the Foreland he was making for? Yes, there it opened out, there it was.

And how black and dreary it was! Always hard-featured, that lone waste, towards night. Nothing for a sailor's woman to look at. There it was, reaching out seaward, as long as life, reaching out far, you couldn't see how far, like dark ignorance into naught. Dave might be there, perhaps, somewhere, and the sea up and around it at this hour. You could hear the strength of the flood, for the hollows and caves of the waste were throbbing with flow and ebb. And that sound again like a warning gun, the tide shooting through one of its blow-holes. She would go along with Killick. That sound was enough to drive her to face Darton himself, if it meant crossing the threshold of his very door. Why shouldn't she? She had sins enough to answer for, but at least she could say she had never lost a ship because she was sharper for money than for the good of men. Let others say the same if they could.

Yet very likely it was wrong to remember ill things of other people. Why yes, it was wrong, especially if you are poor, and they are figures of might. What she thought of it would never change the way of life. There Darton was, sure enough, with his flag over South Spainers, West Indiamen, and schooners for the Banks. He never had enough. He

wasn't satisfied with freights of wine, or sugar, or fish; he
must have all. He was Branton itself, was Darton, you could
say with truth. His word was as bold as soldiers, and his
money was likely to be anywhere, keeping others out, and
keeping in those who peeped over his bars and gates,
wanting to get out. And some said his money, now and
then, was in ships that did not fly his flag, those ships
which loaded more than they were built to carry, when they
were as seaworthy as baskets. Well, well, the less said about
it the better. Not that there was much to say, or only what
you heard from sailors when the rum was talking.

8

Night Watch

THE shipwright stopped. He faced the outer, and surveyed the end of the promontory. "This light isn't enough for finding what doesn't seem to be where we put it," he said.

He clutched Aunt Ruth's arm to get her attention. "But somebody is out there. That will be a man. That will be Mr. Darton himself, surely, out there, do you think?"

Mrs. Penfold could make out a figure which might be that of a man, elevated at the extremity of the point. Was it a rock? No, it moved. She said she thought it must be Mr. Darton. "Nobody would be there at this hour," she added, "unless trouble took them."

Killick waited. Whoever it was must pass them, when returning. This was the only track. He remembered that for them to venture out there in a failing light was chancy, because the ridge of that outlier of the land was a slippery saddle of turf rounding to the deep. It was no jaunt for a woman. It was not safe for a man. They remained merely watchful of the offing in the last hour of the day, with Atlantic weather coming in, and it was uninviting. From where they stood and stared, speculative over a distant atom that might have been a man aloft in the brightness of the sky where the land ended, the track at their feet descended at first into a hollow, and the hollow was then filling with night. The Foreland already was cut off from humanity by the first incoming of the dark. Across that dusky gulf they kept vigilance on the lift of the headland as it stretched seaward. All its craggy bulk was outlined by waters that reflected the translucent sky. It was not easy to keep in sight there a trifle that possibly was one of their neighbours, cut off on a dim ruin that resembled a bygone age of the earth. That place, as they saw it, was separate from the accidents of humanity, was as vague as a fable out of unrecorded time. The monody of the surf and the cries of the sea-mews told of its ancient estrangement. Could anyone who had been caught on that separation from life ever get back? Its increasing indistinction was heavy on Mrs. Penfold's faith in the goodness of Providence, for night, and the booming of the seas, told her of powers that are not kind to men.

The little shape vanished. It might have been absorbed into the shades, or caught up by the wind, it was so insignificant and exposed.

"Coming back, whoever it is, I suppose," said the shipwright.

He spoke as if he hoped so, yet must wait and see. They waited. They felt they had allowed more than enough time for its reappearance, if they were to see it again, when stones were disturbed on the trail below them, and then a man rose before them, too tall and solid to have been the indefinite shape they had seen at the point.

"Ah, it is you, Killick. Any news?"

"No, sir."

"Who is with you?"

"Mrs. Penfold."

"It was kind of her to turn out."

"You see, her boy is missing, too, sir."

" I didn't know she had a boy. Which boy?"

Mr. Darton did not seem to want an answer. He turned to consider twilight over the waters. "The ebb is at two tomorrow morning. You'd better bring Mrs. Penfold along to my house. She mustn't wait at home by herself." He strode away and was soon out of sight.

Mrs. Penfold knew much about that house, yet had never seen its porch. All her life the clump of trees and shrubs within which it was embedded on the hill, and its white entrance gates, and a distant glimpse of its upper windows when the sun was low in the west, were as familiar to her as the chirruping of sparrows at the morning window and the sounds from the shipyard; but this was her first visit to it. The magnolia which had bloomed just within the approach to it every summer since she could remember stood far off, for it was within the border of a forbidden land. Crantock was well above the work of the town, while directing it.

She was lost in the dark when past the pale glimmer of the gates, and round the first bend. Killick had to guide her along the strange and unseen drive, where the wind blustering into the blackness of the trees was a worse worry. It was quite a roundabout walk to the servants' side of the house, she thought, but then she could not see very well. And the noble capacity of Crantock's kitchen, with its floor of stone flags, and a recess for its open fire as roomy as most bedrooms in the town, and more cosy, and the array of polished copper, brass, and pewter utensils on the stone walls, abashed her ignorance and unimportance.

But the thought of young Dave overcame all that while Killick was telling Mrs. Pascoe, the cook, the reason for Mrs. Penfold's presence. The cook, so tall, angular, and swarthy that she reduced the manhood of the shipwright, glanced sideways at Aunt Ruth without curiosity, and with hardly any resentment. Killick, more to be sociable in a domain felt to be wholly Mrs. Pascoe's than through inclination, explained what he thought was Lucy's chance

of survival, if the ledges could be searched soon enough; but
the cook made no comment. She wiped her hands with a
cloth as if clearing them of this business, whatever was the
end of it.

Her visitors stood for some time, not altogether
unembarrassed, before she indicated with a gesture that the
apartment was not without chairs. Aunt Ruth, unable to
converse when she did not know what to say, would have
returned to her own place, but remembered the difficulty
of the journey with rain coming on. Her feelings might be
anyhow, but here she must stay; and the kitchen was hot,
and so was she; her desire for the inclusion of Dave in
Killick's hopes for Lucy was acute, but not gratified; and
the cook's grim calm might have been resignation to the
fate of lost children, or disapproval of an intrusion she could
not resist, it was hard to tell which.

Gollop, the butler, appeared silently at the door, rather
like the impartial and sombre presence of fate in a bad light,
crooked a finger at the room but at no person in particular,
and said, "Come!"

He led them into the parlour, but without announcement.
The company assembled there seemed unaware of their
entrance, and of each other, for that matter, except that an
elderly man, lean and bronzed, whose blue jersey and
sea-boots were inappropriate to a fine apartment, was
talking to Mr. Darton with an ease not right in a fisherman,
however presentable. The man wearing sea-boots glanced at
Mrs. Penfold as in that grand saloon she edged modestly
round a wall, though not as if he knew her. But naturally
Aunt Ruth was aware that Mr. Silcock, the vicar, would
not recognise her. She went boldly to the Methodist chapel,
when she could. Not that she disliked the vicar, because she
believed, in softer moments, that he was an earnest man;
and indeed she did know he was as good as most of them,

for with her own eyes she had seen him take the lead in getting out a boat, and pull away like a bo'sun for the Five Maids, hoping to rescue the perishing, and the men at the quay unwilling, with seas vaulting the mole, till they saw the determination of a clergyman tackling a job not his, and he no better than a Papist.

Mr. Denny sat well back at the best end of the sofa, with his head sunk on his breast, and he might have been grieving, or asleep, or only bored. Uncle Tom stood with his back to the room, studying the fire. The maids were posed round the walls, heads bent, as still as caryatids. All the floor beneath the central crystal chandelier was left to the master and the vicar, until Mr. Darton beckoned to Killick, who went over to them for consultation, holding his hat before his breast in both hands.

That recognition was just. Captain Killick was the only one present, or in the town if it came to that, who knew the secret ways of local tides and currents, and what happened in any cove along that stretch of the coast when wind and water were at whatever conjunction. Though his hat betrayed humility, he did not. At the first question, put to him by the vicar as distinctly and firmly as a text, his bearing was as if it were his lot in life to attend to idle words, yet that folly was nothing much in a pleasant gentleman whose ignorance of things of first importance could be overlooked.

The captain contemplated a distant corner of the room regretfully, for a moment, while the company waited, and then said, "It can't be done, sir, except in daylight, by birds." He rumbled deeply his own opinion and his purpose to Mr. Darton, and departed, while they watched him go, though he acknowledged nobody there.

Flurries of rain rattled across the windows. When a gust was sharper than usual, eyes went instantly that way, as if to witness the entrance of the weather. The torment in the trees sounded like ocean's breakers sweeping the lawn. But in a lull, which promised easement, the watches of the gentlemen could be heard ticking excitedly, each in its fob, the only evidence of anxiety present. Mr. Darton put a foot on the curb of the fireplace, and an elbow on the mantelshelf. He covered his face with his hand. Mrs. Penfold was sorry for him, because she was sorry for herself. The clock near Mr. Darton's head chimed midnight, but he did not rouse to look at it. Only Mr. Denny glanced up in interest, and round. The London visitor was patient, yet glad to hear that at least time was moving. After midnight had struck, and they were in the first hour of another day, familiar household objects, seldom regarded with attention, became personal and significant. They took on that spectral appearance, as though changed in existence, which happens when a home, in silent misgiving, waits an event, and nothing comes to the watchers, except to hear the indifference of the outer dark, an indifference they already knew.

"Let us pray to God," said Mr. Silcock.

They all sought chairs, and went down on their knees. Mr. Denny knelt on one knee, in but partial submission, as a Londoner who could not be expected to show full abasement. Nor did he close his eyes, so while the vicar prayed aloud he was able to follow, through the back of his chair, the sly ways of Crantock's grey parrot, as it explored the carpet. He was also able to see the cook's legs, in white stockings, well displayed by a betrayal of her petticoats, an exposure of which she was unaware, and her calves surprised him. For so bony a woman they were remarkably full and round. The parrot, indifferent to prayer, also noticed them. He approached the cook, and experimented with the tags of her spring-side boots. Now and then she kicked out at the bird, which avoided her furtive thrusts with indelicate chuckles.

There was a pause. They were asked to help with their own silent supplications. When the vicar judged that this had been done, he rose. He went over to a window, watched in interest only by the bird, pulled aside its curtains, and peered out, as if looking for an immediate answer, but it was still dark. The clock continued leisurely to measure time. The wind dropped. Mr. Denny fell asleep, satisfied with absence of noise, if that were all the grace they could get.

Mr. Darton, sitting with folded arms, might have been dozing, but occasionally would open his eyes, quite alert, and turn his head, as if to catch a sound unheard by Mrs. Penfold, though she, too, was intent, though only in the mild way of habitual patience. The windows were showing as faint grey squares, and the vicar himself was overcome by drowsiness, when footsteps were heard outside.

Mr. Darton was up instantly, and Aunt Ruth, without invitation, or show of deference, went after him, unaware that she had bustled Uncle Tom into an inferior place. But the passage was unlighted, and she did not know her way. She heard a question, and Killick's answer in the distance. "Aye. We have them. Here they are."

9

A Word is Dropped

THE early sparrows were brisk at Dave's window. He could not see them, except as quick shadows on the white curtain, but they were happy. He could hear that. They chatted brightly to each other. It was not the sort of talk he had to listen to. Those two outside now, in the ivy, they were whispering in a hurry of a great joke. Didn't he wish he could get about as easily! They were not kept in bed, waiting for Aunt Ruth to come up and ask more questions. He hated questions, one after another before he had time to think, when he knew all about it, but it was a muddle. There is no sense in a muddle.

He was all right. It was wasting time to make him stay where he was. She seemed afraid he would die if she wasn't looking at him. That was why she kept him there; she knew where he was the day long. She had hidden his things, though he knew where they were. But nothing was the matter with him, nothing whatever, except a stiff arm through holding fast to that girl for hours because he was afraid of what a girl might do. They could not have fallen off, unless they went wild. It was only wet and windy and dark, but there was a fearful row going on and it was no good shouting. But you soon found the waves could not get at you. All you had to do was to keep still and wait.

Mr. Denny, who had called to see how he was, said that keeping your head when there was nothing to be done, except watch for a turn of your luck, was something not everyone could do. A youngster who could do it would get on in life. Mr. Denny was cleverer than the others. He knew more, so asked no questions, but told you stories instead. "You ought to go to sea," Mr. Denny said. "We want boys like you."

Dave hadn't thought of that before, or only now and then, but he was thinking of it now. He had been thinking of it ever since. And how much Mr. Denny knew of steam-ships! That was the ship of the future, he said. Not perhaps in our day, my lad, but she's the right ship to better hard times and beat the American flyers, no matter what people say about things they can't see ahead of them because they are looking backward.

Mr. Denny made a drawing, to show how steam drove through pipes checked by valves to turn a shaft round and round, but at that moment Aunt Ruth came in, when she wasn't wanted. He still had the drawing under the bed-clothes. She must have heard something about steam-ships, but she didn't speak. She only looked as if she was going to, and then changed her mind. She wasn't afraid of Mr. Denny, or of anybody else for that matter. She was only friendly, if she wasn't upset. If she hadn't come in when she did Mr. Denny might have told him more about it, more about that shipyard at Blackwall, somewhere in London, a famous place even Mr. Darton had never seen, and didn't want to see, so Mr. Denny said, where big East Indiamen are built, and fast frigates, and now they were building a ship of iron, to go by steam.

Mr. Denny pushed a sovereign into his hand, when Aunt Ruth left the room, and bent down and whispered, "They say it was your doing, but I don't. I've an idea, you young rascal, that Miss Lucy might not have seen her dear papa again if you hadn't made her behave herself. Eh? Certainly. She's well. I think she's quite well. But she enjoys a fuss. Pretty little ladies in bed often do." Then he winked, which was more of a surprise than his visit, and went. He said he was off to London.

Here they came, here came the questions! Aunt Ruth was on the stairs. But there was not much he could tell her. He pushed the drawing deeper into the bed. He had been studying it again. There was nothing else to do. She could always think of more questions than there were answers.

His aunt sat on his bed, comfortable and confidential. "Now he's gone," she said, "that smart fellow who fancies himself a bully boy—no, you'll stay where you are—I know what's good for you, if others don't. Him and his steam kettles! What does he know of the sea? He'd teach them who can use an adze as well as their grandfathers ever did how to build a ship, would he! There's no end to the crafty forwardness of Londoners. And now, Dave, come, I want the truth of it, this day. They're thinking at the big house you were nearly the death of their pretty chit. That's what they say. I don't know how it all came about, for you haven't told me yet, and I don't say I believe them. I've met too many liars in a long life to take every solemn oath that's sworn. But I'll believe you. What did happen?"

"Nothing much."

"I see. You're still going to be undercreepen, so you are. But that won't do for your aunt. Tell me where you met the girl."

"Down by the sea."

"Not near the town, I'll be sworn. She wouldn't look at you there, except saucy. Where was it?"

"I don't know what you call the place."

"Is it true you persuaded a girl to get into that fix, with the tide at the flood?"

Dave was silent. As well as he remembered it, nobody persuaded anybody. The sea did the persuading, and it would be idiotic to blame the sea. He bent his head, and traced a pattern on the bed cover.

"Did she show you the way to the ledge? I don't see how you could have known it."

Dave continued his invisible outline of a boiler on the quilt. A likely thing, to admit he was led anywhere by a girl half his own size!

"Nothing to say? Are you going to be a donkey, and take all the load as well as the stick?"

Dave's sinking sensation was that he would take anything, if only he could be still, and alone, and think of the things he wanted to think about.

"There's something more, and its vexing me. You know, don't you, that nearly all you see from this window belongs to Crantock? Mr. Darton is mostly everybody. We have to breathe his air. This bad job is going to make it hard for me, and that means you. That's why I want you to tell me what you know about it. There's nothing like a cold dash of common sense on a beginning of pestering twaddle. And they should have it, I can tell you. I'm not afraid of the town, though there are some there would touch their hats to Crantock's dogs, and bob to Miss Lucy's pony."

He was troubled by that, inside him, for of course he was fond of Aunt Ruth, but he kept his head bent, and went on tracing a picture she could not see any better than she could read his thought.

She sighed, waited a little, and then rose. "Well, Dave, I did hope you thought more of your aunt than to cheapen her before those who scorn her loftiness. All she owns ought to make her sing as small as the rest of them, and she won't, so how pleased they are, when her day is rainy!"

She moved slowly across the room, giving him more time. Dave did not know how to begin to tell her why it was he and the girl had to stay out in the wind and rain, for it was only what happened. Only the tide was to blame for it. He was trying to find words for so simple a matter, as he continued his tracing on the bed cover. He wanted to call out to Aunt Ruth that they were all off their heads, and there was nothing to cry about; but when she stopped to look at him, she saw how sulky and stubborn he was, giving her no attention. She left him.

He could hear her at work below. There she was, getting busy again. She was always busy, when she wasn't taking more care of him than he wanted. She hardly ever sat down, except to read the Bible at night, while he listened to her. It was the best part of the day. Her voice was not the same while she was reading from that book. You could believe somebody else was speaking, somebody whose voice was never loud, and who never gave orders. One day he told her that she had already done that room once, so why go over it again? And she said, Dave, there's often enough on the mind of a woman, though you'll not know it, for men never know, to tell her that if she doesn't keep busy she'll go mazed. She often used funny words. Did she mean wrong in her head? Sometimes he had an idea she really had gone crazy, for she blew up in a jiffy when he knew of nothing to make a row about; yet very soon afterwards she was as nice as pie. Now she was hard at it downstairs, and he was sure she need not do it. Trying to work off, he supposed, what she thought of him. It was not fair.

He began impatiently to examine Mr. Denny's sketch, though even then he could still hear her below. What could he do? He was glad Mr. Denny guessed how it came about better than the rest. It is some help, if only one person grins at what you did, while the rest pull long faces, or are angry. Do people, Dave wondered, ever get to know each other? It did not look like it. You may explain as much as you like, but you never seem able to clear up trouble so that nothing is left. A little remains, to grow big and mouldy again, as soon as you have nearly forgotten what it was about, and what you said. You have to be careful with words, especially with Aunt. Words change after they are spoken, or else they mean different things to different people. Bother that girl. It was unlucky he met her. He fumbled under the mattress for the round of the sovereign, to make sure of it.

He eyed it. Twenty shillings in that! It was the first gold he had ever had. He ought to go to sea, Mr. Denny told him. Ought he? It might be better to clear out, if staying there would make it hard for Aunt. Then she wouldn't have to worry. If he wasn't there, talk could make no difference.

Gosh, what a smash! That was a saucepan she had knocked down. She wasn't clumsy, either. She must be very angry with him.

10

Impressions of Seafaring

WHEN, a week later, Captain Killick entered the ship-yard, only a robin was there to eye him from the stock of an anchor. He was alone amid the suspended work, but to him a ship on a Sunday was more attractive than home or church. He had a bachelor's freedom and could please himself.

He went to stand under the transom of another vessel on the stocks, to clear a doubt or two about her. She was not yet in being; she was indeed but the skeleton of a ship, no more than an unplanked frame, bare ribs and backbone. The Captain took off his stove-pipe hat, not out of respect for this promising shape, but to wipe his brow; the day was warm. He viewed more strictly the grain of her stern post, and then went up to overlook her in general from ahead.

The only sound in the yard was the shuffling of his feet in odorous shavings of oak. He picked up a bright tool left out by a careless workman, and glanced round sharply before remembering that he had the yard to himself; he carried the instrument along, trying its balance. At a proper distance from the bows of the ship he spread the tails of his frock coat and sat on the gunnel of a boat, still testing idly the feel of the adze, and conned the ship, as far as she had got.

He judged she would do. She was all right, for what she was, but he shook his head over her. It was hard for a ship to satisfy him. This one was only up to specification. That was all. A larger craft would have been better, longer, deeper, and with less beam to the length of her, something to carry bolder spars. She wouldn't be weatherly enough. None of them were. He had told Mr. Darton so. But owners were afraid of anything above four hundred tons, though the captain thought he could see an ordinary ship of a thousand tons. He fancied that if he had the chance he could get a ship to point nearer to the eye of the wind, and that ought to save some miles in a passage of the western ocean. There they were now, sometimes taking more than a month to zigzag over to Baltimore. Such a waste of days! Mr. Darton said it wasn't; it was prudence. All he meant was that it was the custom of his house-flag. Owners always know more of the way of a ship at sea than sailors. So why talk? Keep your mouth shut and take your wage. Besides, think of the boss with that calm prudence of his! As if he never had a gamble when the dark seemed safe enough to hide it!

A gull brought up above the conspicuous stem of the ship to alight on it, wings thrown up for check and balance, and just touched the post with dangling toes before it sheered off abruptly because it spotted the shipwright. He chuckled at its instant departure on a change of mind. That was the way to think and act. But then, gulls aren't humbugged by a duty to keep a strict eye on the job, like it or lump it. You can never leave it as that gull did, come and go. There you are. You are wanted. You must settle on your post.

Killick meditated the edge of the adze. While still mindful of his duty, that tool took his thoughts back to young Bill Bence, carpenter of the *Columbine*. Bence chose such a funny weapon, being used to the feel of it, to repel boarders, one day off Java. What year was that? Now, how long had he been ashore? They all took hold of something handy that day. He himself picked up a cutlass, but not because he was used to the feel of it. It was all he could find. It was the day when last he had a departure from Java Head, and lucky he was to see it. Now he was done with the sea. He had been in this yard six years.

Java Head! He could see that landmark now. Nobody else in Branton had sailed the China Sea. You couldn't say a word about it to a man who knew. They were light airs in the Sunda Strait that day, and the canvas hanging asleep. It was the luckiest of first shots, that, when the Malay pirate was coming along hand over fist. The first ball clean bowled the rowers. Their port sweeps cocked all ways at the bang. So he never had his throat cut. It was a relief. To this day he did not know why that fancy brass gun went off. It must have been frightened. It often refused, when wanted for a ceremony. He made London Dock in ninety-nine days that voyage, though the *Columbine* had always been in the overdue class. And no wonder she had! They reef down, the prudent men, when the wind grows into power, and at night heave-to for safety, whatever the weather. That voyage he found she only came to life when driven. Then she flew. And who but an old petticoat would heave-to because it was dark?

He stood up, and as abruptly as the gull when it fled. That was all past. He pulled his coat to set it correctly, and then brushed from it the curl of a shaving, as though disposing of an inappropriate thought. He put the tool under shelter, and turned his back on the yard, trudging upalong to the look-out tower on the hill. He had a fancy to scan the morning offing. Nobody would be at the tower. This was church time. It was too soon to go home. His house wasn't big enough, and it was dull, when the sea was bright again from the poop of a ship homeward bound on a voyage long ago.

He was nearing the tower when he saw a woman's foot

projecting from it. Somebody was sitting comfortably within it after all. He hesitated. Should he go back? He had no wish for local gossip. Then he decided he would go on past it, right round the hill. It was too soon for indoors when the sky-line was sharp at twenty miles and there were craft about. When he reached the tower he met Mrs. Penfold's eyes. She was just within the shelter of it, sitting on a bench. He greeted her cheerfully, and she nodded with restraint. He was passing on resolutely, for he did not want to talk, yet felt that he was unkind. He paused, turning his head, and asked whether she had word yet of her lad.

"No," she said.

"You can't guess his whereabouts?"

"No."

She was not impolite, but her manner suggested that she was supplied with all the kindly enquiries she needed.

The captain never noticed it. He was patient with tempers unlike his own, a sailor ever suspicious of loose ends, and would frap untidy words, before leaving them, as he would the strands of a rope. He did not walk on, but studied his neighbour. This unfortunate woman was under the weather; but he saw, as he considered her, more than he expected. He doubted she wanted sympathy. She was bearing up pretty well. What was more, she had a good figure for her age, and though her face was comely it showed she preferred to give orders rather than to take them. Her dark eyes met his with an upward glance not unlike a warning of animosity, a glance that sent his own down to note the big cairngorm brooch at her bosom. She was a tartar, when she liked, he had always heard. Well, the poor dear was being tried, and the town was hard. These little ports were always very cruel with the whispers at their doors. He would rather face a mutiny than most of its women.

"Such a lad will be safe. He can take care of himself."

"In this world? Have you found it as good as a nursery for babies?"

Wasn't she prompt with her shot! This woman ought to have been a gunner. He was amused, and sat beside her on the bench. It was likely she was getting no fair advice from the people about. He knew them. They would take their cue from the big house, and she was not one of the sort to angle for smooth comfort.

Mrs. Penfold, however, disliked his comment. "Such a lad!" What did he mean by it? Killick, of course, was of Darton's ships, and knew nothing of Dave except what he was told. She was suspicious of the near elbow of a neighbour likely to carry a hasty word of hers to be passed about. And she was hasty, she knew, in neighbourly converse. She had better not ask him what he meant. She would guess it instead.

"Give him time to settle," said the captain. "He'll see to it."

"How do you know?"

"A lad as bold as that is quick off the mark. Stamp and go, you know, as men say at sea."

The sailor felt his companion move, as if what he had said was sharp; and in fact Aunt Ruth did suppose he meant that Dave, as a young rip, had made the right start from an awkward fix. But before she could speak she could hear people coming along the path, and waited. Then Mr. Darton and Lucy were peering sideways into the shelter with an attendant behind them.

Mr. Darton was unable to control his surprise. These two together? What had they to do with each other? His greeting was ambiguous. He glanced from one to the other quickly, and last on his shipwright, with little lines of humorous doubt about his mouth.

Mrs. Penfold was unaware of his ironic scrutiny. She was

observing Lucy. She was pleased to see that Lucy was a taking little maid, nicer than she had supposed; for Lucy was uneasy at this encounter, and her expression appealed to a matron, because it was forlorn. The dainty little mite! It was a mercy the accident didn't kill the child.

"When do you expect to hear from that boy of yours?"

Mrs. Penfold sat alert at the authoritative voice over her. "Sir?" she exclaimed.

"I've something good for him."

"Do you suppose I know where he is?"

"I've always thought you did."

"So I've heard, but that doesn't find him."

Mr. Darton frowned, and thrust at the path sharply several times with his cane.

"You could soon find out."

"In what way? Do you know of a way, sir?"

"Certainly I know a way, Mrs. Penfold. So do you. There's the police. That is a good way."

"Not for my boy. Wherever he is, he stays, if it comes to that."

"I speak for his good, and for your own. The lad wants discipline, and he'll have it in my yard. He shall go there. We can't have him running loose. He'll learn in the yard what he doesn't know, and what wilful boys must be taught."

"Yes, sir. What is that, sir?"

"His place in life, and the thing to do in it."

Mrs. Penfold rose. She wasn't going to sit and take this, wherever Dave might be. The captain was already outside the shelter, which had begun to feel close, and he judged it might get worse.

"Are you sure, sir, your yard always teaches what is right to a good lad?"

Captain Killick was embarrassed by this affront to an

owner, and feared the outcome. He attempted to ease the matter. "Remember that I'm in charge of the yard, Mrs. Penfold," he gently advised her.

But she did not look at him. She was facing his master. "I'll remember it," she said. "I remember more. I remember another boy who was taught his place in life. His place was in the *Ebenezer*. Where is he now? Tell me that."

The captain began to walk away, to wait at a distance out of hearing. He preferred to hear no more. Mr. Darton recalled him, and sent Lucy home with the servant.

"You stand by, Killick," said Mr. Darton. "You stay here. I cannot allow this to pass. You know as much of that ship as I do."

He turned in reproach to Mrs. Penfold. "That was not a proper remark for the daughter of a sailor, and the wife of a sailor, and the mother of a sailor, to make to me. You ought to know what the sea is."

"Well I know what it is, and the sorrow of it, the sea that is deep enough to hide its secrets till the Day of Judgment. If it isn't right to question you this day, sir, you will hear the question when the sea gives up its dead. For shouldn't you have called me the widow of a sailor? You know that's what I am. My husband sailed, and you remember when, and his ship was never heard of again. Whose flag did she fly? Yes, the *Ebenezer* flew the same flag. Now she's gone. I'm laughed at, I know, because I'm still fool enough to look for her arrival. But I know where she is, and why."

"And why?"

"And why. She wasn't fit to put out, that's why."

She felt, at the moment, much easier, though breathing hard. She had said it at last. She had often told him that, but only in day-dreams, while alone and working about the house. She had given it to his very ears now, and quite loud, and so it wouldn't haunt her from one month to the next, because nothing was done. She noticed his hand was shaking on his stick, and then saw real astonishment on his face. The man's nose was pinched and white.

She began to wonder. Was it possible he had never known what she knew? He felt this, she could see. Perhaps she had done no good with the truth, for he might have been innocent of it, too much of a lord to know what happened to his property. His mouth was a little open, as if he wanted to speak, but could not. Regret came over her, for pressing him so hard.

Then he found his speech. "Killick," he said, "you tell this woman. You knew that ship. You saw her leave Swansea. Well?"

"I saw her, sir."

"Yes, you did. Well?"

"I'm a shipmaster, sir."

"You are what? Of course you are. You knew her condition. That's why I ask."

"Should you ask me? I've already said. There's a report I sent you before she sailed."

"A report? I have many reports. A report?"

"That she was overloaded."

"What? Who said so? Why do you tell me that?"

"You asked me to tell you. That was my opinion."

"So that is all. Anybody else's opinion? . . . Killick, what's the matter? You know perfectly well there can be a dozen opinions about a ship's lading, and yet you talk of a ship's burden like a quayside woman instead of a sailor."

"Sir, there were a dozen opinions about the *Ebenezer* that day, when she was outside and under way. Her freeboard was a matter of inches. She would have been awash, but it was a calm day. I heard someone say, 'That ship will never reach port.' "

"Who said such a damnable thing?"

"The man who stowed her."

Mr. Darton's look of astonishment returned, and was bent now on his master shipwright. It was as though, when his gaze fell, he had to wrench away his regard of his man, for abruptly he went off down the hill.

They watched his swift departure. When he was lost to sight round a bend Mrs. Penfold sighed. The two stood in silence for a while.

"I know what this means, Captain Killick."

"You do, marm? I don't. But I know what some of it means."

I I

Ways of Destiny

As Dave topped a hill late in the afternoon, blisters on his heels pulled his steps. They told him he had walked far enough for one day, and that climbing steeply now was overdoing it. From the height he saw the way he had chosen had led him astray. The halt and the disappointment roused an ache in his shins, for he had driven his legs to put all the miles they could between him and Branton.

What an empty country it was, this Cornwall, and how misleading! The direction of his road had been just what he wanted, south-east. There below him it ended, square on the waterfront of a village. Another of those Cornish gulfs now cut him off. It was a strange land. It couldn't make up its mind whether it wanted to be gloomy moor or frightening coast, and tried to be both, so much of it was sea. A coast is all right if you are not tired and hungry, and know where you will sleep that night. He did not know his whereabouts, and the worst of it was he could not ask. What would the people down there think of him, if he asked the name of their place? Nothing that was helpful. It would only start them off with questions he would rather not answer.

He could see no way round this broad water, nor a means to cross it. As he was a Londoner, he knew how unsafe it could be to admit ignorance to strangers; that sometimes gives them an advantage they are glad to take. He wondered again, standing there, and no help near, what Aunt Ruth was doing then. The remembrance of her voice, at that moment, was plainer than the murmur of women gossiping below him, where the first chimneys were. It was also homely and comforting. Still, he tried at once to think of something else, but it was not easy to do that. His conscience was tender; besides, he had had all he wanted of one day of liberty. He was weary and hungry, and so felt affectionate, and willing to surrender to kindness. That was why he could almost see Aunt Ruth in her hot kitchen, which smelt of herbs, while she rolled pastry, her fat hands floury, her face red, and singing a song to herself. She always did that when making a pie. She said it made it light. A light pie! He supposed he was an idiot. If he hadn't met that girl, or even if Aunt hadn't dropped that saucepan, he wouldn't be where he was.

But he had that sovereign. He turned it again to be sure of it; yes, he had it. Dared he try to change gold? No, the first stranger who saw it would know it was too much for him to have. They would look at it and at the dust on him, and at the hole in his cap, and want to hear how he came by it. What could he say? Nothing they would believe. He hadn't got a likely story, and he couldn't make one up, not one that would go. He didn't mind telling a lie, not if it eased things off, and did no harm, but he wasn't good at it yet. His face always went red, if he wasn't believed straight away, and then where are you? And tell people the truth? Sometimes the honest truth is more like a bad fake than an artful whopper ever is. Dave saw what a tangle quite ordinary life can get into, when you are alone, don't know much, and either you yourself get the knots out of the mess, or you chuck it.

He couldn't do that. He would have to go on. It was too late to turn back. The moors at night would be worse than anything he was likely to find in this unknown village, especially if the black ghost-hounds people talked of were out hunting. Yet the folk below, he knew, would be un-smiling and cunning. The women yarning at a cottage door stopped their talk as he went by. He could feel their eyes on his back. Since leaving Branton he had distrusted eyes, especially if they made a mark of him. These people were suspicious, all for themselves, and when he could not under-stand their queer lingo—and who could, in a hurry?—they let him see they thought their growling dogs were clever and knew a lot. He went without stopping past a baker's shop, though it had a lovely smell of crusty loaves. There was another shop, facing the sea, and he ventured to loiter at its window, though it did not appeal to his nose. It dis-played compasses, tallow candles, grappling irons, fishing tackle, spy-glasses, clocks, lanterns, boat-hooks, a small dark barrel with copper hoops, a marine chart, a book on how to tell your fortune, and many things for which he could not guess the uses, but wished he could.

He limped over to a bollard, and rested on it, with the sea before him. He had a view of its bright level between the stern of one small ship and the bowsprit of another. Their decks were clear. It was a calm evening, and he had no idea of the move he had better make next. He wished he was waiting for nothing but supper—one of those Cornish pasties would do, though two would be better—and then upstairs to bed in Aunt's house, to listen to a wood owl in the dark. Since he had been in the country he loved owls. When you are safe in bed their notes belong to the stars, and to what Aunt had read out of the Bible. He wouldn't care what she said to him now. She could say what she liked; but she was miles away. He could not return. It sur-prised him that the world is endless, splendid, muddled, lonesome, wonderful, and friendless. Since he was resting he began to feel stiff and lazy. Somebody shouted, but he did not look up. Nobody wanted him. There it was again.

"Hey, you boy there!"

A man in a red and black check shirt was standing at the bulwarks of the nearest ship. His beard was black, he was wearing a black fur cap with loose ear flaps, so that only his nose wasn't hairy, though not far from it. The man beckoned to him. Dave limped over.

The man leaned heavy arms on the bulwarks and inspected Dave leisurely. "I'm told ye're a wrong 'un," he said at last, regretfully.

Dave shifted his feet. The comment was almost familiar. How did this man know?

"Where's the ship you deserted?"

Dave mumbled that he had never been on a ship.

"That won't wash. You don't belong here. How did you make it without a ship?"

"Walked."

"Not you. You ran. What had you been stealing?"

"Nothing, sir."

"Call me sir and I'll rope-end you. No sauce here. Are you honest?"

"Yes."

"Right. I think you are, you look soft enough." The man hoisted a demi-john and lowered it to the quay by a cord about its neck. "There's for it. That wants filling with porter. Over there. See the place? Be back in five minutes, or the blood-hounds will be out after you, and me behind them."

Dave was quickly back with it. It revived him, to have something to do. The man appeared, and hoisted it inboard. He weighed it with solicitude, and then gave the boy a reproachful look.

"How much have you swigged of this?"

"I haven't."

The man expressed relief. "No, you haven't. No time for

79

it. Right. Climb aboard and have your whack. You look as if
you want sousing. Always start that from the inside. Wash
afterwards."

Dave clutched the bulwarks to mount, slipped back, and
had to try again. This small ship needed more effort to
board her than he had judged. She was high, substantial,
and unhelpful. It was a long drop to the deck, which was as
firm as a street, and as wide and long as some streets. How
strange! From the quay she had seemed of no account.
Now the vane of the mast was far overhead in the evening
light, and the lower mast as thick as a tree.

"Come on. Don't stop to look at the old cow," said the
man. "She'll be just the same tomorrow, and a bit worse.
This way."

The man collapsed out of sight through a kind of hutch
on the deck. Dave overcame a little hesitation, and followed
him down, though not so fast, into a chamber with beams
that made the man bend his head to clear them. The room
was small, but its far end was in shadow. Three men sat
round a table, at cards. The air was bluish with tobacco
smoke, and that was not the only smell. Dave did not know
what the other smells were, except drains, perhaps, with old
rope, tar, and cheese. He was empty, and was not sure he
could continue to breathe down there, not for long.

The men at the table glanced up at him, but he could see
they did not care who he was. They did not look at him
again. They pushed pewter mugs over to the man with the
beard. They called him Bonser. Dave thought they were not
the sort of strangers he would have spoken to easily, in a
bad light, anywhere, but instead would have been happier
if they never noticed him. They were not noisy, but the
large and easy confidence in their attitudes was worse than
that, and they behaved to each other as if good manners and
polite talk should never be wasted on friends.

Bonser grabbed David, who learned his weight was of no account as he was half-lifted in one hand and pressed into a corner of the bench which ran round most of the room. This put him at an unlucky distance from fresh air and daylight. The man then filled a mug with brown porter for the boy, and brought out for himself a curved meerschaum pipe. He inspected its ripe bowl, which he gave a further polish, in affection, on his nose. Its bowl was carved and coloured as the head of a negress. Bonser cut tobacco from a black cake, ground it to fragments between large brown hands, and then poured the grains into the top of the woman's head. Dave had seen such a pipe in a shop, but had supposed it was only for ornament and pomp, not for use. This one was alight. The smoke from the woman's head became a coiling blue feather of fast growth and unexpected variety. The four men sat so absorbed in their game that the elaborate pipe, pendent from black whiskers, was most that was alive, and all that was elegant, and it took Dave's fascinated attention.

Dave drank from his mug respectfully, but not deeply. His gulps were judicious, as often as he could summon courage for another go. He was too polite to refuse it or to waste it, but he did not like it. He knew of nothing he could do with the inky stuff except swallow it, and that he did with fortitude, in dubious sips. The room grew warmer. That may have been why he had to rub cold sweat from his brow; perhaps it was that, or nothing to eat, or the smells, or he did not know what. He was sure he would never love ships. They were unsympathetic. If he had to take flight suddenly, could he get past these men? No, there was no way out. He wasn't sure, either, whether he could get up. He wanted to run out of it, and at the same time to remain very still, and preferably insensible.

He suspected at length that the fixtures about him were

becoming vague and changeable. There was no sure support to them. They moved about in a sly way. He noticed a little later that the negress's head, like the smoke enlarging from it, had a secret habit of swelling and diminishing. It would begin from the original small image with a trifling feather, and most improperly undergo a peculiar change while he watched. He watched her in fear. Her head would expand, to his great distaste, into a phenomenal face with volcanic brains. When Bonser threw down a card with a shout she reverted to a pipe, but Dave knew she was only waiting till the room was quiet again.

It was quiet now, but a lamp was alight, hanging from a beam. Was it night already? He had not seen anyone get up to light it. The men had not moved. Nothing had changed, except that lamp over their bent heads. The light was a miserable glim. It added to the smells mostly. It made the heat more stifling, and the fog of smoke thicker. It showed him that both sides of the cabin had a row of nooks, and he hadn't noticed them before. They were like boxes, or coffins without lids, for they were the length of men. If only he could climb into one of those boxes, and lie flat! If only he could be alone, stretched straight out! Either he was dizzy, or the ship was. Things were swimming round. The ship was turning about, though the men sat at the table, very still. His head felt no heavier than the smoke floating up to the lamp, and it was spinning. It was like that woman's head. There she was, beginning her tricks, because he couldn't see properly. Her head was growing larger, swelling up. It ought to be stopped, somebody ought to nudge the man in the red shirt to stop it, it was growing larger and larger, a horrid head with flames coming out of the top. . . .

Dave sat up. What place was this? The cabin scared him for an instant. Where was he? The pots and cards on the table told him, and he remembered. But the lamp was out, the men had gone, and at the top of the ladder was a square of pale sky. The air was shivery. Overhead he heard a cry, and boots stump along the deck. The ship was shaking; she seemed to be moving in fits and starts.

Yes, no doubt about it, the ship was moving. He must get ashore. She might be going soon. They had forgotten him. He was up the ladder in a rush, and from the deck saw in dismay a lane of water between the quay and the ship's side. She was clear. In the twilight forward two figures were busy by the bows. A headsail was going up. He heard Bonser's voice near him, and turned.

"Hey, what are you doing here?"

Dave explained that he must have been asleep.

"Asleep? Then you've done a pretty thing for yourself. You've woke up a sailor. That's a do if you like. Once a sailor always a sailor, till you fetch up with Davy Jones. Ever heard of Mr. Jones? Keep your fool's head clear of that boom. Watch it."

Dave watched it. Bonser took the tiller. The mainsail was hauled. A pallor was broadening the waters ahead of them, and it shaped Bonser, who faced it. His long boots, Dave noticed, could be worn only by a very strong man. Dave desired to be near someone who was large and confident, yet not unfriendly. The sea was close to the deck. He went to stand near the tiller. The boom swung over as the great sail filled, and the ship leaned to the wind. The water began to bubble alongside.

"Are you shivering, boy?"

"Not much."

"Right. Breakfast soon. That stops the early morning shakes."

Dave was not thinking of food. He had forgotten that he had not eaten for a long time. He ventured a question timidly. "Where is this ship going?"

"Don't ask. We never know. Sailors only try to get somewhere. As for us, there's a place called the Hole in the Wall. Ever heard of it? But not you. We'll try to make it, but don't talk about it till we're alongside, and not much then. It's unlucky."

It was a port Dave had never heard of. Perhaps it was only Mr. Bonser's fun, though there are ports with names you can hardly believe, and never spell. The ship's head pointed to chilling vacancy, pointed to nothing, for the grey was neither sea nor sky; but low down at one place there was a dull glow in it, as if a small fire had caught somewhere at the back of a drab world, and might soon burn through; so Dave knew they were headed about east, but that was all he knew. Where the ship went he must go, and he was neither glad nor sorry. He was cold. His head felt as light as a bubble, and his feet wandered separately on their own account, because the deck was uncertain. He couldn't guess which way it was going to slant.

The morning was raw and sullen, and he had an idea that a ship should not be steered carelessly where nothing could be seen but the glimmer of a dull flame; but there was Mr. Bonser, braced against the tiller, with his hands cupped before his face over a pipe. The nearest swells were glassy, but they were long and broad. Over the high land to leeward sombre vapours were rolling like masses of smouldering wool, for the fire had spread and was deep in them. The land was asleep. People ashore did not know, though he knew, that day was at hand. Very soon now it might be warm again. He hoped so.

The wind was spurting through his buttonholes. The land is not so bad. You know that when you have left it. It keeps comfortable under you. Some of the swells running after them were so tall that as they swept under the stern they pressed the deck up against his stomach. He had to step about to hold his balance. The land was asleep, not up yet; but is the sea never asleep?—always up, and the men upon it? Forward of the mainmast was a little house, with a thin pipe for a chimney, and the draught was tearing smoke out of its cowl. The sails blocked out overhead a very large amount of sky, rather too much. When she heeled to a stronger thrust, and there was a shout of waters, Dave remembered stories of ships that had turned right over. This one came back again, though, each time, and very easily, as if she were used to it. A block aloft was feeling miserable, and whining. That was the only sound, except the rippling alongside.

There came day. It grew high while the ship was still shadowy, and the silence of its quick coming was noticeable. It gave Dave the feeling that the day had come for him, though he did not know why, and that made its quiet more solemn. He was still expecting he did not know what, when they were sailing up a path of flames towards a crimson arc on a lonely sea. His ship, wet with spray, became a shining stranger, and Dave knew his own face was bright. Never before had the sun looked straight at him over the edge of the earth. Majesty, serene and in a flourish of clouds, rose above his thought and feeling. He forgot he was cold.

"Food at last," cried Bonser. "Down we go."

Another man went to the tiller. "That means weather," said Bonser to the man who took over, jerking a thumb to the scarlet smudge ahead, where a new day had begun.

12

Cabin of a Coaster

Dave was pushed to the far end of the table. He regretted it. He would rather have been next to the ladder. Before him was a wooden platter loaded with fried fish and bacon, and they lost their attractions when mixed on greasy wood. Aunt Ruth never treated food like this. She always thought of those who had to eat it. What was worse, a mug of beer was given to him. The cabin had the smell of the night before, except that the unseen old tarry rope was now on top. He was sure the smells of a ship were quite wrong. They were unlike all other smells he had ever rejected, not bad, but cruel, and there was no escape from them. They hung about to catch him. Even the wind on deck smelt strong. Would this be a long voyage? Bonser speared a hunk of bread and poked it at Dave.

"Come on, now. I've been waiting for this since morning prayers. Haven't you?"

Dave wasn't sure. He smiled respectfully, but his smile was stiff and not exactly real. His seat gently rose, and pushed him up with it, and then they sank together. This was a very difficult meal. His plate went before him as he sank, and it followed him up when up he sailed, yet he could have done without it. If it would only go away, go right away! This it did presently, sliding along to Bonser, who pushed it back as the cabin came level.

"Quick off the mark," cried Bonser cheerfully. "Show proper table manners in a ship. Don't look at your grub or you won't eat it. That's grub, that is."

This appeal to his better nature at least made him pick up knife and fork, but he had to swallow before he could begin to eat, and when he began he couldn't swallow.

Bonser was grave. "Wait," he said, "till you come down to hard tack, and a cut from the sirloin next the horns, and come you will. All proper sailors do, and die of it."

Dave knew nothing of hard tack as daily and deadly food, and cared nothing. In a moment it came over him that fresh air was better, and he left to get it. As he struggled up and out of the companion hatch, the bright morning fell on him. It was more than fresh. Its power and shine were overwhelming. Its flowing shadows bewildered the deck. The wind droned in the rigging, and the bulwarks were wet and harsh and differed from the horizon. The waters jumped to meet him as soon as he showed himself, and he had no time to duck. The spray smacked his face with a spite which seemed deliberate and was accurate.

The large and boisterous world took the heart out of him. He felt very unimportant, and not very well. There was but one refuge left, and he loathed it, but the deck was exposed to the grand rush of wind and light. He could only descend the ladder again. He did not bother about the men below. He had lost his fear of big men. Nor did he wait to be told, but clambered into a bunk as if it were his own.

Somebody laughed. Let them laugh. Let the ship go down with everybody. He collapsed, and kept as still as the bunk would let him. He shut his eyes on life, and tried to forget it, for it was nothing but a giddy-go-round and could not stop at sense.

After that he did not know what happened, or not enough to make a rigmarole. He remembered that a large hairy face stared down at him. And once a cold hand stole under his shirt and lay on his chest. He wanted to move away from it, but he was too heavy. He heard a voice say, "What's his name?"

Once the lamp was bright. It was dancing, and while it whirled about up there, sooty shapes leapt in and out of his bunk. They filled it at every jump, but he could not feel them. Then it was night, with a rumbling that never ceased. He was carried off on rolls of dark thunder. Something bumped about the floor. It trampled from one side to the other. It didn't speak, and it couldn't climb up. He waited for it to climb into the bunk, but it always fell down. Faces were black, and hands were heavy and cold. He was blown up high and fast on the rumbling, and could not catch hold to save himself. His arms would not move. They were dead. The dark was blaring. It was a great black trumpet pealing for ever. He wanted help, and tried to shout out, to wake up, to get away from it, but the noises caught him with a rush and swept him over the edge. He floated up and down on nothing.

13

The White Cliffs

THE hairy face was watching him, but it was daylight now, easy and quiet. It was pleasant to see Bonser there, though he was very solemn about something. He was frowning; but then suddenly he was larky, and winked at Dave.

"Here, now look here. When are you going to turn to this voyage? Haven't you had sleep enough?"

Dave wasn't sure whether he could do what was proper, but he tried to rise.

Bonser pressed him down again. "You're no sailor. What, show a leg till you get the hail? Stay there."

Then an extraordinary idea occurred to Dave, and he out with it at once. "I'm hungry," he exclaimed, to his own surprise.

"Give your orders. We're only here to wait on stowaways. What's your name?"

"Dave Gay."

"Right, Commodore Gay. What's your home port?"

Dave hesitated, not sure whether home was the same as port, but said he came from London.

"Right. That's the little town. London for ever. Do you know you're in the ketch *London Lass*? But I expect you've seen prettier girls. I have, and hope to see more. Anyways, she's come up Channel on a westerly snorter like a lost dog with a firework on his tail. The South Foreland's abeam this minute and it's a grand morning." Then he shook his head at Dave reproachfully. "But

I've thought now and then you'd reach port ahead of us."

Dave knew that yesterday, or some time before that, he would have climbed out of the ship, had there been a way, so he had no honest answer to make. Yes, he hated it then, and he mustn't say he didn't. But something had happened to him. He had changed his mind. How had that come about? He saw with pleasure, as if it were bringing good news, a shaft of sunlight. It slid down the ladder. It came half-way down, hesitated, and popped up again. It pretended it had gone, and then fell the whole length of the ladder and sat on the table. It was alive and playful. A draught stirred a smell of old rope, but that smell belonged to the cabin. He tried it once or twice, and then forgot it. He felt light and papery, and was afraid he'd blow away without feet when he got up.

He intended to get up. On the dark woodwork of the cabin, reflections quivered to and fro. That meant there was a morning outside which must be very sunny and warm, and he wanted to be up in it. The cabin, though strange to him in this light, was only plain, heavy, old, and friendly. Dave noticed its matured beams appreciatively. He rubbed his hand along the timber at his side. It was smooth and honest. He could hear the gurgle of waters on the other side of it. That trembling in the plank came when heavier water swept past. He wasn't going to lie there much longer. The South Foreland? He had heard of it many times. It was in history. If they had reached the white cliffs of Dover he was going on deck.

When he topped the ladder he gripped the edge of the companion hatch. He felt shaky, and on deck it was breezy and dazzling. The morning was a whirl of flashing lights and dancing waves all too quick to be seen at once. There were no white cliffs. The air sparkled as if the vast day were splintering in the wind, and miles of pale green waves were leaving all behind them in their haste to meet the sun. Glowing clouds were sailing fast the same way as the seas. The great world was gay and in a hurry. Nothing was slow and certain but his ship, with her stout bulwarks, her creaking old gear, and her deck seams running up and round into her bows. Bonser stood in the bows, his big figure uplifted and dark against the glitter ahead. He signalled with his arm, and the *London Lass* altered her course; as she did so her mainsail uncovered the land.

There it was; there was Albion. Dave went to the bulwarks, thinking to get nearer. Was that land? It was nothing like heavy earth. It was silvery and bright, like the morning. It floated buoyant and high, like the clouds. Its grass slopes, looping down between the white walls, were as pale as the green sea beneath. It was not old, nothing like history, but new as the day, and as delicate as silk, thin enough for the wind to blow about.

But there it stood. It must have been there, he supposed, and as he saw it, a very long time, unmoved by worse winds than this. Dave's thoughts, as he watched, were tossed about in the breeze, so that past and present, today's doings and stories of long ago, were mixed up with fleeting lights and the rush of wind and waters. Was it possible those ghostly cliffs and tinted fields above were there when the Romans came? Somebody touched him on the shoulder then, and he jumped.

It was only Bonser, who put one brown hand on him, and pointed with the other. Dave sang out. All the ships from everywhere were ahead of them.

"What is it?" he asked in anxiety, thinking of rumours of the French, and of war.

"The Downs," said Bonser simply. "See what a foul wind

does. Those outward-bounders are jammed up by westerlies. You don't often see as many as that. There's a fleet for you, waiting a fair slant."

"Are they all English ships?"

"Enough of them, Commodore, most of them ours." He spoke calmly, as if they both owned them, but were too modest to say so.

Riding the anchorage between the high coast and the Goodwin Sands were ships beyond count. They diminished out of sight far away into a brilliant and quivering distance. There were hundreds and hundreds of masts and a haze of spars and cordage with coloured sparks, for flags were flickering and tiny sailing boats were moving everywhere. It was a spectacle of assembled power. Dave in one long look learned more of ships and the sea than he had been told was there, for those who wished to know. It was too much to talk about. He was held by wonder.

"The best of them will soon be sheering clear of the trap," said Bonser. "They could beat down out of it now."

"A steamer! There's a steamer," cried Dave. "She's going now. Look! She's going fast."

The sailor eyed the little thing, but without a cry of delight. "Calais, that's all. There's nothing in it. She don't have to wait."

Dave watched her, and thought about her.

"So a wind can keep ships back as well as blow them along."

"Can it? It can that. You're learning, Commodore."

Bonser continued to frown at the steamer cutting across the channel, the weather notwithstanding, its tall slender funnel belching a black smother towards the anchored fleet of sailing ships as an insult, its body misshapen with paddle-boxes.

"She's no beauty," he said, "is she? And got no manners. She's throwing soot in the face of her betters. But there she goes, whizzing athwart wind and tide, and no sails up. What do you make of that?"

Dave did not know what to make of a novelty odd enough to take Bonser's eyes at sea, but certainly he could make out a striking difference. The steamer was the only ship he could see on the move.

"That's the way to do it," murmured Bonser.

Dave, still following the origin of the trail of smoke, supposed that his companion must mean the progress of the steamer. He was wrong. He had to be taken by the shoulders to face the anchorage squarely. A change was there. One mighty vessel, a line-of-battle ship, with three tiers of gun-ports, had all her canvas set, and was making off.

It was marvellous. He had only turned his head, and she came to life while he wasn't looking. Unless he had seen it he would not have believed so many great sails could be bulging in a minute.

"There's another," Bonser warned him, "that one astern of the man-o'-war—she's ready for the shout—watch her. Watch her. She's a Blackwaller. She's the ship for sailors—a square deal, and full and plenty, and a crew for the work—didn't I say watch her? There she goes, she goes!"

The Blackwaller dilated into a summer cloud with Bonser's words. Dave could have cheered, only he didn't think of it. At once she was moving and lovely. He forgot the steamer in the stateliness of a noble ship in the wind.

And there was no sound. He could hear only the seething of the waters alongside his own ship. The remarkable show of the sea and its business was silent. It was far, bright, but hushed as a vision of what had been there once on a time, all for him to see from the bulwarks of another day. The wonder of the sea under the vault of sun and stars is its silence. Ships in sight are soundless as the clouds. Famous coasts abeam are mute, are dreams that fade when you turn away, landmarks in history, memories of ages, dissolved.

14

London River

THIS ship, Dave supposed two days later, isn't getting us along. She wanders about. She may have flown straight up Channel like a packet-ship—whatever that is—as Bonser boasted, but he hadn't seen her do it; he had missed that. It seemed to Dave that you are sure to miss a good deal of what goes on in a ship, or anywhere else, however closely you watch. But she wasn't sailing along furiously then. By the look of it, London was no nearer than it was yesterday. Were they really making for it? First she sailed one way. Then over went the helm, and she was off in another direction, tacking about. And whatever she did, at the end of a spell, there she was, still abreast the same mark ashore. That church steeple remained abeam, as if it had the power to stop their ship from sailing farther. Shore marks never drop astern, Dave fancied, while you watch them; they are left behind only when you turn away and forget them. He turned away.

Bonser was bent over the windlass. What an enormous back he had, round-shouldered like a bear! And he could straighten a strip of iron with his hands. He liked Bonser. You didn't have to worry over what might happen when Bonser was about. The other men Dave never spoke to. They never spoke to him. He did not know their names, and he had a notion they preferred to have no names, and to say nothing. Once when he asked at table what the ship's cargo was, Bonser spoke, after chewing a little longer, and said it was fodder for canaries.

He knew now how to belay a rope, and could make a round turn and two half-hitches without looking, and a clove hitch and a bowline were getting easier. Bonser said you are a man when you know the ropes and can jump for the right one while the next chap is waiting for orders. Bonser spoke quietly to the other men, or only pointed, and they did what he wanted without answering. He was so easy you'd think he was lazy and would never get angry, but you'd have changed your mind after what happened that morning. It was just after breakfast, and he was at the tiller. Dave was watching another ship, like their own, drawing close to them. If it comes on much more like that, Dave was thinking . . . and then Bonser's voice went off like a gun. It could have been heard for miles. The other ship heard it easily. There was no collision, but that did not surprise Dave so much as Bonser's eyes and language. They were frightful.

Dave kept away from him for some time after that. He was a strange man. It would be very bad indeed to annoy Bonser. Yet, when next he spoke to Dave, it was only to poke fun at the *London Lass*. "She falls off. Now look at her. She gives way when she shouldn't. The best girls don't do it. That's because she's too plump aft as well as fore. Don't ever ship with that sort, Commodore. Don't take after me."

Dave smiled. He knew he could never be a man like Bonser. Hardly any men were as good as that. He asked when they would be on the Thames.

"On the which? Lord, where do you think you are? We've been on London River since sun up. Where's your nose? You'll not make a pilot if you can't smell your place in the dark."

Bonser went for'ard. This the Thames? Then why blame him for not knowing it? If that was another shore over

yonder, it was too far away, and too near the water, to mean
houses and people. The green land near them on the
larboard side was so flat that the white clouds sailing over
the cows and windmills were in the highest blue. It must
be one of the great rivers, this Thames, like the Nile, to have
so much water spread level with the land. There were many
ships about, though not one was near. And steamers? Why,
once he had only heard about them, and now they were
ordinary. One over there was pulling a ship-of-war along.
It was comic to see the great big thing meekly following a
panting little steamer. If only a steam-tug would take them
the rest of the voyage! The land would not move past them,
and the sky was closed about them for ever/

Towards sunset the opposite shore had come nearer and
plainer. The sun had a last flare-up before he sank up-river,
and set fire to the water, the clouds, and the land. Then he
was blotted out by dark smoke, but the earth continued to
shine with the light that had been left to it for a little while
longer. Astern of their ship the water was a mirror with a
barrel buoy leaning conspicuously on the polished glass. Life
ashore was a solitary heron flapping heavily over mudflats,
trailing long legs. The tide was against them and the wind had
dropped. They anchored. A lamp was hung on the forestay.
The men went below. Dave waited, listening for the silence
to break. There was plenty of silence; but he heard only a
steamer's whistle a long way off, which called over the water
so low and solemn that it was like the voice of the sadness
of things. Down below, there the men were, already at
cards, eyes fixed. They were too intent on what they held to
notice him. He might as well be alone. He would be alone,
for the rest of the night. Cards always did that, it was his
experience. But he liked the smell of a pack of cards, though
he couldn't play, and didn't want to learn. If you can't play
you are left out, and can please yourself what you think

about. Mother and Father used to play cribbage by candle-light for hours and hours, and stuck matchsticks in the cribbage-board to show who was winning. The kettle hummed on the hob, pleased with itself, and Mother was saying, "And one for his nob is nine." He wondered who his nob was, but forgot to ask. He must not interrupt, but ask some other day. He did not know then that the old house had not been always theirs, nor that soon strangers would be living in it. He tried to find countries for the kings and queens, while he was looking on. The best was the King of Diamonds. That was India.

In this silence he would soon be asleep. Even the mumbling of the men was underneath the quiet. It came up to him muffled with the shuffling of the cards. It made him sleepy. They seemed to be expecting something, or some-body. They were waiting. So was everything. Everything was waiting, except that moth, flying round and round the lamp, darting in circles, closer and closer. Next time it would hit the glass. Silly little thing.

He didn't want to see it burn its nose. When he looked again the lamp was out. No moth could put it out. So how long had he been asleep? For hours? He could hear nobody breathing in the cabin. The ship was still. It was very secret. Dave was puzzled by the fact that he was never watching for it when sleep got him. He could never tell whether he had been napping five minutes, or like a log for ages. He might sleep for ever, and not know he was going to. Not a sound above—yes, oars. A boat was nearing them. Here it was. No, it was passing them. That wasn't in a dream, that boat, yet he had been dreaming. It was that queer dream again. He had been flying over house-tops and hills, swing-ing up to clear a roof or a tree when he reached it, following that bird, that heron. It flew ahead of him, and he could hear its slow wings, beat, beat, beat, beat, very plain, and he was after it, rising and falling through the air. There was a bump, and the bird went. He was awake. But now all was still. Perhaps the bump was only part of the dream.

When next he woke it was morning. There was no doubt of that, though it was a woman's laugh which woke him. It ought to have been a dream, but it wasn't. There she was, smiling at Bonser, her arms akimbo, and nearly as big round as the sailor, but younger. Her bonnet was hanging loose behind her head, its silk strings very yellow on her white throat. Bonser reached for her bonnet ribbons and pulled her. Dave shut his eyes. It wasn't his fault he was there. She laughed easily, as if being pulled about was nice.

Dave pretended to be fast asleep. He tried to be more like a dummy than people asleep usually are. He wished he could not hear what they were saying; it was nothing much; it was giddy talk. It turned him hot because they spoke as if he wasn't there. He didn't want to remember Bonser in this: it was very unsuitable. He hoped they would soon go. He couldn't keep up this humbug properly, he was so uncomfortable. Then the woman said, "Hullo, who's this?"

"S—sh. Not so loud. That's the Commodore."

"Don't be a fool. Who's the boy?"

"Quiet. We don't want him about too soon. He's a foundling."

"Is he, though! Left on your doorstep?"

Bonser chuckled. Then Dave knew the woman was bent over him. Scent puffed across his face, and it was warm.

"There's one comfort. He's not as ugly as you. I like his dear freckled little nose." She touched the tip of it, and he sneezed.

"That's done it," said Bonser. "Netty, you'll blow the gaff some day, just to see the ruction afterwards."

She laughed again, with her head back. Her coral ear-drops danced. Dave looked up at her fine teeth.

"Did I wake you, lovey?" she asked. She ducked, and kissed Dave so quickly that in his surprise he was only able to keep his mouth out of it.

Bonser pushed her to the companion ladder. With his hands underneath her he hoisted her up the steps, which in her merry mood she found too steep, especially without a hand-hold.

Dave kept where he was, alert for the next sign. How came that woman there? From the shore after dark? Bonser sang out above. Then he heard that sound again, the beat, beat of wings, heavy and slow. Of course, it was a tug's paddle-wheels. That was what he had heard in the night. It was leaving them. He could hear also another sound, which was quite wrong; the noise of cart wheels on cobble stones. That quite irrelevant clattering sent him on deck.

The woman was not there; but he forgot her at once. The scene about him needed all his senses to take it in. There is not much difference between dreams and the way life goes. His ship was in the midst of ships, ships moored in endless tiers up and down a narrow river. It puzzled Dave that their own vessel had found a way to a berth through that tangle. Ships side by side were moored in a river sunk below the light of morning in a sombre chasm of wharves and warehouses. The grim cliffs rose above the mast-heads. The bowsprit of his own ship was pointing at the lowest window in a dank projecting wall. A little more, and it would have poked through it. They had arrived. This was London.

Still, it took time to believe it. It was too much of a change. The window ahead of them rattled, and a red-headed girl leaned out and emptied a bucket into the river. The splash she made was a certainty. She stared across at

Dave, then banged the window and snapped a curtain over it. That was real enough. So was the smell of the river. It was extremely bad, but not surprising when you saw the tide run by, and the stuff afloat on it.

He looked for the dome of St. Paul's Cathedral to make quite sure of his place, but it was not there. The western distance was difficult with masts and rigging, smoke and broken lights, and ranges of warehouse summits. He couldn't see even London Bridge. But this was London. No mistake about that. There was no other word for it.

A ship at sea, Dave now understood, never seems to be getting anywhere in particular. The sailors never name the place she is trying to make. They never talk of that, they talk of all things but that. Day after day you look at the same waters, and the clouds, and watch her canvas, or a coast so far away that it only thickens the lower sky. Her men do the same work about her deck as if that was what they were born to do, and it was hard luck, but there it was, and no help for it. Then, one morning, you poke your head out of the same old companion hatch, and cannot believe your eyes. It is another world. She has arrived; and you must take what comes in a place where nobody knows you, and nobody cares.

Bonser strolled aft. As if he had the ship to himself he was singing in a jolly way, too loud for a song of nonsense about the King of the Cannibal Islands. He stopped beside Dave, fists on the bulwarks, peering overside, still at it, "Okey, pokey, wankey, wum."

Dave was too shy to speak, but Bonser was hearty, as if nothing had happened just now in the cabin, so Dave ventured to point to the window beyond their bowsprit.

"Is that the Hole in the Wall?" he asked. He thought it polite to say something, and could think of nothing else to say.

The sailor looked down at him, frowning a little. "The which? What wall? That is a rum question, Commodore. Nobody ever heard of such a hole. I've never heard of it. What made you think of it?"

Bonser stood over him, Dave feared, waiting for an explanation of his curiosity. It was very awkward. The more Dave, staring at the deck, tried to recall the exact truth of it, now he had to, the more confused was his memory of what Bonser once told him of the ship's destination. He could not find an answer he dared give. What seemed right was not what Bonser appeared to want. After all, the name did sound like one out of a fairy tale, when attention was drawn to it. He looked up, ready to admit it was a name he might have seen in a book, but to his relief the sailor's attention was elsewhere. Bonser was only watching a ship passing up river.

"That's the old *Sea Queen* as ever was, that is," he meditated. "The old bitch. Fancy hailing her in fair weather. See her flag, my lad? She's one of Miles Darton's little lot. Mark it, and sheer off. He's one of the men who've made England what it is. You'll hear of him some day, if you're dummy enough to keep afloat. Are you? Let's look at your jib again."

He tipped up Dave's face, and studied his nose. "Right. That's the proper cut. You are fool enough for a sailor, just about."

15

In a Shipping Office

I T was in Piccadilly that the cabman, driving his new
Hansom, picked up his fare. It was Mr. Darton. More
promising still, it was as a footman let the gentleman out of
Lord Berrydale's house. The driver was hopeful of good,
because his fare, despite a request for Leadenhall Street—
which is too near Whitechapel, which you can't take on—
looked of uncommon quality. You can always tell 'em.
Drive a cab for any hail, and you learn. The proper toff
don't hail. Not as a rule. That's how. Why should he? He
has his own wheels and a pair o' good 'uns. But did you
notice the rig-out of the nabob inside? Only a grandee
would have the nerve to sport them old-fashioned togs.
Good as an oil-painting. And it ain't the boots and coat,
neither. Did you twig his mouth? Near as tidy a sharp trap
as the Old Dook's own, and a nose nobody ever pulled.
When he's the right sort, you'd fancy he wasn't sure you
was there, and was too tired to find out, and gets in. A good
thing this old swell wanted nothing worse than t'other side
of the city. This new cab wasn't going past Aldgate Pump,
no fear. What, with that inside it, looking over the 'orse's
back with a mug the spit and image of 'is Worship with a
bad case the day arter Sunday? Drive 'im past the Minories?
Ah, and 'ow get 'im out again, quite clean?

That morning in the cab the owner of the *Sea Queen* was
only a few miles from her, and was trundling along in her
direction. Mr. Darton, while noting in sharp disapproval
some changes in London since he was there last, suddenly

remembered that his ship might be docking in that hour. The tide would serve her. Then why not see her first, he asked himself, and the shape she was in? That could fit into the day's work very well. The dear old thing had arrived home in hard times with a freight waiting for her. She could begin upon that contract for railway material to Madras. It was sad she was smallish or she could take more. It might be true that his ships did not compare with the latest. He had never taken that from Killick, who had always wanted to go beyond the mark. Since then he had found that man was disloyal, and his word faithless. What had become of Killick? The yard was at a loss without him. But that man had to go. There was no alternative. Insubordination must be punished. Submit to it, and what could you call your own? A pity, a pity to lose Killick!

Yet in London he had been hearing much the same arguments, and from Killick's betters. They kept on telling him he was dropping astern of the times. By what bearings could they tell? For one thing, they'd all got steam on the brain, all except the best of them. But the confidence of the newer and reckless owners was ruffling. He disliked the speed and uproar of London. It unsettled a gentleman. At the end of the day he never felt as sure of his own mind as he did at home. Give London a chance, stay there till you didn't know how to get away from it, and it would rub out your past: nothing would be left of it. Then what would you have to go upon? You'd be at the mercy of frivolity. You'd get your head full of new ideas, all damnable. He'd even heard an argument for screw propellers for steamships; almost an indecency, that.

Something was wrong with London. Mad? Rather like madness, though perhaps monkeys are not mad because they are never still, and can't keep to one thing for five minutes.

London was full of meddlers and improvers, people who couldn't let things be. No rest at all. Change for the sake of it. Listen too long to their quick talk, and you'd believe, like a ninny, that the land of your birth was taking another shape under your eyes, and not to your advantage, either. You'd be of a mind to believe anything. He'd met Londoners who could believe anything at once; any nonsense, if it was new enough. They talked with long faces of these revolutionary times. But he could laugh at that. He would never see it, never. After all, what was it? Nothing worse than everybody's cowardly fear of the lower orders; of the Chartists, bless you. That was all. This agitation would go, when the wind shifted, like the smell of the drains.

Perhaps he had kept a little too strictly to the good old ways, ships and all; just a little. But the old ways had done what some of the latest notions had failed to do; they had paid. As for the thousand-ton ships they talked about, where were the cargoes for them, with trade what it was? It was hard enough to fill small craft. Mr. Darton then smiled, as if a joke against someone had occurred to him. He had just remembered that a few smart London owners, friends of his, would learn today that he had carried off that sizable Indian contract; had lifted it off their own doorstep while they were talking of trade, instead of making it. That was worth coming up to town to do, wasn't it?

Mr. Darton rested on this joke to get the most out of it. He had overreached the clever ones. Let his ships be whatever they pleased to call them, it was not every owner, when Indian contracts were going, who could breakfast with that irascible old rajah Berrydale. He'd tell the cabman, when Leadenhall Street was reached, to drive right on to the dock. That was the thing to do. His London agent could wait; he'd see Cree afterwards.

He didn't care much for these Hansoms. Anyone could use them. What sort of person was last in this cab? London life was too free. Distinctions are forgotten where things are in common use. The sooner he was out of it the cleaner he would feel. For though Mr. Darton had a kindly contempt for Londoners—they were friendly, but too spry, too presumptuous, even with men and affairs of note, as if the world were their skittle-alley—yet he could not repress a touch of anxiety when present with them in their own place. Why should Thames owners, and a younger generation at that, show so much confidence when most of them would be lost in a shipyard? And he had his own yard, and a good one it was, and it had been his grandfather's. He dwelt on this. What was it they knew that he did not? In London he could not help a suspicion that there were movements not discernible, for which he had no guess, and he never felt that in Plymouth and Falmouth. It was a dangerous place, this city.

The truth was, he conjectured, that it was safer for a visitor not to feel too sure of himself in London. He had to learn where he was. The streets knew more than he did, if he could only get at it. He had best listen at the walls. But, the difficulty was, a whisper might be important, and the shouting of no consequence at all.

London was bigger than the biggest man, and had a drift of its own. It cared nothing for the importance of the Duke of Wellington himself. He had discovered that. You are nobody, or not much of anybody, while there. It doesn't matter if you did win the battle of Waterloo. You are looked at respectfully only if knocked down by a cart. There was redoubtable Berrydale himself, that man, showing nerves over Parliament and its goings-on. The political hocus-pocus dithered even his lordship, or why did he work up into so angry a fuss over Cobden and Ashley? Why take those reformer cranks seriously? It was against nature, against justice; it was a mockery of every proper human instinct that a man's right to do just what he liked with his own ship, or factory, or coalmine, or whatever it was, should be taken from him. What would property be worth, if outsiders could meddle with it, if Jack were as good as his master? And it was talk suitable only to Bedlam, this about making British trade free to all. Throwing the country open for foreign corn and all else. Cheap corn for cheap labour, so they said. What would be the price of land, if bread could be had for the asking? They were talking of making British ports free to the flags of all nations; they would repeal the Navigation Laws; yes, they'd do even that. Moonshine! All moonshine!

Yet Mr. Darton, despite his vehement rejection of the new insistencies, could not get rid of a fear, after his morning with Lord Berrydale, that powers were at large of which he knew little or nothing. Suppose lunacy became general? London tended to lunacy. London, Branton, and Bristol, free to any foreigner who wanted to come in and trade? He knew of one sound Briton who would sooner sink his ships, close his yard, shut up shop, than agree to the ruin of his country.

Mr. Darton's cab checked abruptly, and he was jerked forward out of his reverie to rest on his hands clasped about the ivory head of a malacca cane. A procession of hay wagons was in his path. That brief halt gave time for him to note a further difference in London. A building faced him that had arisen since last he was that way, and its magnitude and gravity were intimidating. A wide ascent of steps led to the Corinthian colonnade of a grand portico. Within its entablature, still incomplete, and overlooking the Bank of England, were graved the serious words: "The Earth is the Lord's, and the fullness thereof." This, then, was the new Royal Exchange? That reminded him of Lloyd's; its headquarters were hereabouts.

His cab jolted forward again. The movement shook him clear of a disagreeable thought which had begun to form. It concerned the insurance of the *Judith*. He must call at Lloyd's to see her underwriters, after he had been to the dock. They had demurred. At least, they had put a question to him aimed straight for the truth of it, in the way of Lloyd's. But Lloyd's underwriters were gentlemen. They never hedged over money matters, not if you could satisfy them; and he hoped he could always do that, please God.

Here was Leadenhall Street. Mr. Darton signalled the driver to stop. He wanted him, he said, to go straight on to the St. Katharine Dock.

The driver appeared to be surprised, but he said nothing.

"Did you hear? You know the dock, don't you?" Mr. Darton was genial and bantering.

The driver shook his head in finality, slowly and ponderously, for it was surmounted by a tall hat. He did not know the place.

"What?" This ignorance was unbelievable. Mr. Darton was astonished, and almost indignant. "I've been told you drivers know every place in London."

The driver stared down at his fare in reproof, as though an obliging and humble servant had not expected this sarcasm from a nobleman, but he did not answer. He regarded Mr. Darton as if his feelings were too good to waste on one who was treating him unfairly.

"Then I will alight here. I was sure any driver would know his London. I've always been told that of you men."

"Some people will say anything. London I knows, of course I knows it, but it's my London."

"Then how many are there?"

"Why, sir, I'm a bad 'and at countin' above a lot. There's lots of Londons. There's one for you, and one for me, and one for everybody, and Aunt Jemima's got 'er own. That's London, that is. And when you knows it, believe me, it's as much as you can 'old."

"And yours doesn't include the docks?"

"Sir, if you know'd what my London was like you'd ask for Turkey. You certainly would. 'Ere, what's this? Beg your pardon, but if you was in my place you'd want another five bob."

Mr. Darton was still annoyed, yet seeing that face above him under its topper, leery but rosy and cheerful, and its body shawled on a day of summer in readiness for snow, he handed up more than the overcharge, while knowing he was acting in weak generosity.

The cabby made a feint of spitting respectfully on the money, and leaned over in hoarse confidence. "As you're a toff, guv'nor, and looks it—and looks it, I say—let me tell you something you don't know. Keep away from that 'ere dock this morning. It ain't your style. Give Tower Hill a miss." He then gathered up his reins, and his horse struck sparks from the stones in its promptitude.

"Hey! What's that? I say there . . ."

But the cab was lost in the traffic. What did that fellow mean? Mr. Darton forgot his whereabouts in his distraction. He glanced sternly round. He was, he saw, by the severe front of East India House; across the street, outside a tavern he knew, was an inviting legend, Pine Apple Rum. He crossed to St. Mary Axe, and turned left into such a warren of narrow passages penetrating buildings so old that men might have been secretly busy there since the beginning of time, and inadvertently had shut in below a fair weight of aboriginal night; or else, in building a city, they had tried to keep plain daylight from squeezing right down to the basement of their activities, as it was not wanted.

Mr. Darton did not remark this. He was on familiar ground. This was the path to his London agent. He did not give a glance to the mullioned windows and oriel of Crosby Hall, did not pause to consider that ancient palace, once occupied by Richard III, and so was not reminded of the odd chance that London has a store of memories so ancient and occult that there is no telling how a day and its generation may be affected by influences of which it knows nothing. He went in at a door with a brass name-plate, John B. Cree, and ascended stairs in twilight to a landing, where a window allowed a little of day to placards fastened in frames to a wall. The placards invited freight and passage in a number of ships, which were conspicuously named.

There he paused. No meeting of importance, no crisis in life, could make him overlook, or treat slightingly, a word about ships. He put on his spectacles to read the sailing-bills, which were as good to his heart as news from home. Those placards, to Mr. Darton, were more than art, more persuasive than pictures or tapestries. They were real. The bills advertised those new and fine brigs, *Whipsiderry, Oxshott, Beulah,* and *Leyton,* of the highest class at Lloyd's some with accommodation for cabin passengers, for immediate dispatch to Port Royal, Santos, Savannah, and the Guinea Coast: apply to J. B. Cree, loading broker, for passage or freight.

Mr. Darton folded his spectacles. He was content. These ships were orthodox. His own best were not outclassed by the finest of them. The only novelty was one whose timbers were kyanized; but in his opinion it was a waste of money to use stuff to prevent rot in woodwork; more than that, it would surprise you to learn how long a ship's timbers will continue to hold together, after they are said to be rotten and dangerous. He knew of a ship, and could name it in confidence, which did not fall apart till on a voyage two years—no less—after he was advised she ought to be broken up. Always risk it. There is less risk than fear ever anticipates, it was his experience. He opened the door to the general office of his agent.

Bonser was sitting within, waiting an audience. The sailor started as if to rise respectfully to a ceremonial entrance, but then remembered Mr. Darton would not know him, though he knew Mr. Darton. He saw also that now he would have longer to wait, but his annoyance was lost in his beard. Mr. Darton, without speaking to the clerk who came forward, inclined his head towards the private room, and the clerk nodded. There is no need for talk where there is privilege. Bonser was left with the mahogany counter to look at, its leaden ink-pot crowned with a circlet of quills; and when he had done with that he could go on to the moon-faced wall clock, and roam his gaze round the shelves loaded with yellow wooden boxes, each box bearing the name of a ship, some of the names suggestive of more than will ever get into print. There were also the backs of three clerks astride high stools under the windows; and a coloured lithograph over the mantelshelf of the clipper *Lalla Rookh*, repelling Ladrone junks off Loochow. A smell lingered in the office of burnt sealing-wax, a little stronger than that of old ledger books, and of the samples of spices and gums on a side table. Bonser did not care for these trifles. He was indifferent to all that pertained to quill-driving. While appearing to be deeply interested in his discoloured knuckles, he was hoping he might hear a bit of what old Cree was saying to old Darton; or the other way about would suit him. But he could hear the clerks scratching with their pens, and the clock measuring the length of his patience, and that was all.

The clerks knew that nobody ever heard what their principal said in that room, except the person he addressed. They had often listened, in hope, but not with good luck. Mr. Cree never raised his voice, even when a mistake or rude ignorance was provocative. Just then, he and Mr. Darton met each other as men who could indicate casually how matters stood between them, without stress. They knew each other well, though the advantage was with the shipping agent. He was not really old, except in the sense that his height and bearing hinted at authority he did not care to use, unless driven to it. The agent's gaze rested kindly on his visitor, becoming stony only when he dropped his eyes to consider an uncertainty.

Darton knew there were times when Cree would take a stand from which nothing could move him. It was certain that Cree knew more than he ever let out, but so plain a business discretion could be approved. He had the odd fancy, too, that his agent was somewhat peculiar, as if he might harden into another person when alone. It was not easy to make him out. Besides, Cree belonged to that extraordinary body of cold-blooded worshippers—if it could be called worship—the Unitarians. How a man of intelligence and high principles could fail to own up to the Trinity puzzled Mr. Darton. But that defect did not count where ships were concerned. The Bible has nothing to say about charter parties and marine insurance. He respected character in another man, though it was weak in religion, if it could be left to work to his advantage. He had often pointed out that you had only to look at Cree to know he could be trusted, unless you tried to be clever with him. Cree would hold to an agreement though he lost on it, and there were unfortunate bonds, Darton knew, that would try the soul of a saint. Every merchant knew what that sort of thing was like. At the same time, it would do nobody much good to try to outsail Cree and make port without him. He had seen Cree indignant once, and once was enough and an eye-opener. He was very amused that day, for it was no business of his. Somebody else was going to suffer for it.

They had arranged for the new Indian contract. Mr. Cree was glad to hear of it. It would be necessary, they agreed, to charter three more vessels of fair size, but the agent knew of a large choice on London River. Tonnage was going begging.

"Begging it is," complained Darton. "What's wrong with the world?"

Cree smiled slightly, as if he had thought about it, and had a notion, but knew the cause of the trouble could be found only by those who would look for it. He did not answer. He clasped his hands behind his head, and his fingers were lost in his thick dark hair. He crossed his legs leisurely, still smiling absently.

"Agitation," went on Darton, "all over the country. Riots in the north. The yeomanry out in some places because the soldiery can't be trusted. Potato famines, ships idle, and of course the money not coming in. I don't know what to make of it."

"Nobody does. But what else would you expect?"

"I? Expect? Something quite different, Cree. I expect a firm government, for a start. I don't expect riots and agitation and other interruptions to be allowed to go on to disrupt our reasonable existence. I want peace and quiet."

"So do most of us. What could be better? But perhaps all good things must be earned, even peace and quiet."

"Earned? Perhaps so. But famines, and hungry mobs howling! What have you and I done to make famines? We haven't earned famines. Quite the reverse. Very much the other way about."

"Then I don't know what to call it, except the will of God."

The cool suggestion did not soothe Darton. He remonstrated. If it was the divine will, then nothing could be done, not even by a strong government. That was nonsense. Something must be done. He was overcome by resentful energy, and began pacing the room. London was getting on his nerves. Here was Cree, too, accepting disturbance and disorder as he would fate or wet weather, just as did Berrydale. There's nothing to be done with wet weather, of course, except put up with it. He paused as if to consider how a supposed superhuman ordering of business affairs could be outwitted, while eyeing a daguerreotype on a bracket. The portrait began to fix his attention instead. That was a remarkable head. He did not know it, but he disliked it, as if unlucky fate were personified there.

"This is a wild-looking fellow here, this," he said. "I fancy I've seen his face before. But where? It's impossible."

"Not at all. I expect you have seen it, without looking twice. It's been in the *Illustrated London News*. But it isn't wanted here." Cree strolled over, took the picture away, and put it in a drawer, saying, "That's Feargus O'Connor."

"Good God! The firebrand? The Chartist?"

"The same. That's the man," said Cree, shutting the drawer on the offending likeness.

"What the devil is he doing here? He's no friend of ours."

"I don't think he is. Perhaps he isn't a friend to himself. But I want to keep reminded of him. His phiz got in here with the unconsidered bric-à-brac." Cree was indulgent with the ill-omened name. "It's better to know the facts that affect our lives, all of them, if we can, though we can't expect to learn of more than a few. O'Connor is one of the facts."

"Transport him, slip him off to Van Diemen's Land, away with him."

"What if we did? He would still be all alive-o under the sun, and his pals would be here. The way of the wind would be no different."

"Then do you take seriously this threat to everything that has been satisfactory to us?"

"Certainly. Our old and pleasant established order is not as steady as it was. By the look of the sky, shipowners and all had better snug-down for hard weather."

To hear a sombre opinion from nobody in particular, such as Uncle Tom, who read too many books, having nothing else to do, was one thing. It could be dismissed with the day's nonsense. That could not be done with what Cree thought. He was big enough, standing indolently there, to block out much of the window light, and had often volunteered good advice about what to do next with a ship which proved to be right, though at the time one hesitated about taking it. Suppose there was something now in what he said? You were told things in London which seemed against common sense, and gave small attention to them, but afterwards wished you had not been so careless. Cree was as disturbing as that cabman just now, who first pretended he didn't know St. Katharine Dock, and then whispered advice about not going near the place today. Why? He mentioned the ridiculous incident to Cree. It was related to his dislike of all that was disorderly in this confusing city.

"Did he though!" said Cree. "Then I suppose they're at it again."

"Yes? I don't understand yet."

"It's nothing. Tower Hill is near the river moorings and Wapping. It's a gathering ground when they're excited.

They get rid of their feelings on the hill—always have done so."

"They do? They? Who are they?"

"The people we never meet. There's a large number of them. They're the background to the show, and if they crowded forward they would occupy the stage and push us off it. Wait. There's a man in the outer office who must have come here by Tower Stairs, I suppose. He'll know. We'll ask him." Cree went to the door and called Bonser in.

"I'm told by my friend," explained Cree, "that a cabman refused to drive him to St. Katharine's today. It wasn't safe, or so he said. What was it like when you came through?"

"Why, not what you would call rough, sir. You could fight a way through, if you tried. Some peelers' toppers were in the gutters, but I've seen more."

"Attacking the constables?" cried Mr. Darton.

"No, sir, I wouldn't say that, not altogether. Not treating them disrespectful. Playful with their hats, that's all. It wasn't a real do. It was only a sailors' outing."

"So my friend could have got through to his business?"

"Ah! Come to think of it, sir, nobody ever knows what sailors out for a lark will do next. It's a bet on a dark horse. I'm sorry to say it, but I've known them go as far as mistake a well-dressed gentleman for a shipowner. I have that."

Bonser gazed sadly at Mr. Cree, and Mr. Darton regarded the dark mask of the sailor with strict attention.

"I ought to know a sailor when I see one," said Mr. Darton, "and you are a sailor, if I mistake not."

"No mistake about it, sir. I'm one all right, off and on. Off, as often as I can make it."

"You mean you don't go aboard when you can avoid it? I'm sorry to hear that from a good man."

"I'm as sorry for it as I can be, but to tell the honest

truth, sir, I'd as lief have something to eat and a dry bed any day as sea air. I don't like an empty belly and a wet back. It's a weakness, and I own to it."

"Thank you," said Mr. Cree. "You've told us all we want to know. I won't keep you waiting much longer."

16

Quality Street

As he left Lloyd's that afternoon, Mr. Darton felt a kindlier regard for a better aspect of London. He was content. He had found, as he expected, that the underwriters were gentlemen. They had accepted without question one of their own sort when they met him. They would pay up. And why not? Thus a slightly difficult matter was overcome. He confessed, without a grudge, that those tumultuous streets radiating from the Mansion House were doubtless of a great and superb metropolis.

Now it was time, perhaps, for him to present himself to Lady Geraldine. This was one of her days to receive, and he was almost in the mood for it, though not quite. Still, it was no good putting it off till he would feel at ease with her ladyship, when she had company. She was an unusual woman; gracious enough, to be sure, and ugly enough, despite her noble lineage, to put a man at his ease. But the world she enjoyed was not his; nothing like it. Who would not feel rather out of it, at one of her receptions? Nobody, except the griffins and queer fowl it pleased her to gather at her Town parties. Yet at least it was his duty to call, since she would know he was in London. A call would be neighbourly, for her husband, at their seat near Branton, was always in comfortable agreement with him; never a ridiculous novelty on the premises, nor anywhere near the park walls. Here in London it was different. His lordship took to his club, not wishing to meet her ladyship's lions on the stairs; he might be at home today, in a corner, looking on genially, but afraid to speak, or he might not.

She was fashionable, but much more than that. For one thing, she might be not long back from Florence, or Seville, from some Italian or Spanish city, and would amiably assume he knew what she was talking about so lovingly. It was too much to expect of a busy man. Mr. Darton felt he would be delighted to see her, if he could be sure her house today was not a den of young and hairy beasts, poets, philosophers, and politicians, that sort of thing, and all the better for it if a smell of scandal hung about the most peculiar of them. She was indeed a very dear and distinguished lady, but she was too tolerant, and knew far too much. The last time he was in Berkeley Square she introduced him, before he knew what was going to happen, to that latest forthcomer, Gladstone, and he felt at once as if he was an idiot child, as well as dumb, though not deaf. It was quite a relief when she brought along another oddity, with a face very like the amusing gargoyle above Branton's church porch, who, she explained, had just returned after five most interesting years on the Orinoco, catching butterflies. Butterflies! Five years of it! Orinoco was written all over him. He did make one remark to the fellow. Why go so far for insects? And the fellow answered that he went because he wanted to, and walked off. Her town house would give you the idea that anything could turn up in London any minute, and it was bad manners to show surprise.

When he arrived, at first he was charmed. Lady Geraldine, he thought, was top-gallant in height as with hands outstretched in full welcome she sailed across to him, in style. This, he knew, was to let others see he was an old friend. She was as plain as ever, yet her billowing silk in her sweeping approach was right, in the space and elegant simplicity of her parlour. Her pale face was out of place at Branton, but the old oak panelling of this apartment, with its austere ornaments and long mirrors, belonged to its mistress. And how many mirrors there were! A man was frequently surprised, and sometimes hurt, as he talked, through catching a distant glimpse of himself that must be real but was no better for that. In that room she could make a nobleman doubt his feet were rather large. But then, she could also give a visitor the idea that, after all, an elegant setting was his by right.

As was her way, she went on to ask in an anxious whisper whether his ships were all safe, and he laughed. Really, she didn't want to know, for she hauled him off at once to a thin man sitting shyly by himself on the edge of a gilded chair taking tea as if he didn't want it, and asked, " Have you met Mr. Lovett?"

No, he had not. All the same, he was glad to rest beside so quiet a fellow, who had nothing against him except his expression of pious melancholy, dress and hair to match, all black, a funeral undertaker; yet who soon was speaking of affairs as they were, quite sensibly. They were deplorable. So they were. The stranger appeared to have the rudiments of intelligence. It was easy to agree with him. Mr. Darton resolved to remain as long as he could where he was safe. Her ladyship had disposed of him, for a change, without resource to a lion as a special treat, and he was at ease. This man Lovett was a friendly person, perhaps a gentleman, who supposed that what the lower orders ought to have was education. That might be going too far, he admitted. There was no need for everybody to be able to read and write, but perhaps it could not do a disastrous amount of harm.

The visitors were beginning to besprinkle the room, and his hostess was busy, but Mr. Darton was careful to avoid showing interest in anybody till he saw Uncle Tom enter, accompanied by Cree. Cree? What on earth was he doing there? And they came over and greeted him, and this man Lovett, as if it were a hopeful sight to find the pair of them confabbing amicably. Even then Mr. Darton had to listen to a length of puzzling gossip before he discovered, with pain, that the guest to whom he had allowed himself to be attached was the notorious working man and offensive outrage who wrote for newspapers of the deepest and bloodiest red.

Damme! This was just like Lady Geraldine. Yet, it was extraordinary, Cree had greeted the firebrand lovingly! Even Tom had whirled a handy chair round and settled down as if he had hit on the right man at once. Mr. Darton was chilled, and left them to it. No doubt socialism and republicanism were becoming prevalent. The subversive stuff was brought out to be examined in the least likely places; but it was beyond tolerance, and below courtesy. It profaned a silver tea urn, footman, and rare china, in a nobleman's house in England.

It showed how this gadding about Europe, where the very thrones, so the news went, were getting shaky on their pins; this knowing your way about Paris and Vienna as easily as Lady Geraldine, when you don't know what bread is made of at home, and who bakes it round the corner, would soften the character of a duchess; and, in the meantime, what became of her ladyship's aristocratic principles? It was lucky there was an English Channel. That would always keep most people quiet and in their proper places. A providential ditch, that Channel. There's no nonsense about the sea.

Lady Geraldine at that instant was indulging her eager fancy that what her guests ought to find that afternoon was not sociability with luxury, though that was delightful, and in her house was natural, but persons and opinions to suggest the enchanting mutability of a marvellous universe. Occasionally this caused an accident to a cup of tea. A lady whose simple devotion to heaven above necessarily put Rome in the place beneath would find, all of a sudden, that the gracious cleric to whom she had been confiding some aspects of her soul was in fact one of the militant Tractarians, and remained a friend of Newman the apostate. That shook the nerves, and the poise of the innocent cup slopped over.

It would have been difficult for Lady Geraldine, moved by sportive fancies, to avoid mischance in her house. She neglected the familiar when eccentricity was present. She took to every new noble cause as by affinity, read the latest books, even poetry, believed in the miracles of galvanism, felt the Bible shake from cover to cover at the touch of a seashell from a mountain top, and helped to spread any scandalous tale she thought pictured attractively a notability out of favour with her. She was a friend, though, to the poor little chimney sweepers, and was resolved not to allow one of them to choke to death in a hot flue of her house. She supported the new movement for sweeping chimneys by machinery, and bore well the ridicule of her friends who owned mansions with chimneys into which it was dangerous, and sometimes fatal, for little boys to climb with their brushes. She had framed and set up in her boudoir in town a macabre cartoon from *Punch,* condemned by all her circle as an incitement to rickburning. It showed a starved agricultural labourer dying on the rags of a pallet, with Death standing over him, and was entitled, His Only Friend. As her husband said, "Give her a stormy petrel for a pet, and she is happy." This was not quite fair, for though she had tried, and failed dismally, to get Mr. Carlyle to call on her, she presented his last work, *Past and Present*, to those who would read it, and to some who would not, because she had enjoyed it herself. She was but kind and generous, though her aversion from pride and cruelty caused her to circulate malicious tales of important people of whom she disapproved.

Unlucky encounters in her house, therefore, were sure to happen, since new and vehement opinions were arising freely from increasing knowledge and awakened curiosity. Not so many years ago there had been an England, and the memory of its calm and assurance was cherished by Mr. Darton and other visitors that afternoon, when change came almost unnoticed, for it could not alter an old way of life. The scene then into which a man was born was much the same when he left it. The cart tracks of his fathers were those he had deepened. He lived and died in one world. That period had gone, while nobody was watching. The speed of change was faster, and was increasing. The world into which a man was born worried him in his middle life because it had become alien and he failed to understand it; and when he was old he had to endure another world, unrecognisable, irrevocable, and inimical to his faith and experience; a thoroughly hateful world, unless he accepted it and lost his spirit. Yet there was stimulation also, an impulse to adventure, in the changed outlook which invention and discovery had brought about. Young people felt it. Vistas had opened full of attractive possibilities as well as of unknown dangers. But even they who enjoyed taking chances in an enlarged and quickened scene did not know to what it all would lead, except certainly to new markets, and greater power, and other sound benefits; and what more could sensible people want?

On her way across the room, Lady Geraldine paused beside her daughter Dinah, who stood by a group where fervour was beginning to sparkle the talk. It was unusual for Dinah, her mother knew, to wait about long if politics or religion or education was all she could get; but the dear child seemed quite patient now, and her mother fancied she saw the attraction. Dinah was listening to young Mr. Barclay, an Under-Secretary of State, or of some office which meant the favour of Sir Robert Peel. He was also heir to possessions which an old Whig family had collected from land enclosures, sinecures, and other spoils of faithful allegiance; though the young man, persuaded by the chance of further good things, was at present in the opposite camp. To a girl, Lady Geraldine supposed, he would be worth attention, with his pleasant voice, easy gestures, and cool demeanour. He had the attraction of a rarity. He was vivid as well as young, for his hair was strangely pale, and his eyes black and lively.

He was then trying to compose the disquiet of the aged Countess Gifford, who had been told—and she wished, she confessed, the fact had been withheld from her—that men and women worked together far underground with hardly anything on, in the galleries of coalmines. If so, it was most improper. Did Mr. Barclay know?

"That women work in coal pits?"

"No, no. You know I mean no such thing. That they are improperly dressed."

"It is very dark down there, I'm told, and very hot."

"Dreadful."

"But," added a testy and quavering voice, "they have their children with them. Babies are down there. Born there, sometimes. Toddlers go on all-fours chained to carts, dragging coal. Is that dreadful?"

Lady Gifford mused, fumbling at a black lace shawl. "That is quite another matter. It is not immoral."

"But the babies are naked too, and when they are smashed doctors and coroners say their deaths are natural. What ought we to say?"

Mr. Barclay showed signs of embarrassment, but recovered. He made a gesture of polite woe. But he did not answer the voice, for a glance in its direction told him it was that of an unknown old dodderer. "You would know all about it, dear lady, if condemned, as I am, to hear the humane crusaders in the House with their facts and figures to prove how base our nation is, how sad our country's morality. And it is certainly true, in a way. The lower orders really have to work hard for a living, as best they can. It has so happened. I assure you that at times I feel almost penitent, and some night in absence of mind may support their crusade, and vote against the Government. Then what would you think of me?"

"We wish we knew what to think," muttered the voice. "It puzzles me how some of you manage to distinguish off-hand between Whig prejudice and Tory bias, night after night, and never make a mistake about which is which, never. I couldn't do it."

Mr. Barclay still appeared not to hear the questioner muttering, for it was almost as inaudible as conscience, though Dinah could see by his hardened mouth that he had not missed its note. She smiled with satisfaction, and Mr. Barclay mistook the fleeting expression of approval in her regard, as he glanced up. It gratified him. It was pleasant to win the bright attention of Lady Geraldine's tall and coldly beautiful daughter as he was about to throw a privileged light on a subject about which most people were talking without knowledge. He fell grave in consideration of things as they are, the nature of which he had seen, for that is the duty of a legislator. He leaned back in his chair, and removed a strayed lock from his forehead, as though it obscured clear thought. He fancied that Dinah would still be mindful of him.

Dinah was, and she was hoping also that that snuffy old

gentleman over there, whoever he was—one of Mama's queer wonders, no doubt—would mumble something more, but was disappointed. She noticed that the venerable interrupter was staring at the carpet now, perhaps trying to remember where he was. Very likely he would think of it soon, and speak again. She did not enjoy eloquence from clever and elegant young men aware of their superiority, and when it met no ridicule she was sorry that proper behaviour must keep her quiet. Mama was always so reproachful afterwards, kind but sad, when she had broken into a conversation with a question she felt she must ask. Sad reproach is most unfair, especially when a few tears go with it.

Lady Geraldine, glad that these visitors, with her daughter favouring them, were sufficiently interested, swept on. The servants moved about with conscious detachment to show they did not exist except when wanted. Mr. Barclay extracted himself from his brief reverie. He leaned forward, clasping his hands. "We had better speak low and circumspectly," he said, looking up and round. "I see William Lovett is here." His smile showed that he considered the danger was small. "It would never do if he were to hear us. He knows too much already. But luckily he is opposed to a violent revolution. . . ."

"Revolution?" exclaimed Lady Gifford.

"It is just a word. Lovett's chief failing is a heart too big for his head. But we won't blame him for that. Tenderhearted rebels can do no harm."

"Revolution!" repeated Lady Gifford. "A very ugly word. Do not use it. We are not the French."

"Nothing like them. And I only use the word because others sometimes do, quite carelessly, but with some appeal, too. There is no call for alarm."

"I should hope not."

"None whatever, dear lady. We shall never see England rise up. Our very poorest have enough sense to refrain from making things worse for themselves. Those women you've heard about, unluckily, they're not positively bad. Their children keep them at work. It is food they want. They don't want to storm a Bastille."

"Then why do they not look after their children, and set them a good example?"

"I think I ought to stand up for them. They are kept very busy, we should remember. They work all day and some of the night. The trouble is, I fear, that lately we've been disturbed by news of what goes on in the mills and mines, and all about the sorrows of the pin-makers—after all, though it didn't occur to us, even the tiny pins have to be made by somebody; and by those affecting stories of what happens to surplus London workhouse children sent north in batches to feed the spindles. . . ."

"I do not understand."

"No. None of us did, your ladyship. It has only just come out that the lower orders not only exist but are indispensable and unhappy. We were unaware till a few weeks back of the sacrifices we must make if we are to succeed in competition with other nations. We have learned more, yet regret it. If we want to keep our peace of mind while facing our country's necessity, it is better not to examine too closely some facts of workaday life. They are sordid and unpleasant. Those recent commissions of enquiry into the mines and factories are largely to blame. They've done no good, and have upset everybody with the news of how poor people have to live, work, and die. The news grieves sympathetic hearers; but what can we do? We cannot help being affected by our humanity and decency. We are shocked to hear that women are forced by the conditions of service to dress improperly. Worse even than our injured sensibility is the fact that the reports rouse expectations in the labourers themselves, which cannot be met."

"Cannot meet a demand for proper behaviour?"

"Eh? Oh, I see! Well, I was coming to that. What we must frankly recognise is that those investigations, so kindly meant, though they have caused anxiety even in this pleasant room, exposed evils for which no remedy can be found. Attempt to change things, and we should get a shock greatly worse than news of coarse manners in coal-pits. We learn of evils while knowing we cannot cure them. It is only human for poor people to dislike fatigue at hard work, and short commons, and we ought not to blame them overmuch. But tell me how poverty can be cured, in a small and over-crowded country? Our national fate is to live by manufacturing. The factory stacks must be kept smoking, or London dies. And—it is very unfortunate, but not our fault—there exist natural laws to regulate our efforts, and we cannot amend or repeal them. They, and not Parliament, govern industry and commerce. To interfere with their delicate operations would do us no more good than an earthquake —or a revolution. Kindly people will always regret the fate of the labourer, born to eat, drink, sweat, and die. But to attempt to improve his state would be to interfere with the principles which operate the machinery, keep the banks solvent, and the ships employed. If we meddled with the forces which rule the acts of men as well as the weather the result would be worse than the squalor which now offends us. Commerce would cease. Our ships rot for want of cargoes. Interfere with the natural order of things to improve them, and the labourer would be without work, and without anything to eat. We should only worsen his lot. Hadn't we better leave things alone?"

Mr. Barclay was addressing Lady Gifford, but he could see Dinah was still there. His argument had come lightly because she was listening. She would know what he meant. If only he could speak in the House as confidently! Dinah herself, as it happened, wanted to ask him a question at once, and opened her mouth to let it out, but the right sound would not come. She was fuming, but did not know why; she hoped she did not show irritation, though her cheeks felt hot. He must be wrong, he must be, for he was so clever and dandy, and far too certain of himself to be right. But where was he wrong? What he said ought not to have sounded like common sense, though it did. Elsewhere in the room she could hear a musical box tinkling a dance, that box with a grotesque doll which danced on the lid to the music. Loud laughter burst out suddenly over there from those who were watching its capers.

"There's some gaiety! Do you hear it? Your answer has just come, Mr. Barclay, sir," announced the old man quite distinctly, to Dinah's secret joy.

His comment broke the spell, and she turned away. Why, Mr. Cree was in the room, and she hadn't noticed him before. When did he arrive? And she hadn't seen him since last May, when he was so helpful to Mama and herself in the packet-ship from Lisbon. She preferred older men, and didn't mind, or not very much, if they were not exactly handsome. They had the good taste not to think so highly of themselves.

Mr. Darton watched her cross over blithely to where Cree and Tom were still talking. The pretty young puss appeared not to see him. He felt out of it, and bored. He edged furtively to the door while his hostess was busy. As moodily he descended the stairs, a door opened on a landing. An anxious face peered out cautiously and saw him. It did not draw back, but relaxed, and chuckled.

"Good, Darton, it's only you. Had enough of it? Come in. What have they been doing to you? You don't look happy.

Come in. No tea here, and no women. Come in. I'm all alone."

Lady Geraldine's husband—that was his chief title to fame—drew Mr. Darton into his study, and shut the door. He was delighted by his friend's downcast expression, and said so. The sombre portraits on the walls of his lordship's armigerant ancestors, some wearing their swords, overlooked severely from the past. Their representative of the present pulled out a shelf of calf-bound volumes, all false, to expose secreted bottles.

"Now there's comfort for you. Don't they look sunnier than anybody you saw upstairs? What shall we have? Come on. You must be as dry as a bone. Aren't you worn out, listening to the clack? I always am. We're safe here, no Christians, no lions. What would you like? Cheer up, Darton, run your eye over those labels. Look, there's one, that's fruity—oh, and I say, while I think of it, don't come back to dinner. Once safe outside, gallop for your life. We've got a bishop coming, and a lunacy commissioner, and somebody else—I've forgotten what he is. Sure to be as grey and solemn as a donkey's behind. But not a smell of that vintage do they get. It's for us. Come on."

17

A Walk through Wapping

Aunt ruth was in doubt. She was more than a little anxious. She was talking to herself. "Woman, it's no good deceiving yourself this way, not another minute."

She was firm with her folly. She was passing through a street somewhere between Islington and London Bridge, and she was wishing she knew where she was. She was lost, and now owned to it. But she walked on, unable to see what else there was to do, and talked to herself as she went. Soliloquy was a habit she had acquired while waiting alone for good news which was in no hurry, well aware that mazed folk talk to themselves, that being a sad sign of what the poor souls have come to. If there is nobody to listen to the tale of your dream, what is to be done but listen to it yourself?

Now you've got yourself into a tangle, my dear, she told herself; you've gone wide astray, and that's not the worst of it. You've always had a low opinion of Londoners, and never troubled to hide it, so you boggle at stopping one of these people for a talk. You're shy of them. You must trust to luck till sure you won't get it. And there's no place to rest awhile in this stony desert, and if there was one you daren't take it, you'd be that conspicuous.

The dun and narrow streets, apparently leading no-whither, baffled her. The day was close. Rain was likely. She was footsore with these hard pavements, and felt shut in by endless walls, all alike. Only her bonnet could see how much of heaven existed above. It was smallish. It was against nature for the sky itself to be skimpy. She hoped the rain would hold off. It could bring no new life where there was no springy turf and no thyme to sweeten the air. With the dust and muck on its stones London would be no cleaner after a downpour, unless it came like Noah's own deluge, a once-for-all to wash away the mixen, the sins of ages, clean the floor bare for a fresh start. But on second thoughts, perhaps that had better not get going while she was there. Filth and dust and heat; and over there was a starved dog chewing something in the road which Christian eyes couldn't look at, a ring of ragged children watching it, as scraggy and pinched as the dog. You put aside what wit you ever had, my dear, the minute you made up your mind you could run into that poor lad in London, and left to do it. For how do you know Dave is here? But here you are, Mrs. Penfold, and now you know what you could easily have guessed, that a woman might as well put to sea looking for her man.

She reflected. How many years, she asked herself, since she was last in London? She gave a wide berth to a quarrel outside a gin shop before considering this. Never count the years past; they add up to nothing but heartache. Which is, she sighed, the very reason we go back to them. What did she know of London? Even when last here she didn't venture ashore. Or only once. She walked out of the dock till she came to a church with a bold white tower. "Then you didn't go far," said Penfold that evening. "That was Limehouse church. A sailor is home again, Ruth; it's all right and good-o when he sights it from Blackwall Reach. That's the last mark of the voyage, and welcome."

A sailor might think it near enough to call it home, after a year of absence in the foreign, but that one walk was enough for her. She preferred to stay in his ship till it put out for Falmouth. She knew where she was when aboard. It was restful on deck, once the cargo was out, and Penfold had only to wait for orders, and run his eye over the gear. But outside the dock it was as heathen as Tyre and Sidon, with all those darkies, and Hittites and Amalekites and South Sea Islanders about. And worse than cannibals about, if she knew one petticoat from another. The dock was quiet. It was lawful. It was what she knew. There was plenty of light, water, and ships, and the warehouses along the quays were palaces, and there was a smell of sugar and spice. She never got her nose over a bowl of brown Demerara sugar to this day without remembering her holiday with Penfold, her first and last. She didn't have to wonder where he was. He was there, and a cuddy servant to wait on them.

As she ought to have guessed before she left home to do this, at her sister's old home at Islington not so much as the name was remembered. She ought to have expected it. She was given no chance to ask more than the question. All she got was, "Never heard of 'em." The door was held unkindly narrow, and then banged. She was left staring at the door knocker, which was in the shape of a billy-goat's head, and it stared back at her for a nanny. Yet wasn't it as likely as not that Dave would have gone back to the only nest he knew, if only to look at it? What else would a stray young creature do? Ah, but if she could guess that she would take to writing almanacs and telling fortunes. To be sure, there was the shipping, and that would draw him to it, and she trusted the street she was in was slanting towards it.

She could begin to remember it all, now it was too late, but from the idle questions with which Dave used to pester her his thoughts shaped like ships. Why wasn't she patient? Why didn't she sit down quietly and hear him out? Now she must pay for passing without proper care the signs which said, as well as signs ever say anything, what she had better look out for. There was the very window, for one thing, she herself had given him. Dave could see from that the sails in the offing, and the far sky-line, and beyond the sky-line is what you want to know. There it was for the boy, and the sun going down behind the ocean. Hadn't she often stood and looked at it herself, while it was there, and felt her inside yearn with the glory of it?

The glory of it! But it isn't always in rose and gold, that west; it isn't always as if the wide heavens were opening, and the silence would break, and the sea would reveal its secrets to hallelujahs from the firmament. Poor Dave was an innocent. He wanted tales of wonder, of course he did, and she had a few she could have told him in the name of gumption, for though he was hungry for tales, what he needed was advice. The thoughts of a boy are a gay raree-show of the fine things to be done in the land east and west of the moon. But she never gave herself time to straighten him. She fobbed him off. If she had given herself a minute to turn the matter over she would have seen that Dave was drifting seawards. True, a doubt had nudged her, she had suspected it, but she had had enough of the sea to satisfy her, so put the worry aside. It's the way of fools, and she had noticed it all her life, ever to turn their eyes from facts too sorry for comfort. But it was her experience that a worrying fact should be looked straight in the face. For her own part, though, she had seldom profited by experience. The trouble is that it is the nature of most facts to be worries, and if a woman can dodge a new one then she dodges it, while knowing full well there it is in the kitchen, watching the back of her.

Well, since here she was in London, she prayed that her boy was not. It would be far better that she had been in too much haste to blunder badly, which was an old habit. She knew pretty well already what the place was. If this mighty uproar and bustle made her feel she was no more free and useful than a scrap of flotsam moving along on the full flood, what help would it give an idle lad? Why, just look at the care it had for its own children! There they were in swarms, and less love for the poor mites than would lift a kitten from a ditch. This endless warren was overrun with nesh young life, left to do the best for itself in the gutters. And nobody cared, that she could see. It was no garden for raising tender and feeling bodies. Nothing was likely to flourish in these by-ways but rank heathen, and the crop of them was greater than ever she had seen of a field of good wheat. It was an offence to God. It wouldn't bear thinking about, that souls should be no more than street dirt, dirt nobody wanted, and cast out, left to heap up with the rest of the rubbish thrown out from the days' passing! London, she doubted, is as cruel as the sea. Like the sea, it doesn't know you are there.

She had come to Babylon. Here the great city was, as ever, and her name was nobody. She was here, but she did not exist. But a saint himself would be of no consequence where life was so abundant and cheap it spilled over into the drains. London could be struck by the seven plagues and still keep on without showing a mark.

At first she was mistaken. After she left the train she had the nervous thought that she was an odd and extra woman just arrived for the curiosity of the street. A foolish body had come to town, and they would be peering at her. She had tried not to be noticeable. She had not spoken to anybody yet. That plunge into the multitude and the noise had scared her; she confessed it had, and it was a sad weakness of the spirit to fear Vanity Fair, and feel submission to its ways. Yet she had not forgotten.

He that is down needs fear no fall,
He that is low no pride;
He that is humble ever shall
Have God to be his guide.

Though it was natural to be afraid when taken by surprise, and to think for a false moment that God must be far away now, not near enough to set up a lowly soul, and guide it through the press of this traffic.

For the real truth was, and it was the most awful thing about London, she was not seen. Her first notion was ignorant. Nobody knew she was there. There were millions of eyes, and now and again a sad pair floating past looked through her but not at her. She was only another wandering soul that had forgotten it was once baptized. There is, she mused, no more charity in London than in the surf when it hurries without rest, and without aim, about the crags and snags of the shore, when the wind is cold at evening; and you watch and wait, and would give all the gold in the world for one small sign of grace. But nothing comes; nothing comes! She had never felt more certain than on this day that but for the promise of the love of God she would give up.

She was near Smithfield; but Aunt Ruth had never heard of Smithfield. If she had been told where she was, that name would have meant no more to her as a famous market and fair ground, and as a place long favoured for the display by fire and sword of man's inhumanity to man, than the name of Rahere himself, the courtier of Henry I, who in remorse and compassion founded a hospital by that field, centuries before the days of jousts and the burning of heretics. She stood, in fact, looking at his old hospital of St. Bartholomew, wondering what the big place was, when there were wild shouts behind her. She turned, and saw a drove of horned beasts charging down on her. But the cattle did not startle her. She was used to them, and knew by their eyes the poor things were frightened. They would part when they reached her. What startled her was the thwacking of sticks on their backs. Why, to drive decent kine that way!

The array of horns came close, but swerved, and the animals slapped past, but behind the herd laboured one worried beast which was lame. A drover urged it on, beating its bony haunches. Aunt Ruth was shocked. She rebuked the man. "Please. Don't do it. It's lame. Can't you see?"

The drover grinned at her, and for reply gave the projecting bones another whack. The animal slipped. It was the slip that did it. The beast's sudden sprawling broke out Mrs. Penfold's indignation. She had the man's goad in her hands and wrenched it from him before she knew what she would do with it. She appeared to be a lusty and resolute virago when roused and flushed, and the surprised drover recoiled unreadily. His hands flew up as he overbalanced and knocked her bonnet askew with violence. In an instant she knew what the stick was for. The figure lying in the road covered its head with its arms against what was coming. "That," gasped Mrs. Penfold, "take that, you ugly you, and that, you evil thing."

Her vigorous blows, loud rather than effective, as the stones took the worst of them, exhausted her rage. She came to herself, breathless. The man remained with his arms protecting his face, and remorse took her. She stooped to help up her victim, but he misunderstood her new movement. He scrambled to his feet and was off, ignominiously, and as he fled unexpected voices shouted their delight. "Go it, mother—after him—he can't run."

She saw happy faces about her, to her astonishment. An instantaneous audience was close around, commending her heartily. It urged her to the chase. Her perception remained as rumpled as her bonnet. She glanced at her eager supporters, and then at the weapon in her hand, which she saw did not belong to her. She handed it gently to a boy at her elbow, and was inclined to precipitous flight, like the man, but was unable. Dignity came to her aid. She pushed her way through tactfully while adjusting her bonnet, as though a duty she had come to perform had been done, and she was going home.

Her agitation did not soon subside. She had to walk cautiously, for her knees were trembling, as if frightened. Nor were they quieted by the reflection that her hasty spirit was always pushing her into trouble, always provoking her into some pranky mummery. That fretted her more than the idea that this great city was as indifferent as tombstones, when it wasn't being cruel to the helpless. But she trapsed on, and at length steadied. When she found, late that afternoon, the river and its ships, she was in a quiet mood, resigned to whatever else adversity might send her.

She was not quite prepared for so much as that river. The ranks of sea-traffickers receding downstream into smoke and shadow told her, beyond appeal, that her long journey was wasted. This river was not like going down to a quay or into a dock to seek a ship you thought might be there. It was very different. Her quest had no hope in it. She understood she might as well talk to the host of stars, and wait out in the cold all night for an answer, as ask here if anyone had noticed a wandering soul. Nor could she see what next she had better do. That wasn't as plain as failure. No help was in sight—in all this busy and terrible city she could not believe there was more of a listening heart than ever there was in the belly of Baal long ago.

Her journey had brought her to that. Nothing was left but to turn back. If the boy was somewhere in that scene

before her he might as well be on the China coast, for what
her eyes would tell her. She continued idly along the street
by the river, unwilling, being a stubborn woman, to leave
at once under defeat. Defeat had only just met her. Defeat,
for the moment, meant that she must return home, and
face the days, one after another; and afterwards would do
for that. She caught frequent glimpses of the ships and the
river between the buildings, but did not go to the water's
edge. She need not look for Dave there; and those narrow
openings, with their landing-stairs, were loud and lively
with boatmen and rough fellows best avoided.

This was Wapping. She had heard tell of it. It had a bad
name. Penfold once wrote a long letter to her about
Wapping because he had lost a crew there, every man Jack.
She was surprised then, but not today. It was a harbourage
where sin was bold in scarlet, and by day, nothing to be
ashamed of, but better than money. A ship could easily lose
all hands here. Nobody would miss them. What else would
you expect? A ship moored, and alongside was a market
street offering men ashore after months of empty sea and
sky what was good for nothing, though they were sure to
want it. The chief shops, almost next door to each other,
and the brightest and best, sold rum and gin. Trade was
roaring. Though pawnshopss were handy; you need not go
far if you happened to want one. It was as mortal bad as
the foreign parts she had heard about, but somehow she did
not feel very nervous. The people were wild and rude, yet
she was sure they would have given her more attention
than she wanted if she had been a constable. As it was, only
the women looked at her, sharply, but not unkindly—
though Tartars they could be, the ugliest of customers, she
hadn't a doubt, once they were suspicious of your business.

Her only business was to get out of it, and before dark.
Well, soon she must turn back. Something she had gained,

if gain it could be called, when it was no more than another lesson of what comes of going down to the sea in ships. The sea, she had long known, has much to answer for, though answer there will be none till there is no more sea; yet she had not properly known that the sea had to answer for such a street as this. Sugar and tea and spice cost far more than is ever paid for them over a respectable counter, that she now knew. The sight of a drunken girl, wasn't that a nice price to add to the cost of your comforts? She could not have been more than seventeen, that child.

So sorrowful a thing, to come so far to see! In all her born days her ignorance had never suspected . . . hadn't the minute come for her to get out of it? If she walked till she dropped she would see only more of the sights to plague a quiet house, when afterwards they come to mind, and a woman can but pray for those who are she doesn't know where in such a world. At all events, it was lucky, her prospect being what it was, she had a house to which to turn; though she didn't think so at the time, not that morning Mr. Darton met her as she was flitting from Branton, with all her sticks. For she wasn't going to wait to be bundled away from her hearth. No, she packed up, and was off. And there she was, sitting at the back of the wagon, on a bale of bedding, when up he came at a canter, out for a morning ride, with his dogs. She supposed, of course, he would ride on. He reproached her instead, while his horse fidgeted. She did not answer him. She felt done. He ordered the carrier back to the house, and to unload, and put everything in its rightful place again, or else keep himself out of Branton for the future. What could she do? She wished to face him to the last, but the cross-purpose of it rattled the pride out of her. Back she had to go.

Aunt Ruth raised her eyes from wool-gathering, and stood. A mob irrupted from a side turning into the narrow

way ahead. She had a glimpse of a few constables march-
ing towards her in the middle of the road, guarding two
prisoners, a man and a boy. They were swallowed up in a
moment. The lad was just such a slip as Dave. She could
only see the scattered hats of the officers bobbing about
above the swirl of the mob. The riot burst open, and a parcel
of women hurried the prisoners away into an alley. Two of
them lifted the lad along as if his feet dragged. If that didn't
look like—but they had gone. Many boys have tousled sandy
hair. The men were keeping off the police. A boy in a blue
serge jacket is common enough, at a bare peep. The constables had taken to the boats: she hoped they got away.

It was all over. But the crowd was threatening, buzzing
like bees that have been upset. Dared she follow the way
those women had gone? Not yet; though it wasn't the first
time that day she had thought she spotted him in the distance. His shape was so sharp and constant in her mind;
that was why. She would be always seeing him. There are
many lads with hair like that. The street was smoothing
down. She wished this hadn't happened. Now she couldn't
rest till she was satisfied. She was haunted enough, without
this. It wasn't right, it wasn't natural, that she should look
up at the end of a wasted day, and see the very moral of
him, and just for a moment. Yet how could it be Dave?
Ruth Penfold, what a soft and gullible woman you are!

Yet, having thus admonished herself, she ventured into
the turning up which the women had fled. She couldn't
keep out of it. Nobody was there. Every door was fast. She
was positive a window curtain twitched now and then as
she went along. Except for that suspicion of a movement
the street was dead, after the hullabaloo. She was alone in
it, and went through the length of it without a sight of so
much as a cat, and passed into another street at the top,
where the people lolling in a fading light appeared to have

heard nothing, and to know nothing, and to care for nothing.

Her scared knees were shaking again. But I'm not scared, she assured herself, though all of a twitter. There was cause enough. Except for the deceit of it, she could have declared that was young Dave. But how could she get her thoughts straight in these twisty alleys? Especially if caught in them at night, and caught she would be. Night was not far off, and it was like her to be looking in the dark for someone who wasn't there. Anyhow, who ought not to be there. Which was it? And though, when a little later night was about her, and she could see nothing through the drizzle— for the rain had come at last—except furtive points of light better not sought out, she was not really frightened, because she had given herself up. I might as well, she supposed, get annoyed with the rain; I might as well blame the dark, or think to turn away from the valley of the shadow. Some- times she heard footsteps, but she saw nobody. Sometimes there were voices, a low grumble of voices. Once she heard a long howl, which was not surprising, of course, when you find yourself in the valley. Yet once you are there you must go on.

In a moment of fright she flinched, and began to grope. The dark was flat against her face, and she fancied a wall was at hand. There was no wall. Then she heard singing begin, and stayed where she was, to listen. It was near. She couldn't believe her ears. What, that old tune, and here, and at this hour? She forgot where she was. It was the very tune which often came into her head at the end of the day, when another day was done, and she had the leisure to recall the length of life, and the hours of it a woman would have back, if she could. It was like a word from one she would never hear again, that hymn. It used to be sung by those round the table, after father had finished reading aloud to them from the good book. Mrs. Penfold's simple apprehension of time and place bewildered her. She was in another year, one she knew, though in the wrong place, and was inclined to weak tears, because life has a contrary way of its own, which you can't make head nor tail of. She then noticed a faint pencil of light lying along the pavement before her, which became a pale wedge on the wet stones when a door was opened and the singing swelled louder for an instant. A figure slipped through. Mrs. Penfold followed it in.

The singing ceased as she entered, but she knew she would be safe where people knew what she knew. There were not many of them. They did not look round at her. They were scattered about the benches of a small hall, its low ceiling dark with rafters. A lamp hanging from a beam at the far end thinned the mirk about it. With its floor of stone flags, its musky smell, and the walls that once had been whitewashed, she wondered whether she was in an old stable. Most of the lamplight fell on the figure of a little woman, younger than herself, standing by a table almost under the lamp, who was looking straight at her. Mrs. Penfold sank modestly on to a near bench, and became as still as the other waiting figures.

Bless us, if the woman wasn't preaching! When aware that this was going on Mrs. Penfold sadly disapproved. It wasn't the duty of a woman. And without a text, too! But she attended to the voice, though a little critically, for it was downright, if quiet and gentle. It might not have been talking to them at all, but to the night, or to the walls and rafters, and not even hoping for the best, but trusting to what must be said. Nor did the speaker look at them, but at the table, or into the air, as if she were remembering, though the truth of it came easily to her lips, which hardly moved.

Mrs. Penfold's disapproval began to go. She merely listened. The lamp seemed to be brighter, for the speaker was more distinct, her pale face clear and sharp when she lifted it up, looking over their heads, talking as if no great city with its ships were outside in the rain and dark, or at most were no more than fears to be put in order. The simple brown dress of the speaker reminded Aunt Ruth of something. She had heard tell of the Quakers, but had never met one before. Perhaps this young woman was one. But was she young? Or was she never touched as the years went by? Perhaps women who are unafraid of what may happen are never marked by the years. Aunt Ruth's own troubled spirit fell quiet, and her own trust revived that she could wait in patience, whoever was lost, and whatever befell. If we cannot change the sad way the world goes, and do not understand it, at least that way shall not change us. As she sat there she became sure that the lamp hanging in that old stable, doing hardly more than light the face of the good woman standing near it, was enough for her, for any man or woman, enough for London. Secure within such an assurance of safety, Aunt Ruth even forgot that she had nowhere to go that night.

Then she noticed they were all on their knees, and she wasn't. The room was silent. The voice had ceased. Her head had been wandering again. Aunt Ruth promptly went down on the flags; but though her thoughts were at rest, not one little doubt running through her mind, which was as still as the room, she could not pray. She could not even think of what she wanted. She but humbled herself, and asked for nothing.

Movements roused her. The people were leaving. She rose, and had turned to go with them, when her arm was touched. "Wait," said the voice, at her elbow.

18

Pool of London: Morning and Night

D A V E was eager as soon as awake. He stole away from
the sleepers in the cabin and crept up to the deck.
In the fresh of the morning the world was as young as the
boy, and they met. Dave was taken unawares. Nobody else
was about. This was all new. It was here for the first time,
and he gaped in surprise. He could see it was his, the glory
of the sky, and London's shining towers; the river and all
the ships on it were his, and he was welcome. That cock,
the gilded weather-vane of the *London Lass,* was high in
the sun, the first aboard to catch it; bright gold, his neck
stretched up, just about to crow and rouse everybody to
good fortune. Dave was sure in that moment that wonderful
things could happen at any hour.

If this was being a sailor he would stay. He would ask
Bonser to let him stay. London was clear and still, like a
picture in a book. It would be moving soon. It was about to
begin. This was the time to be about, before things begin,
the minute before they start off. And there it came, a man
in a ship downstream was singing, though Dave was not
sure it was the right sort of song. Then a rope creaked
through a sheave across river. A dog barked far away. A
mallet began to chant in a creek just astern. A police-boat
rowed leisurely past, and Dave watched it. Always watch a
police-boat, said Bonser yesterday, because if you don't the
devil will have you by the collar. He didn't believe that,

any more than he believed what Aunt Ruth said about those
bears sent by God to kill little children who had only called
a holy prophet a bald-head; but he resented constables.
Everybody said they were tricky; they were up to no good.
Bonser always kept on with the job he was doing, but he
watched the way those chaps went.

The promise of the day began to languish not long after
the police-boat disappeared down river. Bonser put his head
out of the scuttle for a look round, saw him there, wanted
to know whether he never slept, and ducked down. Day,
when it got going, began to dawdle along, like yesterday.
He could watch the men jumping coal out of the hold of a
collier brig, with a shout as they jumped, raising black,
glittering clouds from a barge alongside her. Hundreds of
skiffs and wherries came and went from shore to shore, or
dodged about among the hulls. One good thing was he didn't
think the smell of the river was as strong as it was yesterday. He thought yesterday he could never get used to it;
but perhaps you can get used to anything, almost. All the
same, it was better not to keep watching the running tide
too long, not before breakfast; and the galley fire was
already beginning to smoke. There wasn't much wind.
The blue smoke leaned over only a little way, and the walls
and the river were already bright.

Dave was about to idle from it, uncertain whether to keep
on deck, or go below. When the day is moving on, but your
ship keeps where she is and you don't know when she will
wake up, what is there to do? To cross over from the larboard to the starboard side is all the change you can find;
and that isn't much, when every mark on the ship's planking has become as ordinary as the old stains on your
trousers.

A peremptory cry across the river swung his interest
sharply round again. The rollicking cheer that followed it

popped up Bonser's head from below. A spry crew over the way breasted the capstan bars of a brigantine. Then they broke into song, and began to heave her up to her anchor, pushing the capstan round and round while the incoming cable shook and danced on the water, showering drops, and their ship slid past the marks ashore; and Dave felt sad, for that ship was departing; and to what a lovely song!

Oh, Shen-an-doah's my na-tive val-ley,
Aa-way, you roll-ing ri-ver.
Shen-an-doah is my native val-ley.
A-way, we're bound to go, 'cross the wide Miss-ou-ri.

Bonser was singing it, too; but quietly, he might have been at church, very solemn, as if he had to join in when he heard the choir. The anchor, after many verses, was aweigh. There she went. That ship was free. Her white sails were loose. She was going out with the tide; and Dave dreamed, while watching her dwindle downstream into the glitter and smudge, with the echoes of her farewell song singing in his head.

"You can't watch her all the way over, Commodore," Bonser called out. "She's for Baltimore. Come down and eat. Your turn next."

The *Pochahontas,* for Baltimore! To have heard the names of ships, and of the places for which they depart, was to Dave as good as the silence which follows music. His turn next? He did not, over the sausages and beer at breakfast, connect his turn with names that were as good as music. The boy in the ship next astern, no older than himself, told him they were from Old Calabar, and hadn't he got the fever! He showed him his hands. His fingers were yellow, and their nails blue, and he was shivering, though the day was quite warm. That boy had been to the

Gulf of Guinea. He said he had seen a slaver loading a cargo of negroes. As for his own ship, there she was, and he didn't know why. He had nothing to talk about. If a turn was coming for him, he hadn't seen a sign of it. But how is a chap to know if a sign goes up for him? How can he tell what it is? Nobody had ever told him that. What he did know was that the look of things never gives them away. There they are day after day, always the same; they are only what happens.

He watched from the deck all that went on that day. Only a few strangers came aboard. What they wanted he didn't know, and didn't ask. There was plenty to watch on the river, most of it different. It was like being at a fair. There was the man who pulled a boat between the shore and the ship, nobody with him, except a woman lying down in the stern, but you could only see her wet boots and white stockings, and some of her hair, because a wet sack was thrown over her. He couldn't help thinking of her, whoever she was, for hours; and at last the day turned to dusk.

Lanterns began to show on some ships, but not on his. The water darkened till ships and high walls were the same as night. If there was a sky, it was thick smoke. The only stars were down below, and some were steady, and others wandered about. Though the river could not be seen it could be heard, but not much. It was very much alive, but only muttered to itself as it passed by. Then its whispering would stop for a minute; not a sound came from it. It left you waiting. But it was there. You were alone with it, water as black as night, and old and deep, all ready for you. And even that wasn't so bad as when the water broke into a laugh under the ship's stern, as if it was up to something there; but it smothered the laugh. It didn't want you to hear that.

The night became more secret than ever. The voices of men mumbled over the river, small and low and solemn. You couldn't hear a word they said, yet you could tell by the sound of it that there was danger in the dark, and trouble.

19

The Hole in the Wall

THE night was so black that when a wherry drew alongside he did not know it, though he was not paying strict attention. He was looking away to breaks in the dark, far gleams, trying to guess their meaning, and didn't hear the oars. There was no rumble in rowlocks, and not a splash. Two men heaved over the bulwarks near him and jumped him out of his dreaming. They went below.

Bonser came up soon afterwards. "That you, boy? Stay where you are, but keep a better watch. Strangers were aboard before you knew it. Hear what I say? Keep a sharp look-out. Unfurl your ears and sneak about. If anything draws near let me know and don't wait. You're in charge. Now mind. In charge."

Bonser disappeared. Dave was left on watch, with the topside of the ship to himself. Now he was wide awake, and feeling bigger than he was. He had charge of a ship, and the command lifted him to the height of its importance. Bonser left him to it, and then went away, so he must be up to it, and that was strange. At first he was anxious. He began to see and hear many threats in the dark which were not there. Soon, though, the silent body of the ship, and her solid indifference as he crept about her, was as if she knew him. The night settled into its old place. Its sounds retired to the distance, tiny and of no account. They ceased to bother him as much as at first with the fear that craft were coming, when nothing moving was near. The artful river at night, while he was on the look-out, was what he liked. He would not have changed places with a prince.

Yet he was caught. Before he knew it, another boat was under his nose. A man in it was holding up a lantern, which flashed instantly. Dave's face was as bright as a moon over the water. The lantern played along the ship's side, and then he knew the river police had come.

"That the *Sea Witch*?"

"No," answered Dave gladly. But his heart was excited. He could not run off to report, with the light holding him.

"I said you were wrong," said another voice. "You can see it isn't her. Push off. She's down by Cherry Garden."

The boat sheered off, and Dave went to the scuttle, which was closed, and bumped on it. The men below were slow in letting him in, or else he thought they were.

"Hullo," said Bonser, "sighted the Flying Dutchman? Did she scare you?"

"A police-boat came."

Bonser made to rise, but settled again. The other men glanced sharply at him, and the change in their faces said they expected Bonser to begin first, if a move had to be made.

"Not there, is it?"

"No. It went downstream."

"You saw it go that way, you know that?"

"It went that way. They wanted the *Sea Witch*."

"Is that all? They can have her. We'll go the other way. Now's the time."

The crew about the table made to get out, as if no minute should be lost. Dave squeezed back to give them passage, but Bonser pushed him into the running. "Up with you. You're the eyes. Keep them skinned. Peep about. Don't miss anything that swims. That's more important than you are."

How funny it is, Dave thought, that when something different does happen, there it is, all at once, and you've no time to make it out. What were they up to behind him? They were busy hauling things but were doing it carefully. He turned in curiosity, and then attempted to help a man shove a lumpy bundle across the deck. Bonser was there in a moment, but did not speak. Dave's shoulders were hurt as he was twisted sharply round to face the river again, and a thump in the back sent him hard against the bulwark. Whatever they were doing, it was soon over. He was still dutifully intent on the silent river when Bonser spoke behind him.

"Leave that now. And boy, never cut off to meddle with what others are at. That's for them. Haul your own rope —that's enough. We'll be off. The boat's the other side. Over with you. There she is. Easy. Don't sink her."

The wherry floated deep, though only Bonser and another man were in it. Dave perched on the stern board, and he fancied his seat was about awash with the thin glints on the dark stream, which made him anxious to hold a steady balance. A little more weight this way or that and the water would swill over the gunwales. They went heavily between the shipping and the shore, under the gloom of walls, with no more sound than a log. Dave did not know oars could be muffled. They were gliding into the darkness, taking chances with what could not be seen, so to Dave the shadows were often thick enough to upset the boat, if she struck one. The river, sending up a chill, was next to his clenched hands, and he would have swerved once when it clutched his fingers, but trusted Bonser. If the boat upset they would be found too late, like that woman. He could smell the wet walls. The smell was as old as the river, it was as cold and mouldy as graveyards, and that made it hard to sit as still as a cat with a twisted leg giving him pepper. He could not untwist it. He found he could sit quite still because he was afraid to move.

The boat ran up against a thicker lump of night, which luckily gave way. It must have been a tunnel or a vault. Sharp little echoes sprinkled about, but Dave could not see his hands. The boat stopped. Water was lapping close, and when light opened overhead it showed they were alongside stone steps. A woman stood above them with a lantern.

"You first, boy," said Bonser. Dave hauled himself into a room which was not fit to live in, except rats.

"Come on in, lovey," said the woman. "How do you like my home?"

It was Netty. "You wouldn't take a kiss from me last time, would you, so I won't offer you another." She pulled his hair, and laughed.

"None of that," Bonser called out. "Leave him alone and none of your tricks. He was brought here for safety." Then he caught hold of her, and the pair pranced over the floor. It surprised Dave that a big and hairy sailor could step it out as lightly as Netty, and she lost her weight when she whirled, she only floated around.

The other man's eyes peered over the floor from the trap-door. He disapproved. "When you've done skylarking, might you lend a hand? Or do we wait for the peelers? Better shift the lamp from here, anyhow. Talk about safety!"

Bonser released Netty, and agreed. "Right. I'm the wrong example. But what's duty," he added sadly, "when there's a girl?"

"I'll help," said Netty. "I must see the cutlasses. Would I do with a musket in the other hand? Any good for what's going?" She posed an attitude of haughty defiance.

"You jabber too much," said the man.

"Be off," said Bonser, pointing to the ceiling. "Up you go. But be a quiet little mouse up there. Talk is the way to get us hung, or a passage in a convict ship, and I'd rather be hung."

Netty showed no anxiety. "There's a nice thing to say. Do I talk? But I suppose you'd expect me to gape like a child in a pinafore at a lord high admiral, when that Mr. Cree of yours was here today."

Bonser was bent by the trap-door, but was up and round instantly at her. "What's that? Cree here. What did he want? Was it him?"

"So he said."

"So he said? Who couldn't say it? What was he like?"

"Why, a proper tall man, and he took to me, if he did ask for you. Not well-favoured, but an improvement on you. Very nice black hair and a clean face. Spoke like a gentleman, which you can't."

Her smiling insolence alarmed Dave, who had seen Bonser in a rage. Now she would hear something. But Bonser seemed not to have noticed it.

"Sounds like him. What did he want?"

"I've forgotten, he so took my fancy. Perhaps he didn't say."

Bonser stroked his beard, thinking. "Must be mad, to show himself. Or worried."

"He didn't talk worry to me. The time soon passed."

"It did, did it! I've never seen him get round a woman, so I don't know. I don't know much, anyhow. But there's a name you've never heard of. You've never heard it, have you? I don't know it. Now look at me, Netty. If I'm lagged, that means me, only me. He's different. The magistrates are in a stink about us. They're fair cruel. If he was pulled down he'd bring down a lot with him, and couldn't stop it. You don't know what's going on. Damme. Take that lad away. He's heard nothing, and knows it better than you. Forget how to talk. But not you. What's ruin, when a woman feels gay?"

"Come on, young freckles." Netty gave Dave a squeeze. "Come on. We'll have no truck with 'em, eh! Jack Sheppard is only a low game for ugly customers, and we won't play it."

She opened a door which Dave hadn't noticed, and led him into the dark beyond it with an arm about him. The passage seemed long to Dave, for he wished he wasn't there. Worse than that, she kept her arm round him and it was warm and bare. He wanted no help from her if the floor did sink in soft places. Netty stopped.

"Hear that?" she whispered.

He listened. He had to bring his attention to it, he had to forget he did not like being held in that friendly way. He wouldn't fall. Then he heard the sound beneath the boards. It was the suck of the tide, not loud, but heavy and sullen.

"We're right over it," she said. "My dear, that makes you want company, that does, when the candle goes out. You'd say so, if you knew. It does me, and always will. If you've got to listen to that chuttering in the dark, and nobody to talk to, you listen harder than ever, and that don't do. If you can't go to sleep it's dreary, that noise, it's time running out, that's what I always think, running out to waste, and it's all I've got."

They climbed a wobbly ladder. There wasn't a light in this house, except one the police ought not to see, though you had to go up broken ladders and wander through more passages. Dave thought of Bonser's words, that he was brought here for safety. It didn't feel very safe. If this was a proper house it ought to have a door to a street. He wished he knew how to find it. But it wouldn't do to ask Netty. He must slip off when he could, and say nothing, not even to Bonser. Whatever it was went on here he did not think he would like it. It might be all right, but not for him. She kept an arm round him, and it was flustering to be held tight by a woman he didn't know.

A light was ahead of them coming through a door, and they entered a room which was misty and strong with tobacco smoke. Men sat there drinking. They looked up, and nobody spoke. Dave noticed only a picture of a race-horse, and another of a negro prize-fighter. It wouldn't do to tell Aunt Ruth he'd been in such a place; no, he'd have to keep it from her. They passed through into another room. There Netty sighed, and sat down.

"Let's wait here," she said. "The longer the better. I'm sick of sailors and their rude manners, aren't you? You're not a sailor, so don't tell me you are. Who are you? Out with it. You've got mixed up with a chick-a-leery bunch, if ever there was one. You don't fit in. How did you come to know him?"

It was better, Dave saw with relief, to have too many questions to answer at once. That gave him time to choose an answer to the easiest. Netty talked as if she had not spoken for a week, and somebody must have it. When she asked a question she never waited for what she wanted to know, but went on, and forgot it. He began to think he might like Netty in a little while, if he had to, for she was so natural and easy. She didn't care what she said, either. Now and then he wondered whether she knew herself what she was saying; he wasn't sure he knew what it was she meant. She was as big as a man, too, only rounder, with a lap as wide as an arm-chair, and if her eyes were artful they were kind.

She had not given him a chance to say a word when Bonser came in, alone, by another door.

"Done it?" Netty looked up, smiling and impudent.

"Done what?" said Bonser.

"Hide-and-seek or bo-peep, or what you call it. But aren't you too old and ugly for kids' games?"

Bonser did not answer. He sat staring at the floor, listening, but not to her. "Shut up," he said at last. "Who's drinking here?"

"The usual riff-raff, as far as I know. Nobody worth looking at twice, so I didn't stop."

Dave was alert through mistrust. Something like a row was going on the other side of the wall. He had noticed it. There it was again, and one voice breaking in firmly, with authority. A nervous glance at Netty told him she was not as careless as she had pretended to be. She was listening, her head bent.

"Who is that?" she whispered. "What's he saying? He doesn't belong here."

Bonser rose and Dave imitated him. He thought he had better do the same as Bonser.

"I'll go and see who it is," said Netty, but she was motioned to stay where she was.

The babble out there ceased. Bonser beckoned to Dave, and made to move towards the door by which he had entered, but was too late. He changed his mind, and was leisurely lighting his pipe when three constables came in. They stood and eyed the room, and then fixed on the sailor.

"That's our man," said one of them, and made for Bonser, who stuffed his pipe in his pocket and stepped back as the leader reached for him.

Dave never could recall, not when he tried, or not very well, the way things moved after that. The room moved, and everybody moved too fast and at once. All spun round and was blurred. But the beginning of it was clear and fixed. That never changed. A policeman flew off Bonser on his

way to bowl over the others, which he did. Over went
Netty too. In Dave's eye, that policeman was always off the
floor and on his way. He was following his hat, which
went first. Furniture toppled and a chair smashed, but they
were only noises. A heap of people struggling on the floor
was coming up again, Netty with her arms round a man's
neck screaming in his ear, when Bonser jerked Dave out of
his astonishment.

Bonser shot bolts on the best side of the door a second
before it bumped. Dave was lost in the strange house once
more, but that no longer mattered, as the police were after
him. They banged and battered the door, and the noise was
very bad, as he did not know where he was nor where he
was going. The door couldn't last long at that rate. But he
was not afraid. Not now. It was too late to be afraid. He
was careful to hold on to Bonser, who was in no hurry, but
stood to listen now and then.

"Not yet," said Bonser. "Good door. A few minutes yet.
Stand here, stand still where you are. I've opened a trap in
the floorboards."

Dave did not move, for he felt a cold draught rising, and
knew that Bonser had gone. Stones crunched down below.
The sailor's quiet voice came up to his feet. "Lower yourself
from the edge, and drop. It's easy."

Dave groped for the edge, dangled from it, and began to
think, but he let go when the door crashed. Bonser checked
his fall, then fumbled about, and the trap shut over them.
"They can break their necks where they like," he said,
"but not here. Harm enough here for one night. Smart
now, into this skiff."

Out on the water, well out, Dave breathed at ease, for a
change that night. The river's separation was a comfort.
This was a little boat to be out alone in so much night, but
it was better than the police. They had pulled clear of the

house that was a secret he did not wish to know; though Bonser did not pull very far—not far enough, Dave fancied, as the threat was still only a few minutes behind them. They landed, and went up a gulley into a street lively with people who could not be seen, except when heads passed across yellow patches where lamps were in the windows.

20

Friends of the Lower Orders

A COSTERMONGER in the Minories, at that end of it by the Tower of London, began to thump a drum beside his barrow-load of codlins. Mrs. Penfold hurried to a window in alarm.

Thank goodness! This time the noise meant only apples. What a pleasant sight, and how beamy apples were in that graceless street! Which was empty now. Of course it was. What were apples and the right good things of the green earth to the people there? It was day, so they had all slunk off into hiding. Their hours were the dark, and their joy to make night hideous. The howling last night was as if a herd of hags and hyenas had broken out in full cry, hunting all they could catch and devour. Now look at the quiet of it! Would you believe it? It was just like waking up to see only plain daylight, all calm, with eyes still besotted by the rushing shadows of an ugly dream.

Though she was not taken in. She knew where she was. There were English heathen, now she knew it, who only wanted tattooed jowls to mark them for what they were, and they were capable of war-dance and all uncharity. Their lairs were not far off, either, at that moment. Yet last night Miss Summers had gone on with her Ragged School—and a good name for it it was—as if all you had to do when the Philistines were bawling at the front door was to go on teaching the alphabet to a few poor souls who couldn't spell bread and hardly knew the taste of it.

A funny name, Minories, for an unheard-of place. Mary

Summers said it came from Minoresses, who were nuns, and who lived a good life here in a convent when London hadn't reached this far. Since their day the town had spilled over, and in swarms. The nuns, who might have been as good, though Papists, as Mary said they were, when they settled here, which was getting on for a thousand years ago, had left only a smudge of a name, no more than a wild guess at it, if you were to ask Aunt Ruth's opinion: and whatever those many years back nuns might have considered a proper kind of life to live hereabouts, no history book would ever persuade her those holy ladies had a better thought for it than Mary Summers.

Did one of them ever go into Ratcliffe Highway with a lantern, as far as "Paddy's Goose," which were childish words to hide a haunt of crimps and land-sharks, where the police daren't show themselves, as she did? Do you know, the tales that come out of that Highway would frighten a pirate, if he had any sense left. Usually sailors hadn't, by the time they got there, and no money either, when they were thrown out, if lucky; and if not lucky then trepanned and put on a death ship. But she'd go there, and as likely as not come back bringing home a dismal wretch to be set upright. And what hope of a difference could that make, I asked her, emptying hell soul by soul, if you happen to find a creature not sorry to come out of the lights and riot? Don't look for hope in this world, she said, hope is where we make it.

She had her work cut out to make some there. Even for a saint it was a hard prospect, to bring out a spot of notice-able brightness where you wouldn't know humanity for the canker of it. But perhaps it could be done. Perhaps goodness hardly ever knows the power it has, and that makes it easy for Old Nick to take possession and keep it simply by walking straight in. Besides, the truth is, when you give it

a thought, three score years and ten are not near long
enough for mortals to make out the drift of things, forgetful
the while that to the Eternal a thousand ages are short as a
watch that ends the night. So we can but try.

If she had found a quieter mind herself since that chance
meeting, when Mary first spoke to her, then it would be a
sin to deny a chance to others. If it wasn't Providence that
brought her to a stand, when wandering, to hear singing
voices which took her out of a rainy night and back past
life's mischances into the days of innocence, what was it?
That night Mary said to her, don't look for your boy, you'll
lose your wits before you find him, doing that. He'll come
round to you if it's God's will. Better come with me now,
and wait awhile. And there she was, with work to do, and
she had never known she had the head and hands for it.
She'd say this, that trying to make hope begin to shine
where there wasn't any gave a woman enough to get on
with. She'd no time left to sit and mope and add nails to
her coffin. If only she could be sure young Dave was in the
right hands. . . .

To be sure. Brooding over it tells you nothing. Mary said
friends of hers were coming this night. That room where
the school was held must be cleaned, and it took at least
most of the morning to air the taint out of it, after a night's
education. Still, when schooling starts late from nothing,
when a boy you must bend over to teach him the alphabet
has never slept better than in a barrel or a packing-case,
and was so grateful to her that he picked a pocket to reward
her, and showed her how he did it, who has never heard of
Jesus, and fancies God is no less than the Lord Mayor; and
when a girl of twenty can tell you more of wickedness,
without knowing what it is, than you'd learn from one book
after another, frowziness was nothing for fuss. Where
there's dirt and ignorance there must be bad smells; well,

there ought to be, or else most people would let the dirt rest and leave ignorance to rot.

The first visitor she let in surprised her, though she kept her face. Hadn't she seen this gentleman before, mooning about the heights at Branton? Impossible. That must be her ridiculous fancy. He didn't recognise her, she could see, though true he seemed an absent-minded gentleman, not likely to be certain of where he was, or who was about, or what to do with his hat and stick. Mary called him Mr. Burnham. But that was the maiden name of good Mrs. Darton, and her brother Tom was at Crantock now and then, she had heard, though she knew nothing about him, except the gossip was that old Darton thought his brother-in-law was not so far gone that he would be safer in Bedlam. For that matter, as far as her experience went, there was not much need for mad-houses at all, as the world was big enough to hold everybody. Who isn't a bit touched, when the moon is just right?

The gentlemen, as they arrived, impressed her in a way Mr. Darton did not, well-born and prosperous though he was. They made no difference between her and Mary, as if quality was much the same in each of us, as we are all the children of God; and that make it awkward for her, for she knew the gap there was between ladies and knights and the beauty of holiness. They were a cheerful bunch, that one they called Cree quite frolicsome, but she was too busy at first attending to their creature comforts to pay much attention to what they had to say. You must not be distracted while feeding men. She only knew that never at a Methodist revival, when people you'd never suspect were more troubled by their sins that ever anybody is these days, had she heard men speak with greater earnestness. They not only had something on their minds, but well knew how to get it out. It was when she was clearing away the platters that she saw

Mr. Burnham half rise from his chair, hands on the table, looking thoroughly alarmed, and he said, "Not that, Cree, not that, in Heaven's name."

What was it? Whatever it was, Mr. Cree took it easily. He was smiling at Mr. Burnham.

"Why not? What else is there to do? Does the wolf let go the lamb, unless you take a gun to it?"

"No, no," said Mr. Burnham, in agitation. "That won't do, Cree. You are talking logically, and the human spirit is not kept by logic, not by any standard of the schools, and you know it. Muskets let loose anarchy. You may fire them by logic but the first round summons up all the obscenity in hell. Fears everywhere would come out savage with hate, and that's doing more wrong."

Aunt Ruth stopped while holding a handful of crocks, and glanced at Miss Summers, but Mary's head was bent, and her eyes closed, as if the seriousness of an occasion, long suspected, had come, and she was meeting it as she did whatever disturbed her.

Mr. Cree pushed back his own chair harshly, and stood silent. Then he began to walk the room. Aunt Ruth thought he seemed the best man there, the tallest and most tigerish with that slow movement of his big limbs, and the intent in his face, which still kept the lines of a smile. He stopped and talked at the others.

"That's it. You'll not hold out, Burnham, and here comes the next point on our road. It's close. Dangerously close. This is where many of you are going to turn back. I've always feared it. Though what boldness one hears everywhere, what earnestness, and eloquence, when the Government is being informed of the misery of the people! As if the Government didn't know as much as it needs to know of that. As if it didn't know that when men have not the means to live, then they die. As if we had not been told already by a Government spokesman that it is no man's business to provide for another. Of course it isn't his business. We see that. His business is his iron foundry, or ships, or cotton mill, or milking the great estate his Whig forefathers got by acts of enclosure, that legal term for stealing the people's land. That's his business, and a very good business too. Meanwhile it is natural, isn't it, as the country's wealth increases, for men to die if they don't eat enough? Men have always died too soon, if cold and insufficiently fed. That being so, should we turn aside from our pleasant business to interfere with the laws of nature? That would be to fly in the face of God's word, wouldn't it? Come now, Lovett, what do you think? Do you think it likely that Parliament, unless forced, will ever admit that people are perishing who could be saved? Likely to admit that, when the hunger of the nameless many helps the profits of an important few? Why, are you reluctant too? What's become of reason?"

Aunt Ruth had no more to do. What was he talking about, and what was it he wanted? It sounded very serious. He mentioned ships, and she knew something about them. She rested, and watched, for Mary might want her again. That sad gentleman in black at the end of the table, next to Mary, the one they called Lovett, was shaking his head. He did not seem anxious to own up.

"Come along, Lovett," said Mr. Cree. "Do you still believe we shall persuade what we want out of them with patient words? You can call it educating them, if you like. You do call it education, don't you? I think you'd better be careful, though, lest a Christian upbringing badly misleads us...."

"Misleads us?" questioned Mr. Burnham.

"That's it, misleads us. Misleads us into supposing, for example, that the leopard will change his spots, if reminded of the Gospels when carrying off the baby."

"You're only mocking us, Cree," said Mr. Lovett sternly. "It doesn't help. I've always thought the right way to end darkness is to let in light. I still think so. Your idea of more light is to set the town ablaze."

"Then put it that way. But I say it's better to go up in a good bright flame than to rot off slowly. It's more like life. All right, Mary, looking so grave, I didn't expect you to agree with me, and I don't want you to. You can afford to wait on the revealing of a divine purpose hidden from me. You know something I don't; and that the others don't, I'll be bound. But I'm too driven to put my trust in an unknown eternal power which has never given me a sign. I can't do that, while the world is as it is. Nor can the people wait. How can they wait, when the roof leaks with today's rain, the cupboard's bare, the children have no chance, and they're told with authority that their misery is nobody's business but their own? That means they must rot, or act. They must fight for their lives. Where would be the spirit of the English, if they wait till greed is educated into piety? Who knows when it will turn into that? Lovett, like a gentleman, trusts in slow education and progress and a Parliamentary system. Why, he knows perfectly well that a more cultured and polished lot than the handful of Whigs and Tories which still rules us doesn't exist. Evidently we can't trust such exquisite knowledge of the Classics and the arts to do the right thing, for the cultured have divided the spoils of the land between them since 1688, and lately the new industrial nabobs have not only come along to get their share of it, but can prove by natural law, being practical men, that spoil belongs to those who can take it and keep it. . . .

"Speak up. Yes? Yes, it's true, Burnham. I've done pretty well for myself in the scramble. I know that. But now I'm finding there's nothing in it after all. Success doesn't satisfy.

All I'm quite sure about is that I've lost patience with ugliness. So have you, haven't you? But I've found I can't stand it any longer. I want to get rid of it, throw it out. I don't believe in the divinity of economic laws. That's the hocus-pocus of greed. I don't believe that the cotton trade is more important than human life. Out with lies and liars. And with the bishops whose lawns are never smirched by the waste and dirt of child labour. Where's their trust? Their religion is the same as that of the iron-masters and the land-lords. It's an act of faith in the immortality of personal possessions. They are Christians, yet watch their votes in the Lords. They speak their minds in their votes better than ever they do in their cathedrals. The only holy name today is Property. That's the name they worship. Can't you all see where we are tonight? Our age is the first in history in which science, and the wealth it makes, and the power it gives, is more important than law, religion, and the arts. At every test, far more important. Never before have men had so much knowledge, and so little understanding. To me it is horrible. That's the word for it—horrible. The churches and the universities—yes, Lovett, and even your new working-men's colleges—are more concerned with the sort of knowledge that adds up in pounds sterling than ever they are with wisdom. And don't you call the beginning of wisdom the fear of the Lord? Where's that fear gone?"

"Nor are you yourself wise," interrupted Mr. Burnham, "not if you plan to provoke the unlucky working men into violence. Violence makes only violence. The harvest of the gun is guns. You'll have a hundred dead miners for every dead soldier, and every shopkeeper will swear the miners are better dead. You know what the shopkeeping mind is."

Mr. Cree, still very cool, was about to answer that, when a strange voice broke in.

"My I ask something?" They turned to the speaker. He

was a bent little man, and worried by the sharp interest in the eyes he drew; but he met them, though nervously. Mrs. Penfold noticed that his hands were stiff and knotty, as if they had been broken, and they did not help him, but got in his way now he wasn't using them.

"I'd like to ask whether Mr. Cree knows working men. I don't think he does. I'm one. I began work just after I could crawl, or thereabouts, and I've gone on with it. I agree with all Mr. Cree said, every word; it's just what I think, except that I don't want him to make more bedevilment for us than we've got. I'm sure enough that with all the weapons he could scrape together for us we can't do what he wants. We'd be a rabble. We'd be zanies. We could make trouble for our masters, smash the machinery that puts men out of work, and all that, the same as the other day, but they could make more trouble for us, and worse. Where would it get us? They'd have the army on their side, or enough of it. The untrustful regiments would be shut up in barracks—that's why Pitt invented barracks, to keep soldiers separate from those they know, and would listen to. And there's discipline, that's another thing. It's a gey woeful hindrance to break down, is discipline. I know it. How can Mr. Cree know the strength of the rule of obedience? Doing what they are told to do is in the bones of poor men. We obey because we can't help ourselves. We put up with what we don't like out of fear of a worse tomorrow. We've been bred in fear: fear of sickness, for that means the scrap-heap, fear of losing our jobs, fear of going home and facing the missus when stood off. We live in fear. We find magistrates and bolts and bars whichever way we turn to escape our lot. There's no getting out of it, no way at all, when you're born where we are. Yes, there's one, if we don't mind risking Newgate and transportation. We can become thieves, and the bolder spirits do. For the rest, and that's most, the very sound of the different voice of a gentleman is enough to halt us, when we're unruly, because we never know what to do next. Submission is all our inheritance. There's no sturdy peasantry any more. We're the slaves of the machine. I don't tell you this because I like it. When you know it as well as I do it makes the night darker, it makes us curse the years which have us. It makes us long for the old days of the long bow and the billhook, and the lusty chaps, and they were most men then, who could hit the mark. That's long ago. And there are no preaching friars now sorry for the poor, and hating the pride of the Church, to side with us and rouse the country. John Ball is dead. Faith in God and right is dead. I respect Mr. Cree, and all the good gentlemen who would help us with their influence and better knowledge, but if they suppose we know our strength and have the skill to use it they are mistaken, that's all, they are wrong. That's the last word of truth about us, I think, and I wish it wasn't." He began to fumble for his chair, but turned again, and added, "Give us swords, Mr. Cree, and we might as well stick them into our own innards."

Aunt Ruth regarded the sad face of that speaker steadily and sympathetically. She understood him. He had common sense, and had learned it in the hard school where it is taught. But swords? Swords to take the sorrow out of life? Who would use them for that?

"Don't let him put you out, Mr. Cree," broke in a young man sitting next to the last speaker. He might have been a forthcoming worker, well on the way to be mistaken for a gentleman. "My pal Jim means well. He's stout enough. He's only reasonable, that's all. He was always like that. I say flat out we've got to be as unreasonable as we know how. We shall get nowhere unless we go it bald-headed. We have all the reason we need. We know why we want to make the dust fly, and that's reason enough. Why was the Reform Bill passed? Because threats from men who can use their hands teach quicker and better than the best argument. Fear of what will happen if they don't do something is the only sort of reason governments ever think is good reason. Fear rushed that bill through Parliament. Everybody knows it. Our masters were in a proper funk. So there you are, Jim," and he slapped his elder neighbour on the back, "don't you see we're not the only men to get a sinking feeling in the belly? The old Dook himself, he knows what fear is too, but he don't let on, but faces it out like a soldier. So must we. What keeps you where you are, Jim? Force. What keeps governments in power over us, ordering us about? Force. It ain't love, it's force that makes the world go round, and always was. If you want to get a thing done you must use force, and you have to show it would be unlucky for anybody to get in your way. Is there any reason for making us work till we drop? Yes, and a good one it is. It's because our masters fear they would lose money on a shorter day. But suppose we make them fear they will lose more if they don't let us drop our tools when we've done enough? The meek and mild people like you, Jim, are the support of tyrants. Your twenty-two carat obedience is as precious to the Government as the gold in the Bank of England. It's as good as gold. What we want is not more kind obedience, but fire-arms."

Mr. Cree was frowning as he listened to that young fellow, and Aunt Ruth was not sure, but he did not appear to enjoy him. Anyhow, he sat thinking; he said no more. He was lost in thought. She felt very uncomfortable herself. That house, and fire-arms! What tangled and dreadful talk! It was a relief to hear Mr. Burnham's voice, for it began not much above a murmur, and soothed an after-supper feeling upset by a promise of swords.

"Even if bullets could make truth appear where persuasion has failed," he said, "one thing seems to be forgotten. The Government is of a single mind about the use of guns, for our young friend is right when he says the authority of government rests on its arsenals. Force is its trade. And well it knows its trade. Better than we know it, because as for us, even the few here in this room are not of one mind. Some would, and some would not. The cause of this is simple; the common man is usually more civilized than his betters, being kinder. So what a state the country would be in! The show would be over in a day or two. We may be very certain that force will know better what to do with the weapons of its choice than justice, which merely snatches up those weapons as a last desperate chance. They would be struck out of our hands."

The door bell rang, and Aunt Ruth was on her way to answer it when Mary overtook her, and said, "I'll see to it."

Perhaps that was as well. With such talk in the house, and in that neighbourhood, goodness only knew what awkward question might come to the door. But Aunt Ruth followed Mary with a candle, in case the visitor was somebody two could answer better than one. Mary did not invite the man in, for it was plain she did not know the black-bearded monster, who looked uncommonly rough. He invited himself, closed the door, and peered into the shadows of the lobby.

"Take it easy, ladies," he assured them. "Don't look at me hard. I'm harmless, and always was. Is Mr. Cree here?"

"Why do you ask?"

"That's good enough. Here he is. So take him on one side without waiting for his favour, and say the fat's in the fire, or anything to make him listen. No, I'm not coming in to tell him. I'm in a hurry. The sooner I'm the other side of your door again, marm, the better for you. You tell him

Bonser's been, and that Bonser is on the run, he's making himself scarce, but will wait at the same old place on Tower Hill not more than ten minutes. That's all. Not more than ten minutes. Good night, marm."

Mr. Cree came out of the room when Mary beckoned, listened with bowed head, still with that little smile that would have been unpleasant, only it was sad. He nodded, took Mary's hand in both of his, and was gone. The company fell listless in the absence of Mr. Cree, and the house was soon clear, and quiet; and time too. Mary, who had strange friends and acquaintances, to be sure, though that was known already, said nothing about this gathering. She was quiet and patient as usual. Nothing much had taken place. Perhaps this was what you ought to expect in a life-time, like washing day with a leaky tub, though not so often. She but absent-mindedly bolted the door behind the last, and not as if glad to see the back of them.

Yet Aunt Ruth could not rule herself to that tranquil behaviour. She stood again at her bedroom window, gazing out as if for further news. Now she could see nothing beyond but one large yellow star looking down at her. She wished she knew its bright name, if it had one, for it was far above all this darkness, and steadier than her heart. She lowered the blind, and lit her candle. When that was done she wished she had kept to the light of the star, for it was less shut in than the dip in her small room. For, though late, it was too soon to sleep, with her thoughts still running round after all she had heard, trying to catch up with it, but could not. What was the night hiding? There was no telling. She was never likely to learn. One thing in it was certain, and only one. What a world it was, in which a boy was lost!

21

Signs of Change

His breakfast was late, and when it came it was dull. Never again this new democratic hotel for me, swore Mr. Darton. It could put its choice recommendation, which he had foolishly believed, with its other rubbish. He rattled aside petulantly the brass rings of the muslin window-curtains. Rain was on the panes. He might have known it was. Tepid coffee that was, chicory would make a morning weep though its first intent was bonny. But he guessed where the trouble lay. He had stayed in London well past all the fun, which wasn't much, that it had to offer. But for Cree he would have been out of it before this.

What was Cree doing? What was that man doing? It was over a week since he had asked him to call, but nothing had come of it, not even an answer to his letter. No word about the ships that should have been chartered, though the cargoes must be arriving at the wharves. The cost of delay would be cruel, to say nothing of pillage by river thieves, who kept busy by the wholesale in daylight, so he was told. This wasn't at all like Cree. It was not his style to be silent and invisible when work was about which he was paid to do. Must there be another journey to Leadenhall Street? What, on a day like this, when road filth would be squirting from the traffic in fountains? And the food and smells of London are always worse on a warm wet day. They congeal the liver.

He was not in proper shape to go. He might serve his own interests badly. If he saw Cree, most likely he would

let him have it with unlawful emphasis, and that would
not do. The ships would suffer. He couldn't be sure of himself, for not only was his liver like lead, his head was not
at its clear best. He feared he was losing his ability to see
things straight off and as they really were for their best use.
If he was kept in London much longer he would confuse
good and bad, like other people. Debit and credit would get
mixed up. This city had too much diversity, most of it not
wanted, and it gave a man no minute for choice, so
prudence arrived too late. He had to live at a greater pace,
to keep up with the show, than his Creator built him for,
and his head lost its bearings. Into every hour came a new
idea, the latest fandangle; and, among other sparkling
novelties, there was now a camp of special constables in
Hyde Park, quite near the Throne, let all honest men note,
to prevent one new fierce idea from going too far. A novelty
like that was more of an anxiety than the artful whisper
from know-alls to install boilers in iron hulls. England was
becoming as vulgar and as noisy as the Continent. Gentility
had gone. There was no more quiet leisure, while a
merchant's affairs took their easy and natural course.

Did this mean he was getting old? Nothing like it. He
was still as spry as the youngsters, but he hated the way
they were going, and would not go with them. They could
go their way to Hades, but they would go without him.

It was high time he was home. There was no Killick in
the shipyard now, not a ship's husband he could trust with
the gear. He couldn't get used to the look of that. No
Killick, who knew more than you could tell him, but rarely
said it, to save argument, but let it come out in the job. But
what was a master to do? A halt had to be called, when he
was refused a choice with his own goods. Good Lord, was
his property common? Something worse than insubordination had happened. There was an insolent denial of a

174

master's right; it had come to that. Here was Cree, now, indifferent, by the look of it, where ships were concerned. Think of it! Must the owner himself go to the city to find out how his business stood? Then he would go, and if his impatience with nonsense overcame his discretion, why, Cree was an understanding man after all. A breeze would clear the air.

Mr. Darton's voice, when at the office counter of his agent, betrayed urgency, and admitted no denial, but it did not swing Mr. Cree's clerks round to the brisk attention that was his due, and hitherto had been given. They were idling, and did not move, except to turn their three heads from a close colloquy, in which they found secret amusement, to stare at him. They did not answer.

"What's the matter here? You know who I am, don't you?"

They were silent, as if unable to admit that amount of knowledge. Mr. Darton flung round, strode haughtily to the door of the private room, and thrust it open. The room was vacant. Mr. Cree's table was unnaturally tidy, and eloquent of solitude. Even the waste-paper basket beside it was empty. Mr. Darton closed the door again, though gently, as if he were bemused through the impropriety of an intrusion. It was his turn to stare at the clerks.

"We haven't seen Mr. Cree for some time, sir," one of them explained.

"Ill, is he?"

"Don't know, sir. The police have been here."

"Why? What did they want?"

"They wanted Mr. Cree."

"I don't understand."

There was a little hesitation, and then another spoke.

"We don't either, sir. His accounts are all square. He left money for us. It isn't that."

"What then? Scandal?"

"Not likely, sir, not with chief. Not a word of that ever came this way. The only woman we ever heard about was his mother, and she died six months ago."

"Has he done anything with my contract? Has he put ships on the berth for me?"

"He couldn't have done so, Mr. Darton. That we should have known. He was last seen at an address in the Minories. You can have it, if you like. The police told us of it. They seemed to think we must know it, but we didn't."

Mr. Darton regarded the slip of paper through his glasses, but indifferently. He crumpled it to drop it, yet opened it again and smoothed it, and put it in his pocket-book. It was all he could get, and he determined to use it. "By Tower Hill, this place, isn't it? That is too far to walk. Would one of you please find a Hansom for me?"

When his cab drew up, Aunt Ruth was surveying the street from above. She thought it best to keep out of the way as well as she could. There were important people downstairs this minute, and here came another. The house was all sixes and sevens with a rush of visitors lately, and most of them could have stayed away, for what pleasure they brought. Luckily, she knew nothing of what had happened, so could give quite honest answers, thankful that they wouldn't help. Mary didn't seem to mind any question anybody had to put. They could ask as many as they liked. It was a pleasure to stand by, though nervously, and watch while a simple heart boggled the artful ones. They had never come across it before, and mistook it for a smarter cunning than their own. It brought out their talents. They grew cleverer and cleverer, wasting time and getting nowhere.

As the cab arrived, she was admiring that carriage at the

door, with its spidery wheels, bright yellow, and cockaded coachman and footman upright as idols on the box; and a pair of such lovely bays with foaming mouths, shaking their heads, poor things, hoping to ease their necks of the strain of those nasty bearing reins. How could good people use such cruel harness! That fine carriage had quite an audience, and a respectful one, too, as the police were about. Even this new visitor stopped for a moment to admire the elegant turnout; but as he left it and turned for the steps to the house Aunt Ruth stepped back hurriedly and overturned a chair. She could not be mistaken. That was Mr. Darton, and with his hardest face.

Mr. Darton's countenance was forbidding, just then, because unaware that its habitual lines were inflexible. What it ought to have expressed was perplexity, besides some mixed emotions too rare to show in the lineaments of an important merchant, with an ancient right to find things as they should be. He had not paused merely to admire the fine turn-out, for he thought he knew it, and the heraldic device on its panel told him that in fact it was Lady Geraldine's. At this address? In this rascally neighbourhood? Was the world topsy-turvy? In a moment of hesitation he thought he would turn back. But that would be running away. Here he was, and he must go on. What could she be doing here? If she were here, he must see her, he supposed.

Aunt Ruth, for her part, determined that she would sooner die than go down to admit this visitor. Let someone open the door to him who wouldn't be flushed in such a bungle. She was going to be deaf to all bells, though they rang like the first of a new year. It was Miss Summers who opened to him. Mr. Darton looked down on a meagre figure, who eyed him calmly but not with sufficient interest, gave his name, and asked for the master of the house.

"You may speak to me," she said.

"Is there no master here?"

"This is my house."

Mr. Darton bowed. It had almost occurred to him that this cool female spoke with an air of ownership, and he respected that. "I am sorry if I give you trouble, but I seek a friend of mine, Mr. Cree, and this address was given."

"The police gave it, I suppose. It is all they know. Mr. Cree was a rare visitor. But will you come in? Other friends of his are here."

Miss Summers, remembering that something had to be done and she could not do it, went to the stairs and called up for Ruth, but heard no response, and then took Mr. Darton within. Mr. Darton was prepared to see Lady Geraldine, but not his relative Tom, who was perched on a near corner of a table, with a book in his hand, swinging a leg meditatively. His leg ceased to act as a pendulum regulating his thought as he roused from mental absorption to remark, "What, Miles?"

Lady Geraldine sailed across, both hands thrust forward in confidential welcome as usual, though limply, as if appealing for support and comfort. She did not speak, but regarded him tragically for divination in sorrow. There was nearly a minute of silence, with entreaty in her eyes, and it embarrassed him to support her hands for so long without knowing why, yet he did not see how in politeness he could let them go, for then they would fall.

"Dinah!" at last exclaimed Lady Geraldine. "My poor child. My poor darling!"

Mr. Darton pressed her hands tenderly, but said nothing. Could Dinah be ill? He had not heard of it, yet her ladyship seemed broken-hearted. Not dead, not that, surely? He remembered there was cholera about. He must be careful. He glanced over at Tom, who met his eye, and nodded.

"Gone," murmured Tom, whose voice did not express a grief he felt acutely.

Mr. Darton was shocked. Gone? Not that delightful girl? It came back to him that when Dinah appeared in a room she could give even an elderly man the illusion of youth. They could not mean she was dead. But her mother continued to regard him gravely, waiting for the consolation no mortal can utter in sincerity, when the worst befalls.

Uncle Tom slid off the table and strolled over. "You know what the matter is, Miles, don't you? Haven't you heard? Dinah has gone, run away. Eloped."

"Good God!" said Mr. Darton, partly relieved.

"What shall I do now?" exclaimed her ladyship.

A foolish question to ask me, thought Mr. Darton. "Eloped with whom? You can find them, surely?"

"Not likely," explained Tom. "She's gone off with Cree, and he'll see to that."

This news, with what he had already, was more than Mr. Darton could instantly accept. He had to steady himself. Absent-mindedly he returned the lady's hands to her, while still looking at Tom as if his brother-in-law had become perilous.

"I see," he said weakly, "that's it, is it. I was told the police had been to his office."

"They've been everywhere. But it had nothing to do with Dinah. They don't want him for that. He has been shipping in weapons for the rebellious lower orders. You'll have heard about them. It's called treason, I'm told, or something for the Old Bailey."

Mr. Darton opened his mouth, but made only a slight noise. His lips remained parted. He began a sawing movement with a trembling hand. He noticed with concern that Tom was damnably cool, after tumbling down the verities.

"All?" he stuttered, when he had recovered, "all, is that all you have to say?"

"There's no more to tell, that I know," said Tom. "Isn't it bad enough? Though it might have been worse. Cree might have got going."

"What are you saying? Do you know what you are saying? Got going? How is it you know so much of Cree?"

"I know less than you, I think, but what I know is different. He was worth knowing."

"But treason, Tom, treason! You said treason. It's the most terrible of crimes."

"Terrible it is. Sure to be that. Uproars always are. But as to the wrong of it, that depends on the view of the Government. That's a matter of opinion. Don't forget a government itself will sometimes behave in a way that gets a citizen into leg-irons."

"I don't follow you. I don't know what you mean. I won't split hairs about crime. I won't listen to you if you do it. I say it's terrible, it's dangerous."

"Its danger was pointed out to him, but of course he knew it."

"So you were aware of what he was up to? You really knew what he was up to?"

"Some of it, yes. We tried, a few of us, to head him off. But he had gone too far. If he hadn't, he would have gone on. You can't stop a man like that."

"You know so much, and yet don't know where he is?"

"Look you here, Miles, you are not the police. They've heard what I had to say, though it wasn't enough. Do you suppose Cree would leave much behind him, when he wanted to get clean away, with Dinah, if the gunpowder blew up too soon? And I'm pretty sure he always knew he would fail. He once told me that the keepers of British workhouses and prisons would be found sporting damask waistcoats on the Day of Judgement. You and I are among the favoured keepers. We've nothing to worry about, until Gabriel comes."

"Tom, you are jesting, jesting with death."

"No, I'm speaking about life, the set-out we know. The show will go on here as usual, never fear; but Cree, he couldn't face that fact any longer. He simply couldn't. History moved too slow for him. He had to give it a push."

"A push? And what good has his push done us all?"

"Not much good. Don't you think this isn't bad for me. I don't like it. I shan't see him again."

"We don't want to see him again, except securely in the hands of authority."

Tom shook his head. "We shan't see him." He was trying ineffectively to slip a neat calf-bound volume into a pocket too small for it. Then he began to turn the book about, examining it, as if wondering how he came by it, and what he should do with it. "He's on the water now, I shouldn't wonder," he said meditatively. "We've seen the last of him. He is crossing the Atlantic. The Yankees get him instead, though what they'll make of him or he of them God knows. But he'll be happier in open country, where the impossible is what men are expected to do. Better the prairies than election to His Lordship at the Mansion House. And so we lose him. Miles, you ought to wake up! You haven't noticed what is going on. Look about a little."

He flourished his book to indicate a considerable radius. "Europe is expelling its young. Haven't you noticed it? And you a shipowner! The disinherited of this country, of all old feudal Europe, are clearing out, they're on the move, they're swarming off. Shiploads. All the time. Rough life is flowing westwards, away from us. Today you learn a little more. It is not only the hopeless who can't get enough potatoes that are going. It's a general exodus. Men like Cree, they drop everything and go. Only the police are interested in them here. They're no good to us. Their pity and anger, especially if they have knowledge and invention, are almost sure to break our rules, so they clear out. They take their lively minds to a new world. No bastilles over there, so far."

"But my girl," grieved Lady Geraldine. "I've lost her. I don't want America to have her."

Mr. Darton felt a deeper rage that America should gain Dinah than that Cree would find asylum there. America was welcome to a traitor—let America have him; but it was wrong that a gently-nurtured English girl should be lost amid forests, Indians, bears, and backwoodsmen. Was the good old world he had been proud of breaking up? He watched his relative, who was still moping over that absurd book. Confound the man! How could a gentleman of good family accept the matter so calmly? Here was a shocking pass, and he was idling with an odd volume while talking nonsense.

Tom indeed was still eyeing the gilt tooling on its cover intently, as if for augury. "You'll see Dinah again, dear lady. Cease to worry about it. You will see her. There are steam-ships. There is the new Cunarder. You've only to step aboard. It's only a matter of days after that. But don't stay over there. Have a look round, and come back to us. I'd go myself, but I'm too lazy. Besides, I might never come back. But they don't want leisured bachelors over there, carrying *Tristram Shandy* about with them for luck, standing apart, and marvelling. I'm not as energetic nor as young as Cree either. And Cree, he never had the patience for Sterne. No time to see the fun of it. That may come to him later, I hope, when he has a chance to look backwards, to where we are, or where we used to be."

"I cannot make you out," reproached Mr. Darton. "Tom, are you mad? You talk and act as if you were. The occasion could not be graver, but there you stand fiddling with a book, and drivelling about it. Has it anything to do with our plight?"

"Nothing. Nothing at all. It's only a sign of civilisation."

22

The Ship Star of Hope

Dave was busy polishing the brass of the ship's binnacle. He really was hard at it. This was a real ship. Turn it into gold, was the order. Phew! He ventured a look round. The captain and Bonser had gone. No, there they were, almost hidden by the foremast. This brass had been a beastly green, but when Bonser says change verdigris into gold, that's what you have to do. Was it bright enough? Almost always, far from it. You never knew when he was satisfied, only when he wasn't. No mistake about it then. Bonser was mate, and let you know it.

He was sharper than ever since the ship had a new captain. He says he hopes a sailor has come aboard now, all right, all right. The other captain broke his leg falling down the saloon companion, drunk again; and Bonser, who picked him up, said his broken neck would do more good to a ship than just a leg, which was bandy, anyway. He says that when a sailor is master then you have a ship, and he says this new captain has a proper sea name to start with. Killick is his name.

The new master took over the day before yesterday. He only stood for a minute gazing aloft, when he boarded her, till Bonser came along. Then the two of them mounted to the poop rail, and the new captain pointed here and there, and Bonser agreed, and told him the charterers were greedy sharks who cared as much for the ship as they did for the emigrants, or the rats.

The captain said nothing, but walked away. He stood

over the compass for a spell, thinking about that, but did not see Dave standing by, though you'd think his eyes saw everything, and it made him tired.

This brass would have to do, it was as bright as he could make it, until he was told it was the shame of the ship. He expected he would be told so. Dave gazed aloft, as the captain had done. He couldn't help staring up quite often, and in a little fear. He was afraid he'd never find sense in that dizzy raffle of ropes, never be able to read meanings in that monstrous webbing stretched high on the sky. He doubted it was true that every single line up there had its own name and use. You couldn't name every thread in that complication, nor ever find out what each stretch of it led to. The three masts rose to a frightful height. They made the head go round. And the wind was in the rigging as usual. The ropes were humming a tune just for themselves, not for him, it was too faint to make out what they were singing about, perhaps of Port Royal and flying fishes. The dock basin was small for this ship. Her heavy lower yards were above the roof of the shed alongside, and her topmost spars were under the clouds.

Dave frowned again into the upper light, sad with the thought that he would never find sense in that mixture of standing and running rigging. Which was which? All he could be sure about was the shrouds. And it seemed quite beyond the ability of men to work this great ship away from the quay, round the corners; and out safely to the Mersey. He wouldn't believe it till he had seen it done. After that, in that height of yards and ropes, many sails had to be set, all true together, and giving their full pull and no loss, Bonser said, and the body of her to come alive at the shout, and answer to the turning of that wheel. Yes, all the way over to New York!

It was hard to believe it, unless you shut your eyes, like a miracle in the Bible. But Bonser says it's as easy as love when you were used to it. He wasn't used to it. So far he could only remember the names of the masts and yards, and then had to give himself plenty of time for it, and perhaps forget the spanker gaff, or the mizzen royal yard, or something more important, and worse. Then Bonser swore and called on God for help. Lifts, braces, halliards, sheets and downhaulers, bowlines and reef tackles, and bunt and clew lines, to say nothing of stays and preventers. Look at those cobwebs of lines streaming down from each top to the deck! How could he be expected to jump at the word for one rope out of the lot? Where was it? Bonser says that when you have to jump for your life you soon learn which way to jump. He says that when you must hang on or die, then it's one hand for the ship and the other for yourself, or else Davy Jones. Davy's locker keeps wide open for the next duffer. Bonser says he was right inside the locker himself once, but before the lid shut he popped out again, because full of rum and fun.

Dave watched the captain—he didn't like to say the Old Man, though that's what Bonser called him—descend the ladder to the quay. The captain did not stop, did not pause to admire his ship, as Dave always did when on the quay. He strode away without looking back.

But Captain Killick did not give his ship the deference due to her because he had gathered all the information about her he could tackle for the moment. Today was near to the day of sailing. Her passengers would be aboard before the week was out. He was off to raise a din, though doubting that good would come of it. His ship was seaworthy, but ill furnished; and he could not complain to her owner, who was not interested; nor to her charterers, those distant specu-lators who smelt money in cargoes of humanity, now Europe was pouring away its life to the western continent, for the charterers were probably a group of tallow-chandlers or brassfounders, or something else as briny. The only man he could go to was the Liverpool agent, who knew too much, and didn't care what happened to a ship after she was out of sight of the land.

The captain, as he went off, was judging the possibilities of his voyage. He had no time to give to the beauty of her lines. Four hundred emigrants, and his ship was sure to be loaded beyond capacity. More than enough. She would provide water for them, and that was all. They would have to feed themselves. Bonser, who appeared to know his work, and had talked to a few of them, was delighted because they supposed America is just out of sight. Only out of sight. One day on the water and they would be there. They think food enough for a picnic will see them across.

The ship's stores he had inspected couldn't keep them alive, if the usual westerly winds muzzled the ship all the way over. And that could happen. Poor devils! Change to them was not a risk but an opportunity. And there might be a month of it, especially with a crew of agriculturists bundled aboard drunk or drugged at the last minute by a boarding-house blackguard. No wonder England had failed, so far, to persuade gentlemen to take charge of her merchant ships, except a few East Indiamen. But for the fact that he felt pretty sure his mate was a sailor, and a driver at that, he would throw in his hand. He never cared for the North Atlantic passage, either. It was a dark, cold, heavy, and turbulent ocean. Eastern waters for him. But a sailor must accept the first thing that offers without looking at it twice. He'd never go to sea at all if he looked twice at his work. And then? What then, in hard times?

Oh, cheer up, man! For now he came to think of it, and he must admit it, whatever a ship and her venture might be he was never fully content with life except when in charge on the high seas; alone in his own cabin where he could meet himself at last, and no more bickering, free to judge for the best, and responsible for his decisions. That was no more than the sense of power, of course, and no different from old Darton's, but it did drive a man back on his soul when he remembered, within the round horizon, and under heaven, and no help near, that the safety and happiness of a company of fools and innocents depend on his knowledge, and the use he makes of it; to say nothing of what happens to his nerve, should the outlook turn ugly. It was as much as he was fitted to do, so he had better see it through.

That medicine chest, though; that was another thing. He must keep it in mind. It had been carried about for years, evidently, and never replenished. The bottles that were not stale or broken were empty, and the mess stank like the poisonous accident it was. The ship's surgeon had not complained about it, and that was a bad sign—one of those surgeons, very likely, who have to look up the difference between sternum and cranium. Ship-fever was bound to come, more or less, to the miserable wretches in those crowded alleyways below, battened down when the decks were awash; and he had heard of worse sickness in these ships, and more than once.

If this trip wasn't going to be a nice basinful for him, then he could thank his lucky stars. What was it that blackbeard of a mate said just before he came away? "What's a corpse or two? The fishes could have the lot of us, and no questions asked." That man Bonser had the cut of one who had served under the Jolly Roger. All the better if he had. He would know the use of discipline.

The captain had to check his steps when nearing a dockside gin shop. A lively mob stretched across the road, its centre bobbing about to the jig of an invisible fiddle. A wild-haired wench flinging a leg bumped into him, but her wink put matters right. Blue eyes, with that black mane! Those eyes explained the miracle of dirty rags showing so gay a spirit. Irish, of course. An irrepressible lot, the Irish, and they swarmed here. But not all were dancing. Others were past that, looking on glumly, or attending to a cheap-jack who was as eloquent as a pill merchant, but who had a ship's sailing-bill hanging to the wall behind him instead of a quack's usual chart of the human bowels.

He was selling ocean passages, if you please, the new cure-all, and the captain had not seen that done before. No specific for a gummy inside slow to action could match the glowing benefits that salesman knew were to be found in the west, the Land of the Free.

Captain Killick listened. He heard that you were a full and free man, for the first time in your life, with no more than a passage ticket in your pocket. All for three sovereigns! Haven't got three? Then what about two pun' fifteen? Dirt cheap that, to bring about a change of view as gay as Cinderella's. Two pun' ten, then! No? Think it over, you over there, you with the dudeen in your hat! Haven't you had more than enough of this old country? D'ye want to spend y'r life breaking stone and picking oakum for a spoonful of skilly?

That Irishman started energetically to elbow his way forward through the crowd. He had decided.

Bonny for you, Pat! But all Pat could manage was to fish up some silver from the deeps of his breeches, and he offered that, together with a broadcloth cloak, which he must have stolen.

The sailing-bill advertised "That elegant emigrant ship, *Star of Hope,* 600 tons, copper fastened, Captain Tom Goodenough, now loading in the Waterloo Dock, for New York direct. The best chance of the season for a safe, short, and easy passage." You paid your money, boarded her, and were released from care, as a beginning to a nobler existence.

The captain went on to his agent. So it was this way cargo holds were filled with voyagers who knew less than a ship's cat! Tom Goodenough must have known something, when he went and broke his leg. These were the simple people who would be shut in down below, when she was lurching scuppers under! Rations short, and no medicines. If he couldn't get what he wanted from that agent he could leave a piece of his mind in the office, and no whispering about it either. And what good would that do?

Bonser came to the binnacle, and eyed its brass. Then he eyed Dave slyly, and walked away, without giving another order. Dave scrambled down to the quay, for only there could her figure-head be admired, a white angel with half-folded wings, holding out an arm, with a finger pointing ahead, and a golden star in her coronet. He walked the length of her to her square stern, with two windows in it, and the words in gold, *Star of Hope,* Liverpool. She was his ship. He was sailing in her, the day after tomorrow, or pretty soon now. The quay had a nice warm smell of tobacco and treacle.

He climbed aboard again watchfully by an outboard channel, which was the easiest way, for it projected over the quay, and the shrouds helped to hide you. Bonser said that if he caught him so much as staring overside longingly, like Susan at Handsome Jack, he'd know the taste of a rope's end; and if he stepped ashore he'd stay there, and go to prison. But he hadn't been caught yet.

23

Outward Bound

THE *Star of Hope,* bound towards New York, was out
in the Mersey. She was nearly free of the land. How
she contrived to reach the river from the dockside was more
than Dave could say, though he had watched, all eyes. Her
movement into the stream was as imperceptible as the
drift of a ghost. There was no fuss, and hardly a sound.
Only her flags were excited. They were very excited. Now
and then came a shout, but Bonser's voice ruled, the best
one to sing out in an expectant hush, for it knew what it
wanted, though how it knew was surprising. A hawser
splashed as soon as he called; even the ropes obeyed him.
Yet it was not the ship that moved, as well as Dave could
see from behind the high bulwarks, with the fine rain
dripping from the peak of his cap, and tickling his nose. It
was the buildings that moved slowly past the ship, as if
the roofs swung round gradually, changing places.

The sailors were slack and lazy. They were brought
aboard that morning with their sea-chests and canvas bol-
sters, some of them as helpless as dead men, and had to be
dragged forward along the deck out of it. Packet rats, the
second mate called them. Several of the brutes cheered just
now, when a rope tautened and flung a passenger head
over heels, and knocked him out. Captain Killick stood
above at the break of the poop, and didn't seem to have
much to do with it. The emigrants, who came aboard in a
great mob just before the ship moved, lumbered the deck,
like stacks of dummies, and did not speak; they had no

voices, except when one of them raised a miserable song which nobody wanted. They gave no heed to the ship and the work. They stood and gazed shorewards, and only moved when pushed. Some of them were weeping.

She was in the river, and nothing held her but the hawser of the steam-tug, and that was slack. Was she moving? When Dave raised himself to peer over the bulwark, the water was uncoiling along her side, and some chips of wood were bobbing astern. She was moving, she was under way, though she still seemed too bulky to go of her own accord. The white sea-mews sheering overhead and around, crying as if they wanted to rest but could find no place, might have been sorry for that woman there, crying, holding her arms to the shore. It was no good doing that. She couldn't see a soul there she knew. They were too far off. The water was growing wide between the ship and the people ashore who were watching her; but the emigrants still gazed at the dockhead, though not at their friends, only to where a blotch of black and pink was slurred by the rain, with a few handkerchiefs flickering in it.

Why, thought Dave, we're off to America; here we go, yet these people would make you feel it was the end of all. It was only the beginning. He was as excited as the flags, and nearly as shaky, though he did not stir from under the break of the poop, because he wanted to watch unseen. Not even Bonser would notice him there, it was all too important for him to be seen in it. He felt like this at his first and only pantomime. There the lighted stage was, when the curtain went up, and nobody on it, though it was certain something would happen on it very soon. This was just like it. It was like a pantomime, but more of it. Ahead of them was the sea, and the steam-tug had really got hold of them.

"Set the stay s'ls, Mister," said an easy voice above him.

Here it came. Bonser raised so cheerful and rolling a cry that the men roused. They jumped to the halliards with lively shouts. The fore-and-aft canvas fluttered aloft in spurts, and then the sheets steadied it. The ship knew at once. She was waiting for this. You could feel it in her timbers; the deck made a difference for the feet. She was alive. Another order came, and men mounted the rigging at the word as if the wind blew them aloft. They might be drunk, some of them, but that didn't matter. They could hang on by the toes. Her square topsails bellied and her heavy weight had gone. Her head grew light and lifted, and the water roused to chant and murmur alongside. She chased the tug, and was overhauling it.

"Let go!"

The hawser leaped overboard. The crew of the tug cheered as she passed, going fast in a confusion of shouts, running men and tackle flying, and more of her canvas going wild, flapping and banging; too much of it, Dave imagined, and the foresail far too big for safety, while the noise of waters grew louder. The barefooted sailors, with sheath knives on their hams, threw themselves at it, and sang, as if it were all a great joke and they didn't care what happened. That was how Dave began to feel. It got into him. He didn't care. Let go all. Danger is splendid. Give her royals and studding-sails, give her everything. Let her fly. Hang on if we can.

That burst of liveliness, with the wind and wet, cleared the topside of most of the passengers. When Dave's eyes sought the deck again it was almost free, except for the sailors making fast and coiling ropes. Only one woman was left, the one who gazed shoreward as if she couldn't let go the look of it, and held out her arms for what was only getting worse every minute. Now she was clinging to a stanchion at the main hatchway, afraid to descend steps that would not keep still. She'd fall down the lot if she didn't make up her mind. Dave ran to help her, and found that to persuade fear that it has nothing to fear will make a fellow hotter than hard work at something useful. He guided her below without a tumble, though she was still at a loss. She didn't know where her berth was, nor whether she had one. She didn't know anything. He had to prevent her from returning to the upper deck. She said she was used to the country, not a dark prison. She couldn't breathe down there.

"Is it breathe?" said another woman standing near. "Come now, darling, you try. It's as easy on you as a tinker's curse if you'll not think of it. Never a thought do I give it, and me in poorhouse and prison more than you'd believe, and what you'd breathe there would take the nose off the face of you."

Dave left them talking. He didn't know where the women's quarters were, and wasn't going to find out. She must look after herself. He'd look well, if seen there. Bonser was very particular about that; he said they had no Royal Marines in that ship to guard the right people from those who haven't been found out yet. "So watch it, Commodore, there's nothing to start shindies down below here. This is where you'll berth, and you'll enjoy it better than you would the Old Bailey. That was a close shave. No room this voyage in the fo'c'sle, and that's lucky for you. Those men for'ard are not fit to live, let alone live with. But while they live they'll work. They'll work. They'll work till I break their hearts, and yours too."

The good luck in sleeping below wasn't very plain. Perhaps these people who had all this deck would sort themselves out presently. A London street crowded at night was better than this. Above a crowded street is the sky, but here it was beams next to the head. Most of what light there was stayed about the steps of the main hatch. It didn't travel far, and it couldn't turn corners. Those small plates of thick glass set in the ship's sides did not help at all. They only showed that a green day was outside. The smell below was strong of new wood, like a cargo of raw packing-cases; and that in truth was what it was between decks, a catacomb where live bodies were newly boxed and stacked in recesses.

The narrow alleyways with their tiers of bunks faded into gloom for and aft. The rough woodwork, hastily knocked together, was already complaining of the movements of the ship. Its creakings came sharply through the babble of the people there. Would things, Dave wondered, ever settle down, or get worse from day to day? They didn't know what to do with themselves, these emigrants. The sweepings and refuse of all lands, someone called them. The shadows were so thick that he could not help bumping into them. bruising himself, stumbling over boxes and bundles on a deck that it was hard to see.

Faces peered over at him from upper berths. They were real faces, when he was used to it. They were pale, and had eyes. Masks without bodies hovered about. It would be fresher and more open up above. He knew already he would be up where the wind was, and as often as possible. The air down here would not change all the voyage except to get thicker and hotter.

Was he in the women's quarters now? It sounded like it. Women were everywhere, chattering in the gloom, and children were howling.

"Will you stop that snivelling, you little bitch you? You'll get a bite when I've found the bundle. Is that the bundle you lost, Bill?"

Men were here. Then did men, women, and children all sleep together in a general huddle? There seemed no doubt they did. Bonser hadn't told him that, Now, there was a man, breaking the first of the orders, smoking his pipe in a lower berth, the fool. Dave hesitated, then bent down. "No smoking allowed below deck, sir," he said.

The man leaned leisurely on his elbow. "An' who'll stop it?" he asked. He then went on to tell Dave of the frightful things that happened to anyone who tried to stop him from doing what he liked. A woman laughed.

Dave moved on. That fellow hadn't met the mate yet, but a meeting would come about pretty soon. Bonser had given strict orders about his duties below. He had to watch it that there were no naked lights, and no smoking. No lights, even when all was battened down in hard weather and it was dark as the inside of a black cow. But a glim was to be kept at the main hatchway after sunset, only that.

"If it'll burn," Bonser had remarked. "Usually it won't, or only burn blue when the weather lasts, and the hatches can't be lifted. When it comes to that, Commodore, you'll have to choke with the rest, to save the ship from foundering. That's the proper thing to do. All the same, wet or fine, middle watch or dog watch, no fighting down here, and no gambling, which is the same as fighting, and no lovemaking, which is worse than gambling for shindies. Stop it, boy. Pull 'em adrift.

"And another thing. The passengers are to sweep all alleyways clean before breakfast. Clean, mind, if they are sick, and sick most of 'em will be till we lift the land, and after that. No litter, no dead infants to be left about for more than a day. For me, I'd sooner berth with the cables than turn in with your crowd. And they must carry up their dirt, and cast it overboard, to loo'ard. Show 'em which is loo'ard before they let go. What blows inboard you'll eat, for learn you must, somehow. But I'll say you are coming along handsome.

"Though mind this again. When you come across him, and you'll do it, a passenger dying isn't so much odds as a man smoking. A dying man can wait till the sailmaker isn't too busy to measure him, but I'll be down at the word, and I'll strangle the man who won't put out his pipe when ordered. We'd look grand, flaring up over the deep in a snorter. Why, this ship with its lumber would catch light as quick as a crew diddled of its rum and rations. Quicker. She'd blow away down wind, smoke and sparks. Hurricanes and cholera if you like, but fire aboard here won't bear thinking of. Shiver me, but I dream of it. I had it once. I can see this full cargo of ignorants breaking loose once she began to burn. All panic-struck loonies at the hail. And where could they go? Why, the only boat is for me, you, and the Old Man, and we'd never hoist it outboard in a blazing riot. Do you want to die?"

As it turned out, the difficulties were not as hard as Dave thought they would be. Most of the trouble disappeared after Bonser had been down to persuade sense into that passenger who always had his pipe alight. The man began to argue. He said he'd do what he liked, he'd paid his money, he wasn't a nigger or a sailor, he was a free Englishman.

Bonser didn't talk. He moved at once. As he twisted the pipe out of the man's mouth it popped like a cork. The furious passenger started to scramble out of his bunk, but he was helped out, and faster than he could have moved by himself. To save the kicks Bonser held the man off at arm's length by the throttle, and for so long that the kicking died down. The women began to scream at Bonser for a murderous bully, and the men threatened, but he took no notice. The smoker fell limp and was bundled into his bunk again. He didn't move much then.

"That'll put him off his pipe for a bit," said Bonser. "But that's nothing. You'll see what I can do when I try if I have to drop in again. You don't understand yet, none of you, and that's what made me easy as a lamb with that hulk, him not knowing what it is to be in a burning ship. What's that you say about your rights, that man there, you there hiding behind a woman? You'll come to me about those rights, my son. There's no rights aboard this packet only what I allow. There's no rights about a burning ship, only hell's doings. Mark me. You'll go by orders, not rights. My orders. Break 'em, and there's me to break. I'll be here for it at the call. What I want is what you'll do. And don't force me to show you what you're made of before the women. They'd not like it. It's going to be shipshape here, I tell you, and you'd better all learn what that is. Do it soon. You want to see green grass again, don't you? Right. Then act as I say, and there's a chance you may." Bonser picked up a loose batten, and snapped it across as he pushed away.

"Bones," he said, "are softer than that."

He had no more trouble with them, or only when they were ill, and couldn't help it. They meekly obeyed even Dave. They would do what anyone told them after they saw the sea itself. That frightened them. What they wanted was comfort. They were easily scared. If the ship lurched suddenly there were screams that the end was coming. A louder noise up above made them stare, waiting quite still for the next thing. The sound of the wind rising was more than they could face, and it was a cold and melancholy sound, the wind in the rigging; Dave himself admitted that. On the morning when the land had gone, quite gone, and only waves were moving under the clouds as far as they could see, and they heard the plunging overfalls, the poor people supposed they were lost for ever. They clung together. Some of them prayed, kneeling in the alleyway.

Small blame to them. It was a wide and lonely waste, after all, and Dave felt himself subdued by it. It was nothing like the English Channel, which was only rough. He could have believed the ship would never find her way out of this wide emptiness to the right place, if he had not seen the captain at the rails, talking to the two cabin passengers as if all were well, and looking like a man who knew that better than anybody else on board.

Dave saw the face of the deep, as it was when light came on the first day of the earth. It had not changed. There the firmament was, in the midst of the waters. While he gazed over the solemn billows he almost wished he was home, and it was just before bedtime, and he was listening to Aunt Ruth reading that part. He could not help feeling, in a way, that it was better to have it read to you than to see the thing itself. While hearing her quiet voice, as she read, he could believe that God was present, above it all, saying: Let there be light, and dividing the light from the darkness; but it isn't so easy to believe when there you are, and the sea is getting up, and you are hanging on, and if you let go it is all over. Dave wondered why there should be that difference in the way one felt about it. But he could see for himself how vast and awful the ocean is, for there it was to the sky-line; but the sky was empty, nothing was there except evening clouds as black as iron, so he could not make out the greatness of God. He had to believe that, or go without.

After dark, the sea was stranger still. Then he could believe in what he could not see, and easily enough, because it was necessary. When night was falling fast, and he was lonelier than ever, and the upheavals of the waters in the twilight were more monstrous than by day, and the sounds of the ship herself, alow and aloft, seemed to tell him that she was fearing the coming dark, then Dave believed in God, because he had to. He didn't want to be alone then; it was too much for him to understand, when alone.

At last the sails were black shapes, and the ship snored

along in fair weather, and no need, for a change and a miracle, to touch a rope. That was when the sea surprised him. He saw it as though he had never known it till then. This was called calm, but it was not. Under a thin moonlight, and not much wind, there were no waves. There was no broken water. But there was no rest. Upheavals grew slowly immense without a sound, silent as shadows, and rose higher than the lower yards, quivered in the pale light for a while, and were gone, but not before you knew their power. The ocean was alive. Men were nothing to it. The great rise and fall was everlasting, and a mystery, as if the Spirit of God was moving upon the face of the waters.

24

A Dog-watch Yarn

THE wind was fair. Not a thing had started in the ship so far, not a rope. That morning the surgeon had been below, for the first time, because one woman was more gravely ill than some others; but he went to the wrong passenger, and left in a hurry screwing up his face as if he were about to be ill himself.

Chips, the ship's carpenter, was sitting at the bottom of the ladder at the main-hatch in the second dog-watch, as he did sometimes. He was sitting in a good light, where the air was not as thick as it was farther in. He was yarning, of course, to the men and women standing round him. You couldn't help listening to him, because he had a voice like Punch's. Those emigrants knew he was no liar, for he told them what they wanted to hear, that their ship was doing fine, though ignorant landsmen wouldn't think it. Not many more days to starve. New York soon. No more dry oatmeal and a little cold water. No more hard tack. Rare beef-steaks and onions every day for all, and beer that poured about.

The children stood close up to Chips's feet. The bandanna covering his head fascinated them. It was a yellow silk handkerchief with white spots. He said he wore it when he was a pirate, and it was given to him by a princess of Madagascar. It had four knots in it, one at each corner, to keep him reminded of his wives, so he said. He took it off to show the children his bald head, as a treat. He lowered his head, to give them a full view of the top. It had a blue scar across the shiny dome from back to front, sunk in. He got that, he said, at Trafalgar, through chain shot, just as he was picking up poor Nelson.

He shifted the bandanna comfortably into its place again. The children begged him to take it off, but he told them that if too much sea air, which is very strong, got at his head, the pressure would burst it open, and he would lose what brains he saved after the battle. Then he would have to stuff his head with sawdust. He had plenty, but it didn't work well in damp weather, except with some people, who never used anything else.

Bonser said, that the captain said, that Chips was the best insurance against fire the ship could have, and cheap at that. His stories of disaster brought about by folly at sea were as good as keeping everything soaked. A child screamed now if she saw a light struck below. Early that morning the men had kept the pumps clanking for more than an hour, and Chips told the crowd that meant their old *Star* was as sound as an empty rum puncheon, though not so sweet. She was doing as well as a Black Baller under a Yankee cracker-on, and a knot better. They had found the best ship there was, and the best navigator that ever knew where to find the right wind, so don't look for another. Go ashore, when you get there, and stay ashore for the rest of your lives.

"She didna look as dry that the morn," said a man.

"It's a fact you don't know what water is," Chips told him. "You want to be in a ship that's pumped to float her over, day and night. I've been in a ship down to her scroll work a week out of Bristol, and all awash with the water over the hatches when we were off Sandy Hook. That's what bent my back and I'll never straighten it. It was the mooring lines of Pier 11, East River, New York, that held her above the surface. She tied up in the last minute, though the weight of her broke a rope or two. You don't know what pumping is, when it's ten men against the ocean, putting it all back again as it flows in. That or drown."

Some of his audience did not know what he was talking about. They were Scandinavians, Bohemians, and Germans, mostly. There were people from all over Europe in that crowd, and they could not make each other out, except the hardships they had been through. That was the same in all languages, from Irish to Greek. Those people were running away from stint and grudge, but hadn't got far yet, and looked it. They were escaping from famine, landlords, prison, princes, margraves, hospodars, bosses, bailiffs, potentates, lieges, stadtholders, gubernators, protectors, electors, debts, judges, and archdukes, but the sea and its weather were there, and short commons still had them. They stood patiently listening to Chips, and took him for a safe man, because the sick and pale ones who understood his language kept faintly smiling. The barometer was unsteady, but even Chips didn't know that.

He was talking to the children. He could hold their attention without trying. There were gold rings in his ears, and they thought that was because he was a pirate. But he said no, he wore them so he could see what was going on after dark. His round red face had a roll of grey wool from ear to ear, passing under his chin, and his thin lips were tight and hardly moved as he spoke, for a quid of tobacco had to be kept clear of his words. That was why he wiped the corner of his mouth with the back of a brown paw, now and then. But his eyes puzzled the children. First they looked at one eye, then at the other. The lid of the left eye was half shut, and fixed that way, and its eyebrow was dead. The other eye was round and lively, and its tawny brow often arched in surprise the rest of Chips did not feel. He kept it raised when he surprised everybody else. It was only that eye that talked. His bare arms were quicker than his face, and they joined in the conversation. Though his hands were brown, as if all the tar could never be washed out, showing hairs like fine golden wire, his arms were of smooth old ivory, with blue veins, and the muscles slid about and bunched as he pointed or waved. One forearm was tattooed with a woman's face in red and blue, and the other had an anchor with the name Lizzie over it.

The ship heeled, and a toddler fell against Chips. The audience clutched one another for support. The sudden complaining of the timbers was noticeable. "She's talking to us," said Chips.

"Why, can a ship talk? I thought it was only the boards moving," said a girl. "I listened to them last night."

Chips regarded the child gravely. "Some men I know say of their ship, they say it of this one because they like her, that she can do anything but talk. I heard one say it only yesterday. That's because they don't know. They live with her but she's laughing at them. Of course she can talk. She has a lot to say, from the kelson to the tops. Why, there was an admiral I sailed with, when he didn't know what canvas to carry, would go to the mainmast and whisper to it. Then the ship told him what he had better do, and she was always right, was that ship. So that admiral never lost a spar till he went to another ship that was either dumb or wicked. He lost that one and serve her right. She never said anything. Now what do you think of that?"

"A wicked ship? I've never heard of it. This ship isn't wicked, is she?"

"Our ship? She's nearly as good as you. She's so good she falls off her course if there's gambling or bad language on a Sunday. I've noticed it. Someone, says I, ought to know better down below, troubling the heart of a good ship like that. After this, m'dear, you keep your ears open for what she says to you. You'd never believe how touchy a ship can be. Nor how much she knows, either. One frigate I was in would sail after a Frenchman, when she saw his flag, faster than after any other. Off she goes when she sights his colours. Her captain would promise her a coat of paint and some gold leaf if she would overhaul, and she always won that paint."

A man laughed. "Did you ever hear the like of it! Go on now, say a ship has a soul to be saved, same as parson says we've got, and we've only to try."

"Stow that," said Chips, as if he were going to be angry. "Don't mention parsons here, mister, no black coats, not if you want to see land. That's the sure way to call up dirt. The weather backs into the wrong quarter when you monkey with words aboard ship. She didn't hear you then, or she'd have shivered her timbers at a mistake. That shows whether she's got a soul or not. Live long enough, and don't get pride in your parts, and you'll learn better. You'll know then of the bad ship, the one with a bit of gibbet post about her somewhere. She's the devil's own, that one. You can't get anything right with her no matter how you try. It's always a headwind with that ship. She's the ship with foot-ropes that break when they're new, and you're done. Keep off a ship like that, or you'll be cast away on Coffin Island among landcrabs and no water. Why, if ships haven't got souls, how do you account for ghost ships, tell me that?"

"I don't account . . ."

"Not another word, or you may have to this night. I say there's no teaching people when they're sure they know. As for me, I know nothing to be proud of, and know it. I've lived too long over the deep for that, and can believe anything now, when sure a man ain't clever that's telling me. Wait till you know you don't know, then you come to the right way of looking at it. No ghost ships, says he. You said it, didn't you? You want to be on the look-out some night in the middle watch, you do, and all quiet. You want to sight her dead ahead, coming down on you fast, but no sails set, and against the wind, tall as a hill and black as a funeral, and see her fade, and the one black man on her quarter-deck, as you shout. You'd have to account for that."

There was silence for a time while all looked at Chips, and he grumbled to himself. Then the girl spoke again.

"Mr. Chips, those ghost ships, are they all black and bad?"

"That's a fair question, m'dear. That's the thing to ask. If you hold on the way you are you'll be a bright shiner. There's always good with the bad, the same as day and night, and fair weather and foul. You take the fat with the lean, if you can get any lean. It's with craft as with men. Most shipmates you can trust when it's too dark to see your handhold, but there's those that strain your eyes in daylight. Watching them about is harder than work. I've sailed in all sorts of craft, and it's my belief there are more good than bad by many. Though I'll say this, to leave some of the good craft is better than another voyage in them. Much better. That's plain, ain't it? So it stands to reason it must be the same with those ships gone missing, ships done with articles, don't you see, done with lead-line and compass, and no more watches to be stood. Breakers ahead or deep water, it's all one to them ships. Storms don't matter, nor fire, nor what people say, nor what owners want. They're unmoored from all that holds timber in place. And there's good with the bad. That's what I say. So if you see a ship come full sail out of a cloud in the offing and pass inland like a thistle-down, which she shouldn't, don't think the worst of her. She may have a good log. Perhaps you'll feel like screaming, only you can't, when she doesn't run aground on the church steeple, but holds a straight course right through it. It looks unusual, does that, and I admit it. Most things are rum, if you look at 'em honest. Some of them ships it's lucky to see. Only the best people see 'em, but not till they deserve it, so it's not often."

"Have you ever seen one?"

"Ah! Have I! I'd like to tell you, so I would. But you'll find it don't do to say what you've seen, that you will, when it's a thing like that, or worse. There's those that can't take truth, when it's agin their natur. I've seen many things, and not all for putting into pot-hooks and hangers for my old mother at home, either. So I don't do it. What I've seen is mostly to keep me minding my eye, not your eye, and not Jimmy Brown's.

"Anyways, between you and me and the mainmast, there's ships, and not only ships, that puzzles us till we can't make out how much we don't know and can't learn nohow. There's the ship called the *Mananono,* so I've heard. I've never met a man who knows where she hailed from. She was a great craft. Most people have heard of her, though she was only seen once. She was so big that she stuck fast, for a tide, between England and France, but she scraped through, and that's why the cliffs there are cut straight up and down and clean white. She lightened herself of ballast, and that's the Goodwin Sands. As she lay, her spanker boom was over Calais, and her jibboom poked into Dover and swept a regiment of soldiers into the sea. Sailors who went aloft to her royals as boys, they came down the shrouds afterwards growing beards. She was as tall as that, and the captain went about on horseback giving orders. It took a year for her to tack. After she shipped green water, same as a ship will do when the going is hard, and her decks were afloat, you'd find whales washing about in her scuppers, as it cleared. I don't think I'd want to sail in her. She'd be as hard to steer as a kingdom, and I always like to know where I am, and what to do next, as near as may be.

"Then there was the *Ship of Stars*. Perhaps there still is. It would be good-o if there was. Her captain wouldn't have had me on her, though, nor the likes of me. She was manned by children. She used to be seen now and then, once or twice in a hundred years, but mostly by your sort. Sometimes by women, but hardly ever by men. I never saw her, not me. That ship cruised only by night. She never hove-to at night, but only by day. She made herself snug, at sunrise, up in the middle of a good cloud, where she wouldn't be sighted, for she called on the stars. The stars are better seen at night, and she didn't want to run aground on a tiny one in daylight. They had the best of music aboard, fiddles, and flutes, and Jew's harps, and that music was most that was ever known about her. It was sometimes heard when she was passing over, late at night, about two points abaft the starboard quarter of the moon, the sky clear, all quiet, and people and birds asleep. Most people, but not all. Then the one who heard her aloft knew it was safe to shut-eye. You mightn't have been thinking it was a fine night and you were lucky, but you knew it then, when you heard her on her way.

"My old grandmother told me she saw that ship once. She had her in full view. It was a week before my mother was born. It was a cold winter morning, with enough light to see the tops of the elms plain on the sky, and she'd gone to the chicken-house to look for an egg that wasn't there. What should she see, coming back, caught in the stone wall across the road opposite her door, but the brightness of a small anchor of gold. A fluke was stuck in a fault, and the wall held. She was very surprised, but not frightened, when her eyes followed the anchor's red silk hawser to a ship under the clouds, all yellow sails set, just over old Mrs. Morgan's cottage, about as high as swallows fly when wet weather is coming. It was sparkling with lights, that ship, like a diamond necklace. It didn't belong to the country, and never had, so my grandmother went over and worked the fluke loose. The anchor flew into the air when free, no weight in it, easy as the first lark, and when she looked again the ship was making off with a row of cherubs at her gunnel, their faces rosy, though the sun hadn't topped the hill, and the whole crew of them looking down at her and laughing, while music played. She said . . ."

There was a shout from forward, and Dave didn't hear what more was said by Chips's grandmother. He had to cut and run. That was a call for him.

That sick woman was worse. He thought it would end like this, and now he could see it. She could never be persuaded to go up to the galley for her share. Besides, everybody had to fight for it at the galley. She wasn't able to fight, and she couldn't have eaten much for a week. She wouldn't take food from others, but always smiled and shook her head. All she'd ever take from Dave was water, when he had the luck to get it. You had to fight for that, too.

25

Battened Down

DAVE returned, and in a whisper warned Chips, who shook his head. "That's the first. Tell the mate. Stamp and go. Don't tell old Bones. That surgeon's the same as nothing, if he is a surgeon. Tell the mate."

Dave was halfway up the ladder when the mate's whistle screamed, and Chips was behind him in a jump. All hands! That shrill pipe bustled them. That screaming whistle was the beginning of it. It struck while they were yarning comfortably. As Dave tumbled out on deck a sea washed inboard, and he swung on a stanchion to save himself from the lee scuppers. Down there the water was dancing. It was beginning to blow, and it was bleak. The change had come in a breath, and she was just saved from being taken aback. The watch had been too sure of its luck in the hold of fair weather. The captain came to the poop rail, and Dave didn't know he had such a voice. It carried into the confusion, through the worry of the frantic sails, sure as a trumpet.

"Aye aye, sir," cried the mate. The canvas was flying wild, and it was pale in a queer light, as if day had sickened. The men were hurried and quiet, trimming her into shape for it, furling royals and top-gallants and hauling her wind.

It was no good going to Mr. Bonser now, or he'd find trouble. It would have to be the surgeon. Away to the west was a loom, as if night were closing in on the ship long before the hour, approaching like a high wall, blue-black. Before it scurried a few low clouds, spooky as that woman's face, and underneath the livid sky the seas were heaving a sour green with flashes of white, like the flags of an army riding down on them. Something was coming. It did not look good.

Dave mounted to the poop, and as his head was level with its boards her stern rose steeply to a sea while he held fast, looking up at the helmsman's head, the first thing he saw there, and he never forgot the moment and that man's face. Under a mop of fair hair which the wind was tugging the man stood with his wheel against the clouds, too high to keep his place, with more than he could hold though he daren't drop it; his stare showed the strain of it, but the captain was with him. "What do you want?" said the captain; and Dave told him his errand.

"Out of this. Get below and stay there."

That was easier said than done. You can't run about on the pitch of a roof. And as he reached the rail again a squall broke, and hail was bouncing on the deck below, but only as a brief surprise. The deck vanished before he could drop to it. The hail increased in a moment as if the whole white load of it was shooting out of a cloud turned bottom up. It flew straight across the ship as sharp as splinters of glass and as thick as blindness. It cut and numbed his face.

It became a long and hard journey to that main-hatch, with the men only distant shouts in the pealing of the wind. She was laying over to it, and he had to decide, while holding on he hardly knew where, with no feeling in his hands, that it is better to fight it out than to give way. The savagery of the blast astonished him into anger and energy. He fought it. A good thing, he thought, it's a hatch and not a royal yard. Could the fellows aloft hang on in this? He found his place just in time. Chips had nearly closed it.

When shut in below in the dark he heard a shout on deck, and then a heavy plunge of waters. What was that? He listened, but there was nothing to learn, down there.

He began to fancy before very long that he would rather be topside where the men were busy than battened down with the helpless passengers. They only cried and groaned. It was worse to listen to that than to be out with men hitting back. A storm can be fought, but not the miserable wailing of terrified people. He was scared himself for that matter.

That was a wallop. She was struck by another heavy one. She was rising again though, she was still there. In the dark, there is no telling what the thumps mean, nor where the large and swift movements will end. When suddenly she lifted and kept on rising as if she had lost weight it gave him an empty inside. The sea was getting up, by the feel of it. She began to decline again, and he waited thoughtfully. How far down this time?

What he'd better do was to light that lantern. It wasn't much of a job, it wouldn't go far, but it helped. It took up some of the time. He remembered what Bonser said of the way that lantern burned, if they were battened down too long; for want of air it burned blue.

He cheered himself. Very likely the hatches would be opened again at daybreak. That was the way to see it. This careering was too bad to last all night. He got the lantern going, though it made but little difference, except around the ladder. Its light showed that girl near, the one who had been talking to Chips; and its shadows, as the ship rolled, flickered and jumped about as if the hollows were alive with black frights. The child was on her hands and knees where she had fallen, and was looking up at the lantern too surprised or alarmed to move. He took the lantern and led her to her people. Anyone out of their corner now would have to stay out till daylight was let in again.

When he had put that child in her place he went

wandering with his light, because that was better than to
sit down doing nothing, waiting and listening to sounds
he didn't want to hear while watching shadows leap about.
His lantern lit up vague heaps of sea chests and bundles in
his journey. Over some he had to climb, where there was
only enough space to crawl between the top of it and the
overhead beams, while the pile was still shifting towards
another avalanche. Where he was able to walk he was
never sure whether it was clothes or bedding that had to
be dodged, or bodies. There were plenty of bodies. Passengers had been flung out, and where they dropped they
stayed, all the go knocked out of them. It was easier to roll
about below than to climb back, and no use climbing back
either, though they might be brained by another charge of
mad boxes if they stayed where they were.

That hollow darkness echoed with a continuous low
rumbling boom. When only a bucket broke loose it went
off in a hideous clatter, as if a bucket could stand it no
longer; and that started a woman screaming. Scream after
scream. The children wailed to hear it. It was through
being imprisoned, that was the trouble. He felt it himself.

He hated that woman. Her shrill cries made him seize
hold of himself to stop the burst of fright in his own inside
which she had started. Part of him wanted to run away at
once.

There was no running away from this. Hands shot out
of the shadows and clawed him as he passed, clutching
him with questions nobody could answer. How did he
know whether they were all going to die? He hoped not,
fastened down and no way out, a nasty way to die, but the
awful bumps and echoes were not good. You'd think the
worst, if you stopped to think. He tore himself away, and
struggled on.

Then he remembered a duty. He ought to go to that

sick passenger again, though he didn't want to. Nothing could be done for her now. He had better go, though. He stepped over a man flat on his back, his big chest a black mat of hair underneath the lantern, his eyes shut, babbling away in a foreign language, all on one note, as if chanting without stopping for breath. The ship lurched again, and loose oddments racketed off in another alarm, and the howling broke out afresh.

Dave dragged himself along, his sense of his whereabouts not perfect. Wasn't this about the place? Yes, this was it; and there she lay. Somebody had lashed her fast.

No wonder. They wouldn't want her bumping about loose now. Though there was nothing to frighten anybody in that small yellow face. He used to think she was old, but she wasn't old. She was as young as his mother was. It was the calmest face in the ship; no fear in it. She only looked asleep and satisfied. Dave clutched an upper berth and held up his lantern.

He forgot the storm, looking at her. Well, if that woman could, so could anybody. Well, now he didn't care as much as he did. Another woman, her long grey hair wild as a witch's, hobbled over towards him and gripped him for support, looking down at the still figure. She swayed in contemplation, and presently she spoke.

"Will you look at her now," she said. "The creature. Rest her soul. I declare to God she's as innocent as a baby, but there's nobody to say a word for her, there's nobody knows the name of her. May the high and holy court of Heaven hear us, all hidden from pity as we are this night."

She dropped to her knees, and lifted up one hand, holding to the berth with the other, mumbling words Dave could not make out in the endless racket, but he gave them both the light of his lantern.

26

Mid-ocean Ceremony

AFTER that, Dave was lost with the others down below, where time had ceased to count. Whether another day had come, or another night, was more than a fellow there could be sure of. For all Dave knew it might be next week. There was no way to tell. Time had left them. All thick darkness is alike.

He couldn't be sure whether he had been asleep one night, or part of it, or a day and a night. He dreamed he heard noises, or perhaps thumps heavier than usual shook him into attention now and then. He would listen for a while in case he really had to move; a new thing might have happened. But it never had. There was only the heavy dark. There was nothing between yesterday and tomorrow, and he drowsed off again. He was always drowsing, and when he wasn't asleep he wished he was.

If he came to, all he was sure about was that he was thirstier than ever. Let this go on much longer and he wouldn't be able to swallow. Once he was so hungry that he felt he couldn't wait another five minutes, but now he could wait for food for ever. His tongue felt too big and dry for his mouth.

There was no dream about that. That was a big sea overtaking them and sweeping the ship forward till she settled again; and that was feet padding along the deck overhead just afterwards. So somebody was still on the job. And more than one man; the pumps were clanking. It was a very long storm.

The lantern failed long ago. That certainly meant many hours had passed. The passengers were quiet. They could all be dead, but he supposed they had only given up; all they wanted was to be still. So did he. He wasn't going to move to find out how they were. If he went along he couldn't see them, or do anything. He had heard nothing of them but a groan or two for he didn't know how long.

He'd have a look round if he had a light, but the lantern was almost done long ago, when the man came begging for water. He said his girl was crying for it, and he must have it. When was that? She was ill. Dave went round everywhere for it, but nobody had a drop, or said they hadn't. It was natural to tell lies about water. The light was going out then. He could just see the child, it was the same one, the one who had been so bright with Chips. He thought she might be only stubborn when she paid no attention, though she didn't look very spry, with her black hair plastered to her white face with sweat. It was very hot and close then, though he hadn't noticed it much since, except when he woke with a start. He didn't wait there long. He'd brought nothing back, no water, and he couldn't help it when her mother bent over her, calling her, though she didn't open her eyes, even when shaken. All you could do was to hope people were all right.

The sea wasn't an easy place. It could do that to you, and keep help far way. He supposed this was what he had asked for, though it was more than he expected, but that girl only came and was caught. She wasn't to be blamed for being here, but her face was beady with sweat. He had no idea ships could be like this when he was glad to go to sea. But he wasn't going to say he was sorry: he wasn't anything in particular. He couldn't think about it; he could only wait. If he kept still he thought he could wait till he was told what to do next. One thing was sure: Bonser would not forget. Bonser would be down the moment he could. The idea down there was that the mate of the ship was a cruel brute, but Bonser only pretended; he would not forget; if he was alive, that is. Some of them were alive on deck. He had just heard an order and then feet running again.

He fancied he could make out that round of glass in the ship's side, but now he was sure of it. There it was. He kept his eyes fixed on the place. Yes, it was some day or other. After a while the round grew plain, with its watery green light, though it was at once blotted out as a sea swept over it. All the same, day was outside. The green cleared again. It grew a little brighter. He began to count the number of times the waters swept over and darkened it, but gave up that game when he had to wait too long for it to go.

Not long afterwards a row broke out, loud and immediate, as if the ship was tearing apart. That put him on his feet. Boards aft were crashing. A bright lantern appeared down there, where the bulkhead was, and several men stepped through a gap in the boards. One was the captain, and another was that swell the cabin passenger, Mr. Cree. But they stopped as soon as they were through, as if still hindered. They hung about at the beginning of it longer than rescuers should, Dave thought. Mr. Cree put his handkerchief to his face and turned away, as though he were going back. You could see the captain was telling him to go back, but presently he came on with the captain, still keeping his mouth covered.

The captain led with the lantern, holding it aloft to the upper tiers, both sides of the alleyway, peering into holes and corners, quite unconcerned, though the gentleman with him showed signs of being unable to hold out, turning away from some berths, and then coming round to them once again, as if he must see this, anyway.

Hardly a passenger bothered to notice the visit. They were quite changed from the early days, when a panic broke out if suddenly she heeled. She could heel now as much as she liked, and nobody cared. Here and there a face lifted to stare at the light, and that was all. Once there was a voice, and the captain answered.

"Yes, be easy. Think yourself lucky to be alive. Water is here, it's coming now, but you'll get only a little now and then or you'll be ill."

"We're ill now, your honour," said the man. "We want the doctor."

"He's ill too, he's pretty bad."

"Then we're done for, sir."

"Not you. Cheer up, man. You'll see blue sky in a day or two and like it. You'll pull through."

They came to where Dave stood, and the captain regarded him. "So you're on your feet. Good."

He felt Dave's wrist. "Take a sip of this. Do you think you could carry this lantern round? Try it. You know your way about here. Let's see you walk."

Mr. Cree made an unpleasant remark about the ship.

"No," said the captain, "it's not the ship. This isn't her work. She wasn't built for it. None of them were. They're too small, too crowded, and take too long. Steam-ships is the answer."

"But the Americans are building great and fast clippers."

"I know. Grand ships. But it's the wrong answer."

Dave continued to carry the lantern, holding it up for the inspection, but not feeling very curious over what it exhibited. More than once there was hardly a question. Two women and one man paid no attention at all to the light; if they weren't goners they looked it; and the last one, a woman, was as far as Dave could manage to walk.

"My God," muttered Mr. Cree, "what is it? What's its name? Are we to find any more?"

"Possibly. You'd expect it, packed together this way. Jail fever. Ship fever. The same thing. Typhus, I suppose. That and starvation. The hatches will have to come off, whether or no. The ventilators are worthless. We must risk it. Boy, what's the matter with you?"

Mr. Cree took the lantern from Dave, who was sent back to his place.

That day in the forenoon watch the hatches were opened. Dave was the first to get out of it, and giddiness seized him at the height and purity of the wide world in a dazzle, but he was not too weak to notice in alarm the state of the ship. The main and fore top-gallant masts had gone, and men were clearing the tangle. A length of the larboard bulwarks had been carried away, giving the waters there a much too familiar nakedness and liveliness. The deck was wet and cumbered with wreckage, and the men were busy and grim, and seemed used up.

She rose and fell to the running of a heavy sea, forlorn but proud. She wasn't done yet. She was on her way. While he gazed, he was taken by the shoulder from behind, and spun round. "So it's you," said Bonser. "Why, Commodore, I made sure you'd been dead a long time. That hatchway smells as if you had, but you're walking about. You'll be a man yet, if we get the right slant, and get it we will."

The weather lifted all that day. The next day was brighter still, and warmer, though the sea continued to heave immensely, but without breaking. Dave felt better already, keeping to a patch of sun as well as the clouds allowed. When the sun clouded over the wind seemed to blow on his bare bones. It was then eight bells, the morning watch. There was a muster amidships, crew and passengers. The Red Ensign was run up halfway to the gaff, and the main yards backed. Way was taken off her. She rolled in the long swell, without progress.

It was mid-ocean. To larboard, quite close abeam, a Mother Carey's chicken drifted up the long hills of water, then scooted down the valleys, dragging its toes just off the rippled glass, a tiny mite to be there alone. The ship rolled, and the spars complained sadly. The undertone of the wind was in the rigging. All stood to attention, and she rolled.

Seven figures were laid out in a row on the deck, sewn up in old sailcloth, their feet towards the water where the bulwarks had gone, on the lee side. The sailmaker and Chips had been busy fixing them up. Bonser whispered that the stout party this end in a canvas overcoat was the surgeon, but who was that ha'porth at the other end?

Dave knew, but he didn't say. He couldn't say. It seemed such a pity now that she never had that drink. Captain Killick came forward, a book in his hand, and with him were Mr. Cree and the tall young lady they said was Mrs. Cree. The captain tucked his cap under his arm. The men uncovered. A block swung and creaked overhead, and the surge of the ocean sighed as it met her; but when the captain began to read his voice had command of all other sounds. At last he lowered his voice, and came to it. "We therefore commit these bodies to the deep. . . ."

The men lifted each canvas bundle to the sliding board, tilted it, and the shape dived off; one after another they plunged. The last to go was the small one. The waters swelled all alive to the deck level as it went, and met it. The splash it made jumped in Dave's throat; the waters took it and vanished. Mrs. Cree was weeping. The group stood without moving, though it was all over. That block was beginning to whine again.

The captain slapped on his cap and walked quickly aft, but stopped and turned his head.

"Why don't you fill away that mainyard, Mister?" he called out sharply. "Away now."

27

Cabin Conversations

THE cuddy, in the stern of the *Star of Hope,* was flooded by a calm and bright morning through the skylight. Under the skylight swung a brass lamp, highly burnished, and in itself a minor sun. It was but leisurely pendulous, so comfortable was the weather, over the captain and the mate at breakfast. The cuddy was more like hope than the rest of the ship, for it was panelled in mahogany, and that gave it a warm and luxurious glow.

The mate was telling the ship's master about the difficulties with the gear, but could report that most of it had been put right as far as the stores and spares allowed. "She wasn't provided for western ocean doings," he explained sadly.

The master meditated, and answered that the man would know a lot who knew what the Atlantic would do when it was all out to do its best.

"Ah, and specially, sir, if he judges it between the curtains of a Liverpool parlour."

The master did not comment on that. He looked absently at the skylight. "I never liked this passage," he said.

"Nor me. Summer nor winter. When it isn't gales it's fogs and icebergs, to say nothing of cracking-on till you half hope she'll be pooped and done with it."

"How about the fresh water?" asked the captain irrelevantly.

"We'll about manage, sir, watching the half-pints—that

is, we'll get in on the last barrel, supposing we meet no more dirt."

"If this slant holds today we may make landfall the day after."

"Ah. Then all right. And I'd say that after this little trip any landfall would be nearly as good as a Blackwall pub I know."

"I don't know that pub, but we're doing better than I expected sometime back."

"Same here. There was a night when I wondered where I'd go when I died, but here we are at breakfast. As we shape now we'll make her underwriters happy. After all, we've only jettisoned twelve passengers, the surgeon, and one sailor; though a useful hand Billson was. It might have been worse. It's better than expected, as you said."

"The sea is still a problem. We haven't learnt to manage it yet. There's much to learn."

"I've learnt all I can hold. What I want more than a long fair-weather voyage is a little farm. Or a cosy pub would do, perhaps better. All the same, it's long odds old Davy will look me up and down one night and grumble because I didn't come sooner."

The master smiled. "He'll think himself lucky if he gets you. You know too much for him."

"Thankee, sir. It's the first time since I was a young shaver that the cabin has given me a testimonial, so I'd better go before I lose it."

Mr. Bonser pushed away his plate and rose as Mr. Cree entered. They politely exchanged morning greetings, showing no more than that familiarity which eases constraint while at the same mess table. They were, to others, but compulsory shipmates, otherwise moving in different worlds.

The mate stepped back, however, as Mrs. Cree also came

in. There was no constraint or formal manners about her. She was cordial with Bonser, and he responded. When he was not about she called him the Great Bear, and had explained, when challenged, that this was certainly not because of his hairy bulk, but because he was as dependable as the stars you could most easily find when you looked for them.

She inclined her handsome head, standing behind her husband's chair, as she asked the officer quizzically whether he had now relented, and would allow the ship to let her have this one breakfast in peace. She gave him no time to answer, but went on at once, "That's a pleasant lad you call Commodore. I've had a nice talk with him this morning. He knows a place not such a very long drive from my home. It is remarkable, but he has been to Branton in Cornwall. Think of it. It was delightful even to hear the word, with the sea wherever you looked, and going far away from home."

"Then he told you more than he ever told me, though I don't wonder at it."

"You'll not make me believe he is secretive. Ginger people with grey eyes and freckles never are. I expect you are not sympathetic."

"Why, nobody ever called me that, either, so I expect Branton wasn't what he thought I'd care to hear about. With you it's different. Did my smart Commodore name any other places he'd been to that I don't know?"

"Branton took up all our time, because we didn't have much. It is such a good place we couldn't leave it for another in five minutes."

"Branton?" exclaimed the captain. "If you'll sit beside me, Mrs. Cree, I can remind you of more of that place than the ship's boy. I've known it for years, but don't remember seeing him there. But it's full of boys, and they're all alike, unless you fix on one of them. I thought our lad talked like a Cockney. He's not Cornish, I'd bet. Nothing like it; and I'm only Devon, and that is a foreign land to the Cornish, and so you'll tell me straight out, I know."

"Then come along," said Dinah, sitting beside him. "It's you that's secretive, knowing so much and never saying a word."

"How could I? A man may know a lot, but when he lives on deck as well as he can, and doesn't know which will go first, his ship or his sick passengers, how can he gossip? You yourself at one time, so Mr. Cree complained, wouldn't listen to anything from anyone, not even a tiny word of hope."

"Oh, let us forget that. It has gone by. It has gone, hasn't it? We'll begin on something better. It's such a nice morning. What shall it be? Now, as you know Branton, you must have met Miles Darton. He often drove over to stay with us, when we were at home. My father was very fond of him. So was I, sometimes."

"Of course I met him. I must have met him more than once, I fancy."

Mr. Cree chuckled.

"Why do you laugh?" asked the captain. "I doubt you always found him a laughing matter."

The passenger stiffened and glanced sideways, but did not speak.

"I never met Darton's London agent, Mr. Cree, but I've often heard of him. And it seemed to me now and then you had considerable news of ships, from a quayside view, not to name a craft or two I myself saw off the slips at Branton. I could only wonder. Not that it kept me awake."

"Come now, captain, what else do you know?"

"My own business, the rest goes down wind. Where are the winds of last week?"

"Now I'm out of it," grumbled Dinah. "Instead of what I wanted the captain to tell me I'm to hear about ship after ship. I know. You men never mention a ship without becoming sentimental and talking like pretty valentines. But go on while I eat. Don't mind me. Anyhow, I'm hungry and shan't listen."

"Men are under fate to be talking of ships, Mrs. Cree, though it bores you. Ships, luckily, are just as variable as the funny neighbours that keep ladies talking when they meet. And if ships, then politics too, and the rest of the tiresome stuff that puts ships on the move. Each must dree his ain weird. It's our lot in life to keep fleets moving about somehow, or the world would go bad."

"She's in quite a good humour, captain, I assure you. She likes to hear you talk. But she doesn't know, she turns away if I mention it, what free trade and the rest of it will mean at home, and soon, although furious shipowners and landowners say those reforms will sink poor old England. Yes, you laugh. You would laugh. I've told her, whether she is pouting or not, that steam-ships, and all that makes the Chartists talk as they do, are going to contract the coasts of the world, draw them closer together, liven them up. That's it, and especially liven them up. But when I warn her of a new book of life opening, she only says she likes the old one best, and goes on reading her blessed poets. What's to be done with her?"

"Better let her stick to the poets, I suppose. I wish I had nothing else to do. The book of life, as you call it, the old one, was more than I could ever spell out. You're right about it though, I guess. I'm sure new moves are on, but to where, I'd like to know."

"We shan't live long enough to know where we are being taken. But there's an uprising. There's a surge forward."

"I should say there is. It puzzles me. Watching the shipping was enough to tell me that something is up. Europe is exporting more people to America and Australia than pig iron. The departures from the home ports, with the roguery flourishing about them, were enough to say that unusual ideas are stirring. This voyage is as strange to me as it must be to you. I can also see how steam will help presently, when we learn how to keep high pressure in boilers without funerals. The knots that will raise! That's all pretty plain. But I can't see beyond it."

"You don't need to. There's the facts, and we'll have to use them. I've had to be about Europe, of late years, and from Hamburg to Vienna the old dry bones are stirring. This is resurrection from feudalism. It has come at last. Even in Berlin there was a sort of revolution, where nobody expected it. Paris is another matter, always was. Quite often it wasn't safe to be about where not long ago you'd have thought that nothing would ever interrupt the dance and the popping of corks. It is all over! The curtain is rising on another play, and we're in the stalls."

"What's this new play about? When you say we don't need to know, that the facts are enough, I won't have that part of it. Facts can be damned awkward. Damned is the word. I use facts for the safety of this ship, but it's no good puzzling out the weather, and measuring the sun and stars, without knowing where I'm going, and what to do when I get there. Facts can be hell itself unless we get them right, and know how to use them, and what for."

Mr. Cree stirred his coffee. "When was the point to which human affairs are drifting ever known?" he asked.

"How solemn you both are," murmured Dinah. "The conversation sounds like the wind in the rigging."

"Perhaps it is only that, Mrs. Cree. Perhaps there is no more in it. Men have always gone on like this, you know, and see what has come of it! But I have a recollection, since you compared this easy little talk—and it's the first we've really had, remember—to the emptiness of the wind. There was an old man I met in Cornwall—that will give me your attention—who once said, in my hearing, that no good ever came of anything we did under the sun, unless it made men kinder. But he was only a wandering Methodist preacher."

Mrs. Cree said nothing, while considering the oscillation of the lamp. Her husband asked the cuddy servant for another cup of coffee.

Bonser's voice was heard above them with an order to the man at the wheel. "Steady."

Then the steersman's reply. "Steady it is, sir."

28

Landfall

A PRIVILEGED few of the ship's company, having been confided with their approximate position in space, ventured to count the hours to landfall, but they forgot to reckon fog. The incoming of a chilling and enveloping indistinction, when all was going full sail, reminded them of the vanity of enthusiastic estimates. More men were posted to the look-out, and there they stood, fixed shadows, intently listening to blind silence. At the poop rail hovered uneasy spectres, yet up there it was that the actuality of sure guidance should have been.

The ship faded to an unsubstantial apprehension; she was subdued. The fog was silence itself, visibly swirling through the rigging, trailing across the deck, a cold and white apparition. Voices were lowered, even when giving orders. No shipman would raise his voice in full authority while this stalking fear was about him. The white silence swirled on, without end. Dave caught himself in a foolish attempt, while peering outboard, to fan away the frustration; for it seemed to have little in it, no more than a film over the eyes to be rubbed away; but the world was false no farther off than the transient glints and shimmering of the waters at the ship's side.

Then as quickly the fog went; it appeared to go the moment they were resigned to it, as though only waiting to be accepted in apathy. You could hear the ship's sigh of relief as first faith returned, and then weak sunlight cast shadows on the deck.

"I hate fog more than the rest of it," said the captain to Mrs. Cree. "An enemy that blinds you is fiendish." He then gave an order to the mate. They were to take soundings.

Soundings had been taken before, but this duty, to those who did not understand, was no more than the rest of the ship's routine. They knew only of another tedious day to be pulled through. There still was the unhopeful and wearying ocean unchanged, except where distant areas of it were missing under luminous wraiths and white banks of mist. Nothing else was in sight. They were alone and lost as ever in the waste. Not all the voyage had they sighted another ship. Nothing was there to tell them that they had not wandered aimlessly clear of the inhabited world, were beyond its bounds, and in waters man had never sailed before. Lassitude and regret were upon them. They paid scant attention to the men who had stationed themselves fore and aft, while way was off the ship, the main yards backed, with coils of line, and who now sang out to each other to watch, watch, watch, as the line was released from one man to another.

The lead went. Bonser, after a pause, raised his head, and called casually to the captain, "Forty fathoms, sir, sand and shell."

His call turned a few heads to stare at him in surprise. Then they had reached the other side, they had crossed over? Sand and shell! It was America.

They looked round. The new land was not in sight, not yet, but it was under them. The name of the ship took on a cheerful meaning. Her figurehead, pointing forward, had known the right direction all along. There had been nothing in clouds roving within a fixed horizon to advise her; but she had known it. And how easy it had been to doubt that, on some days! Now the sunlight, though it was frail, was but the beginning. It was shining where the old life could not touch them again; it was shining on all things new.

The good news passed around. There was stir and hurry. It was vain, of course, to crowd the bulwarks to see the new land, but all who could rest elbows there watched the sky-line for the first veritable mark of the future. On a first voyage, each one of us is Columbus once more. To Dave a miracle had happened, and he knew who had brought it about. He glanced aft shyly and respectfully to see how the captain was taking his triumph, but that great person was not looking for America. He and the two cabin passengers had found a subject to amuse them.

The ship was pressing on with all canvas for the discovery. She had as much as she could hold, and the watch and the steersman kept her full. There was confidence in the wind's song in the rigging, instead of melancholy. Her ensign was brave. The wash was leaping past; it was gambolling now. But what they would discover ahead was as vague and various, if as full of promise, as the hopes of westbound voyagers two centuries before.

America remained mythical. It was still dream-like and without frontiers to the westward, a region open for romance. It had grown far beyond what it was to the men who first sighted it on the horizon; then it was only a stage towards Cathay, or it was only an unexpected hindrance in the search for Terra Australis, that other country more desirable where saints could dwell in everlasting summer nearer heaven, as Columbus supposed. Nobody now wanted to go round it in search of a better land. It was a tremendous entity in its own name and right. A passage to the North-West round it, a shorter way to China, was still being sought, but only as an old observance, and somewhere then beyond

Hudson Strait two ships under Sir John Franklin were seeking that route; but the possibility that had moved early adventurers up the St. Lawrence, hoping for an outlet to the Pacific that way, was long forgotten in the treasures found inadvertently by the shores of the Great Lakes. There newcomers were swarming from Europe, destroying the forests, founding cities, building railways towards the prairies, and making canals to take wheat, timber, and steel direct to the Atlantic. Primeval earth was surrendering to men as it had not done since they were but hunters and pastoralists, coming out of prehistoric darkness to grow crops by irrigation, and to form kingdoms by the rivers of Asia and the Nile.

But America was more than corn, metals, and labour. It was an emancipating idea. It could provide visionaries with auspicious faiths. It continued beyond farms and industrial tumult, Baltimore, Philadelphia, New York, and Boston, beyond the axes of pioneers and the camp-fires of buffalo hunters, to the remote speculations of dreamers. It was lost over the Mississippi among fabulous tribes of Indians, where rumours of prodigies hidden in deserts, forests, and mountains were superior to books and geography. The West was an incantatory word. It started men off with their eyes fixed, they did not know where, nor why. They were released, at least, from the compulsion of old spells and circumscribing enchantments. This freedom itself was a wonder in a life accustomed to a narrow plot confined by the bans of antiquity.

Men escaped from the past. Notions that had become exhausted in the East, spirit that was flickering out on soured and tired earth, revived and found courage and resolution when moving westward. The drift of humanity from the beginning has been towards the westering sun. The sun drew men after it. For men are destined to go forward, they seldom know to what, though cherishing in some form or other as a secret of the heart the fable of Atlantis, or of the city of Manoa, or of God. They ridicule Utopia, perhaps because they know they are unworthy of peace and joy, but they will never cease to believe in it, and on any pretence they can invent will stumble towards the point where they trust it could exist. Columbus told the Spanish monarchs at Granada that he proposed to reach the East by the West; but in secret he was not looking for Cathay when he happened upon a new continent not knowing what he had found; he had set course for Paradise.

Not that a matter so august and mysterious was known or suspected by a soul aboard the *Star of Hope,* though the eyes of many of the ship's company were looking hopefully for America. They could see only the waters, bright and quick, distant sails, and one large ship nearing them; for common sight is deceptive as well as hopeful, true but for the moment and what appears to be in it. The vision of what resides within a prospect, a task, or an adventure, and will grow out of it, is not for those who are eager in the present scene of life; as for the changes to be related to it by and by, and as sure as that approaching ship would soon be abeam to leeward, even the eye of faith would have to be very long-sighted for that. What did the gaolers guess of the destiny of Imperial Rome, because of their interest in the persuasive words of their prisoner, Paul?

Captain Killick stood by his helmsman. All he was sure of now was the position of his ship in that moment of time; he was sure of it within a trifle. He could not be far out, he knew, for he trusted his judgement, since the lead line confirmed it, though a sight of sun and stars had been infrequent during the voyage. Experience, patience, and resolution were now justified. By dead reckoning mostly, and keeping a good heart, he was expecting as a reward to pick up the marks that would lead him to Manhattan. Then he could relax, his responsibility discharged.

What surprised him was the number of ships in view, ahead and to the south, after a hard passage in which he had not sighted another sail. He was again in the midst of life. There had been hours when the appearance of the wilderness assailed him with the black doubt that he had taken his ship and her people right off the map while following an unascertainable error. About him now were the ships, mostly outward bound, of an abundant metropolis. Each was crowding on, doing her best, as if the city had released an impatient fleet that had been confined by adverse weather.

Killick watched that big craft closely. Here she came, twice the size of his own, cutting it fine. The man that handled her knew the way to do it, and was flying a towering cloud of canvas that would have frightened some sailors he knew. An obviously bold and handsome Yankee. Here she was, and in a tearing hurry. He could read her name, *Reuben R. Kimball*.

They hailed each other. The voice of the American came across to the English captain with the timbre of good news for the ignorant and unlucky.

"New York to San Francisco!"

That's a voyage and a half, thought the English master. California? What could a big thing like that do there? Nothing was there but shacks for hide merchants and sealers; and foul Cape Horn was mid-way.

"Good luck!" cried Killick. He knew they would need all of that.

"We've got it," returned the American, sweeping his arm to include the other outward-bounders. "All California."

"What a noble picture that ship is!" Mrs. Cree exclaimed. She went to the taffrail to follow the snowy cloud with her eyes.

Captain Killick turned his head to watch, quite puzzled. All California-bound? Why? What had happened?

29

Return to Tower Hill

AUNT RUTH came out of the house in the Minories, a
market basket on her arm, and paused to lift her nose
to the weather. She always did that, though she knew she
would be deceived. Once she could declare at breakfast,
after a turn in the garden, a glance at the sky, and a sniff
of the wind, what the heavens would let fall before the day
was out, and make as good a guess as any sailor. But not
here. London beat her. It would beat the best. Its horizon
was itself. It made its own weather, mostly of coal smoke,
and fattened on it. She supposed her own pipes by now were
as black as a kitchen flue, after these years by the Tower.
Her very inside must be dyed London colour. She was
claimed.

She looked about without moving, approvingly. The air
was broody and mirky. There was rime. It smelt of soot and
frost, and had the proper feeling of a few days before Christ-
mas. It was as still as a contented child. You'd fancy the
place remembered to be quiet. It was composed, and was
waiting; it knew a secret. She loved such London days.
They came now and then. She must be a Londoner herself
by now, taken in by it. She shared the secret. This place
wasn't naughty on a day like this, but satisfied, good-tem-
pered, and comfortable. We are all of the family. The
family has been here a long time, a very long time, and
worn it smooth for us; if we ourselves can't stay for longer
than will help wear a doorstep a trifle nobody will ever
notice.

She had to visit Aldgate market. That way she always turned, not towards Tower Hill and the river, if she could avoid it. Sometimes she couldn't; she had to go. Go that way, and the sight of topmasts and sails aloft stirred up things best left asleep. Then she went all adrift. On Tower Hill you run straight into it. Then men just ashore, or about to leave—there they are, at every corner and post. There was a day, while she was still on the look-out, that she'd stand and chat with one of them, if he seemed to be a likely customer; but when a sailor steps ashore he knows nothing but mistakes, he is the most aggravating, amusing stupid alive. The land under his feet makes him lightheaded and giddy. He comes to himself only when aboard again, and hanging on in a blow with no friends about. No, she wouldn't turn that way any more, to watch what was going on by the water-side. She knew what went on, and was sorry for it. She'd look well, asking such a fool question, whether any ship in the river was just arrived from New York.

Still, without more hesitation she turned towards the river, she didn't know why, except that the morning was her own. Perhaps the season of the year helped; the street itself seemed thoughtful. Perhaps the past nudged her that way while her thoughts were idling. Sometimes there is no telling what takes hold of us, but we go. It's no more than another sign of middle age, and should be expected. A woman who is getting on has the right to be a trifle touched, a little queer in the hat; it's a privilege. If you happen to know you do look a bit funny to other people, where's the harm? Time's fair wear and tear is nothing to be sorry for.

And after all, she reflected further, when by the Tower, and could hear the cries on the water—after all, why not be like the others? If she was slightly cracked, just a wee bit chipped through seven days a week, who would notice it among the rest of the crocks? One among many, that was all. Why, the world itself, you could tell by its excitement, wasn't quite all there.

Just take a look at those shipping bills, stuck on every wall! Enough was there to tell you without asking for more. Each advertised, with the same old picture, the best ship that ever floated, with the fastest passages, at the lowest rates, and it was either for Australia or the West. There was the wildest talk, words had gone mad, over the discoveries of gold, a new field of gold once a week, if you please; and not a clown but was sure he could make straight for a fine fat lump of it by bilking his landlord, selling his bed and sticks, and buying a passage, with half a crown left over between himself and the pit. Ships were leaving the Thames every week for the ends of the earth, full of hope and confidence, but with no more gumption than would run a baked-potato can.

Not a man of them knew what he was in for, when he went up the gangway, and never asked. There was nobody to ask. All believed the same. It was unsettling, the common uproar, once you allowed a sound of it to get inside, mixing noises in the head. A touch of the excitement of the street would spoil the morning, if it only made you go about impatient and scornful. Is there no end, she asked herself, to the happy confidence of fools? Life itself is so like a gamble, one promise of better days after another, but usually a cheat, that a new way to fortune, all flags, with trumpets and drums to lead everybody on, gathers the town into a daft processsion.

The truth was, very likely, that anything that would take the taste out of everlasting drudgery for a while was as good as gin. It is natural to fool yourself. If you don't, what are you to do?

Today the idea was that the world was soon to have its pots and kettles of gold. No more than that. The millennium was just round the corner, with steam-engines to take us, to save the trouble of walking. This would pass, of course, because sooner or later we find after all we must stick to black pots, and wait for them to boil, if there's anything to cook. Still, when this excitement was over, what next would come over the town? For another there would be. Just when you begin to think a nice, long, dull time is coming in, and all quiet, there it goes again, more commotion, and over something a sensible dog wouldn't smell, having had his nose blistered before.

She might be mistaken about it—she couldn't rid herself of a nagging doubt that she was. Perhaps the world knew better than she did what it was up to, hard though it was to believe—and how very hard it was!—that the world ever knows what it is doing, and the trouble it is storing up for itself. She remembered, all the same, that she had been mistaken before. Well, God would judge that it isn't always easy to tell His divine purpose from one of Old Horny's encouraging whispers. For the worst of the business is, and she saw it sadly, that before long a new lump of public ugliness, a monstrosity pouring smoke and stink, another bout of deafening lunacy, one more clever trick of bedevilment to bamboozle the gulls, which she had refused to have at any price, which she had flung off in a temper, becomes as ordinary as the cat next door. There pretty soon it is, part of the street, all comfortable. Like everybody else, she no longer noticed it.

A day there was, she recalled, when she had never seen a steam-ship, didn't want to see one, prayed they would all blow up, and some of them did. Now look at it. Here this river was, alive with them, and if one of them gave a far-off whistle, late at night, while she was lying awake thinking, then the sound was no more than an echo in her memory of the days that had gone. It was a trial to the soul, to feel sure the latest uproar in town was only another boil-over of the wickedness of the pit, where the imps never cease preparing fires to burn our pride, and yet to remember how often she had been scornful, but wrong. Perhaps an answer will never come. Perhaps there is nothing to quiet the heart, when you are nagging yourself over high matters, except to submit and say with the psalmist, My soul is even as a weaned child.

She strolled along towards the entrance to the St. Katharine Dock. That dock, so the gossip went, was packed with ships, it hadn't a berth for one more barge. She had been almost tempted to go in herself one afternoon, like everybody else, to see that American flyer the *Oriental,* with her cargo of tea, the first to arrive from China, setting all the shipwrights and riggers of London desperately over-hauling their old-fashioned moulding floors and sail-lofts. So what was she grieving about? She ought to rejoice. The river could never have been more abundant than it was that year.

After the lean years a while back, when thousands were dying for want of bread, and the ships were idle, she should be glad of this bustle and noise, though she was too short-sighted to see God's hand in it. But why look down when things are looking up? All the gloomy prophecies of Darton and his friends, which had seemed to have truth in them, that the country would pine and die because of cheap food and free ships, had no more in it, except fear and fret, than the tin can rattling at the tail-end of an ownerless dog. In-stead, the land flourished. You need go no farther than Ratcliffe Highway to see that. The taverns and painted women had no apologies to make. They never felt better, they had never done so well. Of course, the Ragged School

had grown, it was coming along, if not so well as the
gin-palaces; not yet. Not yet.

Above all, there had been that letter from young Dave a
fortnight ago, put beside her plate at breakfast, and left
there. It wasn't opened till after the first cup of tea, which
was what she really wanted; not a letter that gave the notion
that it wasn't meant for her except by chance, like a hand-
bill. It was so uninviting on the outside, as if it had been
knocking about over long. And who would want to write
to her? She never thought of Dave. She'd long since given
up waiting to get a word from him. She was expecting
nothing that morning, except the baker. It was only another
morning.

She was no wiser when she opened it. From New York,
of all the strange places on earth! Suddenly she understood.
That upset the cup. In an instant of time, there the boy was
talking to her. You couldn't blame her for being so dense
till she was well down the first page of it, still puzzled. At
first it didn't read like the boy. After he went, the days remained empty so long that the clearest picture of him, at
last, came only in a forenoon moment, now and then, when
the sun was young, and she could see him in that far-off
window seat, his head bent over a book, and the light in his
hair. That was all that was left of him. Then in a moment
of time his voice was at her ear, and over went the cup. He
was about. He was somewhere in the world. He was safe,
so far. She might see him again, some day . . . but would
she know him if she saw him? If he came along this minute,
would she know him? Why, that letter was written by a
man, or by a body very like a man. Anyhow, it made her
feel that an easy and salty fellow quite tall was talking the
sort of nonsense to his mother that would blarney her into
a good humour.

It was worth waiting for. Yet the boy must have seen

miracles, to have learned to make light of dark days. Perhaps it was better for her ease of mind that he hadn't been plain about it. It would teach him much, no doubt, to have seen first and last things with such a man as Killick. It was her experience that a man who has looked death in the eye, without turning away, is good at a joke. She doubted, though, whether it was all quite such fun in that emigrant ship. No, she wouldn't swear to the truth of every word of news in that letter, even now; but it was worth all the gold said to be out there, where the sun sets, to know her lad had been saving up that for her, to let her have it when he felt he could speak out. Is there anything in the world more important than personal relations? If there is, what is it?

Well, this wouldn't do. It was time she turned about and got to work. She made to return; but opposite, across the way, outside the entrance to the dock, was a lively group of men. She wasted another minute watching them. They had just stepped ashore, she could see. Their assortment of odd toggery would have said that, if they hadn't been so glad as well. One had a parrot in a cage, and was singing a song of woe to the others. When men are happy, what makes them sing melancholy ditties? Through the doors of the dock entrance behind them came a person who was passing them, but the gang stopped him.

They wouldn't let him go. The stranger was embarrassed, but good-humoured. Down went the parrot to the pavement, and its owner shook hands long and solemnly with the newcomer. The others pressed round. He looked like a ship's master, that man, and shy of a fuss; but, if he was a master, it was uncommon for his men to greet him with admiration in the street. Quite uncommon. Aunt Ruth smiled; plainly he did not relish it. Then he broke away, waved an arm in farewell, and was crossing the road rapidly towards her.

It is a wide road, there. She had time to observe him. There was that in his build and gait which she knew, and she fixed her gaze. If it wasn't Killick, then he must have a twin brother. He was about to pass her.

It was Killick. He went by, it seemed to her, without a glance her way, and she turned to watch him while making up her mind to go after him as fast as she could. In a few paces he stopped, and looked back. There they stood, fixed for some seconds, staring at each other, as if they were slower than their eyes. While the thunder of a passing heavy wagon enveloped them she shook hands with him as long and as solemnly as had that sailor, for she was trying to find the right word to say, and it wasn't there. The wagon was past, and he spoke first.

"It is you, Mrs. Penfold? You are sure of it? I must believe it, for there you are, and not a day older. I must be in luck. If my owner had been waiting at the quay for me with a bunch of flowers I shouldn't have been more surprised than I am this very minute."

"No?" said Aunt Ruth.

"You see, I meant to find you somehow, not knowing where you'd be, before I sailed again."

"Yes?" said Aunt Ruth, and smiled. "But you hurried by."

"I did. Of course I did. What else would I do when the first person I meet away from my ship is you yourself? Come now, one doesn't look for luck like that. What do you make of it?"

"It really is very fortunate, Mr. Killick." Aunt Ruth had wish to call it the hand of God, but judged that might be too strong. "Is Dave with you now?"

"No. But I should say he will soon be here. I have news

of him for you. I was hurrying, when you saw me, but I was on my way to the Custom House. That cannot wait. You know that without being told. After that comes the owner in Mincing Lane, which isn't far away. Owners ought never to be kept kicking their heels, either. And after that, where do I find you?"

30

Past and Present

As she was lighting up late that afternoon Aunt Ruth saw the parlour lamp, though doing its best, was a poor supernumerary. The fire was giving light enough to animate the room. Every panel of the sombre wainscot was quivering with reflected flames. Only the portraits above of forgotten men remained obscure in the dark to which they had gone.

It was a hearty fire, happy in its draught. She had seen to that, for the haze had not gone with the sun, and that meant the frost would hold till morning. She also knew as well as the next woman what a sailor enjoys when home, especially after a western ocean passage in winter, which men hate, and the night outside no better than a middle watch with the wind and the sough of the deep for company. He loves a dancing fire, and no argument. That keeps him contented in one place; and while the poker is at his hand to jump the flames and help his yarn as well he will go on telling you all about it, and that was what she wanted.

It takes more than an evening to fill years of expectation, all silent. But she hoped the sweets and pastries beforehand would help, as he must almost have forgotten the sight and smell of them; though if the sirloin turned out tonight as she wanted it, that would be enough to put the harness cask in its miserable place. So would the spiced ale afterwards. Mary Summers had smiled at that touch, but Mary had never been married to a sailor, and this was important. It was her experience that a man's cheerfulness comes entirely from the hour and from nothing that makes a soul Christian, and he must be accepted as he was made.

There went the bell. Not here yet, surely? But it was only Mr. Burnham, and she wished it wasn't. She respected Mr. Burnham, who came now and then, at unexpected hours. She was even in some awe of him, for he seemed very simple, and yet could interrupt with knowledge she wasn't aware existed, and as if he'd known it since childhood. He seemed to live in a separate place where there is never a sound, or only when a page of a book is being turned over, so was odd and lost when he entered the day to mix with its goings-on. He would never get used to us. You felt you were bound to be helpful to him and keep an eye open for his pipes and spectacles, usually under your feet on the floor, but she'd rather not be helpful this evening. It was her evening, even if she couldn't claim it. She was also a little jealous. An intruder so important would take most of the conversation, and tonight she wanted as much of it as she could get. This was a special night; there might never be another like it. But there you are. Time is for everyone, like air, and we can never claim a length of ten minutes of it because it is plainly stamped with our name.

"Ruth, what a fire! I like that one, the right December cheer."

"Good evening, Mr. Burnham."

"While coming along I was thinking how drear and vacant all was, no hope in sight, and here's a merry heart to a dim world."

"It is a bright one, isn't it? We are expecting a visitor, someone you used to see at Branton in the past."

"Indeed? Expecting a guest? Then I'm sorry to intrude. My visit is only an escape from solitude in Half Moon Street. But you say I know him?"

"Yes. You remember Captain Killick? He'll be glad to see you, I'm sure."

"What, the mariner who used to be right-hand man to Miles? Is he still about? How pleasant to see him again; though I think I remember we never had much to say to each other."

"He never spoke unless spoken to, did he?"

"Was that it? Perhaps so, but I used secretly to admire the easy way he could overcome difficult matters that would have left me helpless. Coming tonight, is he?"

"Yes."

"He'll be just back from China, I suppose, the lucky man, some Xanadu of a place too distant for ordinary eyes. You and I will never see it."

"No, I don't suppose we shall. I met him on Tower Hill today just after he stepped ashore."

"Good news. He'll tell us something we haven't heard before, tidings of another world. If you can find a place for me, then I'm glad I'm here. But will he talk? Perhaps he won't. These sailors think nothing of what they've done."

"No."

"It's the same with us all, I suppose. There cannot be anything interesting for other people in our day's work. You've noticed that, haven't you?"

"Yes, well, so we each think, Mr. Burnham."

"Of course. Should I expect Captain Killick to feel the slightest concern in what I've been doing today?"

"I don't know. I don't know what it was, sir."

"Between ourselves, it isn't worth mentioning. But I've been trying to discover what there is to show that Cæsar Tiberius was annoyed with Pontius Pilate for ruling the Jews with too heavy a hand."

Mrs. Penfold laughed. "I shouldn't think he'd want to hear about that. That's all over. It's so very long ago."

"Long ago. But is it all over? Sometimes I wonder whether there is ever an end to the things we do while alive. Dusty old history is as brisk to me as today's traffic in the streets, if you can believe it."

"That's a dreadful thought, Mr. Burnham, isn't it?—that we die, but the things we do, never?"

"No, not at all, not if life has a meaning, and we must believe it has. It puts us on our merits . . . there goes the bell, Ruth, and here comes your guest, I suppose. Allow me to make myself scarce for a while. You must greet him."

It was like him, it was most kind of Mr. Burnham to disappear as he did, allowing her some free minutes, especially as Captain Killick moved straight to the fire, spreading his hands to it, as if it had drawn him over into confidence. He stood silent too long trying to make out whether it was a man peering out of the gilt frame over the mantelpiece, or a woman. After the lamp was alight you could never tell which, as it was only part of the unlighted dark; not that it signified, for Mary herself said she didn't know who the person was.

"Who is that?" he asked. "There's only sharp eyes staring down at me."

"That's all it ever is at night," said Mrs. Penfold, "eyes looking down at whoever is on the hearthrug."

"It makes me feel we are being watched. I hope we are approved."

"It's the portrait of a young man, but he must have grown old, long ago."

Captain Killick considered the flames. "Well, I hope they don't always watch us as closely as that." He turned to her. "It wouldn't do, at every minute of the day, would it?" He added, after a pause, "Have you heard from David?"

"Yes, I've had a letter from him, a long one."

"He promised me he would write, and I believed him, or

I would have written myself. I saw him last in New York, only a month ago. Not till we were well into the voyage out from Liverpool, and that's a way back now, did I know the ship's boy was the youngster you were troubled about one Sunday morning, because he had gone astray. He confided in a lady passenger we had, who reported to me innocently. I began to wake up, and had him into my cabin. He was your David. I'd have given him a wigging, only he was contrite."

"It was a nice letter, but he didn't seem to be sorry in it."

"No, it wouldn't be right for a lad to be sorry all that time. But I don't think there is much in him to regret. He has the makings of a fine seaman, I can tell you that."

"That part of it doesn't make me glad."

"I don't suppose it does. That's the way the shore always looks at us. It only means I would trust him where I wouldn't trust others."

"That is better. I've never heard better news. No, I haven't."

"You ought to be prepared, though. Your recollection of him is not like mine. He is taller than you. In fact, I know a bold hand who tackled him roughly, but regretted it."

"Dave came of stout stock."

"He is beginning to look like it."

Mrs. Penfold was silent. She put out her hand to clutch the mantelshelf. She said, after a pause, that it was worth living so long with a fret at the heart to be told that. "I used to fear he'd never come to anything, never do much, he was such a moody, pale-faced slip. I'd say that to myself while wondering what had become of him."

"Not do much? I don't know. Anyhow, when I left him he was beginning to overtake me in navigation."

"Yes, but what is he doing now?"

"This minute? Let me think. At a guess, he's below keeping watch in the engine-room of a steam-ship, crossing over to you. Coming fast. What do you think of that?"

"I don't know what to think of it. That isn't a place of my choice. Still, it is comforting to hear that he is on his way home. I want him to do the best for himself."

"Then rest easy. We must remember, especially when we don't want to, that what was best for us doesn't always suit young people. There's no doubt he has picked up more about marine boilers than I know, and if that doesn't mean he'll leave old hands far astern I don't know what it means. He'll reach a point, if he goes on at this gait, out of my reckoning. Not that I want to reckon it."

"No? Why not? Isn't it much good?"

"That isn't what I meant. I expect I'm only feeling easy on my mooring ropes tonight, for I must say my last round voyage was overlong and more than enough. This moment the idea takes me that I've had my fill of blue water. That's all I meant."

He turned to her, reassuringly, or with something more to confide, but saw she might not have heard his last words. It was she who was now gazing pensively into the fire, and as if she could make out there an augury that had a shape promising fulfilment.

She roused slowly, and left him. Someone else had come to the street door. Perhaps there would be more than one intruder; but she was resigned. She would have loved a long comfortable chat with one who knew the place and the people she used to know, but she must be thankful for the word she had got. She let in Father Lawless, who was as immediately jolly as if she were a handsome young body; but she wasn't altogether in the mood for happy nonsense. But tonight she had almost forgotten her first astonishment, of a year ago, that Mary Summers should welcome indoors a Papist, and what was worse, a priest.

"You're not pleased, Ruth, and I see you are not. Who has put you out? Show me that man. I'm his foe."

She assured him that truly she was very happy. It was easy for her tonight to accept this enemy of the faith as a friend who was but perverse if you mentioned sacred things. After all, he was only Irish, and an Irishman of authority was very useful there.

"You'd not push me back into the cold," he said, "now would you, and me so starved I declare I've not tasted real food since you fed me last."

She took his hat and coat. Put him out again! She could have blessed him, but wasn't sure of the worth of her blessing to a priest of an idolatrous church.

"It's a friendly smell this house has, but there's a housekeeper I know who was sent to try my soul, I tell you, and she remembers more fast days than a saint, which I am not."

"We'll see about that," said Aunt Ruth. You couldn't be hard on him. Where he came from in Wapping it was positively dangerous to be about by night, and not only by night, yet his old face kept as fresh and dainty as a baby's. How he managed it she didn't know, but she knew his people were afraid of him when they were on the rampage caring for nothing and nobody. This round little man would go among them, and they wouldn't fear a lion more when he bullied them for their cruel ways. He'd pour their drink on the earth, smash their bottles; he'd do that, and live to tell the tale. They'd only beseech him in tears, when they'd leave another man to the coroner. She squeezed his arm kindly as she was taking him in, but he stopped.

"Whist," he said. "It is that terrible man Burnham I hear? Yes, that's his voice, the insidious heretic, but before God I say I'll have no word of metaphysics this night. I will not.

You hear me, Ruth? I will not. If free will is mentioned, destroy it, there's a darling. I'm tired out with folly."

She whispered earnestly that, on this occasion, if a subject were started that had no more sense in it than the wind in a keyhole, then she was afraid she'd play a trick to end it.

"Don't be afraid at all. Drop a plate, drop two. But I'm sure I hear another voice now, and I don't know it. Am I in danger?"

"Oh, no. That's an old acquaintance, a sailor just home again."

"A sailor, is he? Then Burnham is done. I don't understand these sailors, and he does not. They're queer men."

"Surely they are not as queer as all that."

"Are they not? Isn't it lies they tell us? I never know whether the world they know is one I ought to know or leave alone. After a talk with one I'm like a child in the dark, fancying there's things moving about me that I'm afraid to see. Come along. If he's your friend I'll risk it."

When a little later Mrs. Penfold glanced at the heads dim and afloat in the candle-light, for Mary preferred candles to light her dining-table, she saw she might have spared her prayer to have this evening as she wanted it. The thoughts of those four people were nowhere near her. No matter where you are, she decided, and what you wish, you have to remain as lone as a sea-bird in the winds of heaven. Mary and Father Lawless were confidential together, and very serious; but then they always were, as if the deep difference between them made no difference when they forgot it. The other two were picking up things of the past to look at them again, and not always as if they really wanted to. It was unlikely there would be a call to check a disturbance. Aunt Ruth found she had no more to do than to watch the serving maid, that good things should come to the table in the right shape, and get on with her dinner. She heard the talk brokenly.

"Mellowing, of course; but all the dictator still," Mr. Burnham was saying. "Miles is just as confident as ever the truth is with him and not elsewhere. No change is right, except he makes it. Branton is where you saw it last, or thereabouts, not an iron plate in the shipyard. Iron for Miles might still be the stuff of witchcraft, and he's an honest Christian man. He is full of a plan for a line of fast schooners to Spain, for passengers in a hurry, and fruit."

"I thought they existed," said Killick.

"No, not the real thing, not the better shape in his eye. He went to Leith from London by water, and fell in love with the ship, the *Nonsuch;* and that's what she was, to him, by all accounts. Have you heard of her?"

"I know her style. She's the famous London and Edinburgh Shipping Company. She's an Aberdeen novelty and a fine design. All her sort have good length and concave bows. You know the old full-bosomed bow Darton used to insist on? In these schooners it is turned inside out. I explained that clipper prow to him long ago, but he thought it fantastical and dangerous. Those fore-and-afters can beat up to weather in a gale."

"So you know them. Well, that's his latest, all for the future."

"As to that, I don't see much of a future for them. They can outsail most craft, they've gone past me handsomely, but the year has drawn clear ahead of them. They've been passed already in the guesswork of quick thinkers."

"Is that your opinion? I don't know what you mean, but it is regrettable that you can't talk to him about it. I'll admit he doesn't flush now when you are named, and tighten his mouth, but he never forgets a grievance nor examines a prejudice, never. I know he is sinking a little fortune in those ships, and with his usual energy, the stubborn man. But he has been losing money of late on some large ventures, and he can't afford to lose much more."

Aunt Ruth listened, yet with loose attention. What did it matter, that a man should drop his money into a bottomless place because he was a stubborn old fool? The more we all talk, she thought, the more certain it is we never get near to each other, except as far as you can see in a mirror.

She left them to overlook the heating of the spiced ale in the kitchen, and when she returned they were sitting round the parlour fire. Father Lawless had his crossed feet stretched towards the fender, his head on the back of his chair, eyes shut, as if in a cherubic sleep. Mary and Mr. Burnham were leaning forward listening to whatever the captain was relating, and Mary was frowning in concern.

"Had you no surgeon aboard?" she asked.

"I had, but he was an early victim."

"Which means," said Mr. Burnham, "you had it all to yourself."

"That is in the articles," said the sailor.

The priest opened his eyes to gaze at the ceiling. "Dear God," he said, "but birth and death! And they my people, some of them, Irish they were, and dying. The sorrowful creatures, and nobody with them. Is there nothing you do for them on a ship?" he asked, sitting up. "No rite? What is it you do?"

"Put them overside," said the sailor. "There is a rite, the last. It is all they can have, against death and the sea, as well as I know. It was all I could give them, while getting the rest along as well as wind and accidents allowed. It's no fun."

"It is not," said the priest, "it is not. It is misfortune in the grain of it. I wish I'd been with you, but from what you say it is better I was not, to add to it and all. I shall

254

never understand. The longer I live, and the more I hear, the more foolish I am. It is not compassable by us, the lot of the destitute."

"Could a rite help the destitute?" asked Mr. Burnham.

The priest shook a reproving and restraining hand at the doubter.

Mr. Burnham ignored restraint. "Whatever we leave un-done, it is vanity to think it is lost. I refuse to accept finality. We see our work cut off at a raw edge, and can't help feeling sad, remembering our short lease of daylight. But that measure isn't enough, though it is all we've got."

"It is not," said the priest brusquely. "I tell you again, Burnham, it is not, though maybe it is all you've got."

"Shall I drop a plate, Father Lawless?" asked Aunt Ruth.

The priest chuckled. The others looked at her inquiringly, but she had the tongs, putting a few knobs on the fire, kneeling with her back to them.

"However you look at it," said the sailor, "it gives us a jolt, if we don't know why, to see men dying, and to leave them to it; yes, and to look on the destitute as if they were dunnage. When my men were bundled aboard at Liverpool by the boarding-house master, all swinish and useless, some of the drunks without much more than a shirt against what was to come, it looked as if we'd loaded more anarchy than we could carry. Yet I was in luck. That was only the beginning. They proved to be what I call good men. I left them to the mate. I don't know what rite he used, but it worked."

"I know that rite," said the priest. "It can break bones."

"The mate I had then wouldn't worry over that incon-venience if it helped the ship. The men jumped to it when he shouted because they knew he knew. He must have been born on a gun-deck. Not much of a navigator. He only knew the Pole Star, and nothing of compass troubles, though he was a good guesser at dead-reckoning. But he was as stout a seaman as ever faced it. He could smell trouble before it came, and was ahead of it. But I lost him."

The sailor glanced at Mrs. Penfold, as if by chance, as he mentioned his loss. He wondered how much David had told her, in his letter; but she was silent, with her face partly averted. She knew that men could be lost on a voyage, and that no gratification was to be had by asking for particulars, so she did not ask. If you are concerned, you are told, and then must take it.

There was an interval, and only a hissing coal to be heard, and then Mr. Burnham said, "It seems to me you must have landed friend Cree on the other side about the time when everyone began to talk of California, that land more attractive than the gardens fair of Hesperus. What became of him?"

"What a terrible pity it is, Burnham," said the priest, "that the Holy Church did not take your attention when you were a happy innocent, if ever you were one, instead of the extravagant tarradiddles of paganism. 'Tis a pity. Such a vast disturbance to our life as there is now, and all because of a yellow metal with a false value, and there you sit, without a word for it, with nothing but a mention of a child's fable."

"I didn't expect you to recognise a quotation from such a cove as Milton," said Mr. Burnham. "Can you reach that jug?"

The sailor smiled at the priest. "There wasn't much of what I'd call a garden about it, either. I've never heard a garden could loosen the wits. San Francisco did. Stolid people went demented, right off the earth, at the mention of it. Quite mad. Common sense ceased to work. It was all over in a minute. I was there. You'd see another ship come in, hear a harbour furl ordered, and then away her people would shove off for the shore and fortune. A fleet of ships—I counted three hundred, and gave it up—was on the mud. All abandoned. Some with cargoes, too. Nobody would unload them. A loafer could state his terms like a prince for breaking out a bale of goods. There the ships lay, at all angles, their yards canted anyhow, rotting. Not a man aboard. Sea-birds perched on their rails. A junk from China was near me, all alive, but that was rats. In a wind at night that junk's loose gear made the sound of a crew of the damned celebrating shipwreck. It was desolation. Duty had come to an end. But Cree wasn't there then. Couldn't have been. No time for it. Neither was he in New York when I was back there again. I didn't expect to find him. Nobody over there stays in one place for more than a week. And it was lucky for him that he wasn't in San Francisco then. One night I saw the whole jimcrack town go up in flames, a regular hurricane of fire, and I must say I watched the fine show in admiration and some satisfaction. Only fire could give that place a clean bill of health. You didn't feel charitable yourself where the simple rules for fair dealing are the same as set-outs for mutiny, kidnapping, arson, and murder."

"But your men, were they there, had they run away too?" asked Mary.

"Two of them. Two made off one night. I don't know what happened to them, and perhaps they don't. You could turn a street corner beyond the Golden Gate and be lost to daylight. I couldn't replace them, but I was lucky to get out of it so cheaply. We were under charter to Americans, but the rest stood by the ship. They were affected by the stir ashore, but we had a first-rate counter-influence aboard. The crew looked on more than once, and I think with pride, while the mate tackled crimps and suborners from the land. His strength and tricks were wicked. If those

confident boarders cared nothing for law and order, that
suited him, for a few minutes. There's no doubt things
would have been worse for me, but for that man."

"You didn't let David go ashore there, I hope," said Mrs.
Penfold.

"What? Ashore? Why, no. He only looked towards the
hills with longing eyes. So did I, for that matter. You can't
help doing that, after months without sight of permanence,
on food which makes you dream of things to eat, and
Cape Horn ahead, to be rounded again. That sticks up
black in the mind, that headland. Months of cold emptiness
to come, before you can allow yourself a thought of eggs
and bacon in peace, not to mention a dry shirt."

As if helping the story-teller to point so great a journey
to felicity, a kitten by the fender stretched its belly
luxuriously to the warmth. The sailor noticed the little
thing as it moved, surprised to see it there, and stooped to
smooth it.

The priest put a difficulty; and the sailor told him,
bending over the kitten, his anxiety about fresh water and
provisions. San Francisco was only a bank of smoke and a
smell of roasted muck, and he wanted to be away. "I
hauled off, trusting to luck for what I needed on the coast
further south. The day after doomsday is not the time
to wait for fresh meat, or orders. I hadn't the first word of
orders. I got out of it."

Mr. Burnham peered over in short-sighted curiosity at the
sailor, and his frown was the puzzled estimation of the
student for the man who can make things go the way he
wants; who can take hold of that world beyond the cur-
tained window, a world hostile and infinite, as casually as
if fondling a cat were part of it. The sailor's manner was
gentle and deliberate; and it may have been only Mr.
Burnham's fancy, but his eyes seemed to show what had

happened while he looked on, directing other men, clear and slow in shadowed pits, but absent in expression, as if seeing beyond the foreground, with the skin about them wrinkled through half-closing them against an excess of light. He did not look sad, but only as if he could turn to the next thing without much reluctance.

"All very well," said Mr. Burnham, "if a fellow has only himself to think of. If he fails, then there is not much in it. As for me, I shouldn't care to carry other men's lives about. I'd dodge that."

"We can't dodge it," said the sailor. "Come to think of it, we are always doing it, and don't know it. A sailor must put on that responsibility with his cap. His messmates' lives are involved in almost every move he makes."

"But does he know it?"

"He can't help knowing it. The facts teach him. If he forgets, there's the ship's mob to remind him, and they'll do it. The Lord help him if he forgets where he is. But I'm afraid the shore knows nothing of the sailor, except when he is in the gutter near where we are now. He isn't always in it, and, when he isn't, of course he is far out of sight, very likely beating round one of the two bad southern corners of the continents. That's where you want to see him as he lives. I've had a lot to do with that fellow, and there's nothing amusing about him, nor in his job. The seaman is only a man trying to earn a living the best way he knows, that's all."

Aunt Ruth assented with nods, made absently in a reverie. The others had their eyes on the sailor, alert for more, but he was silent for a time, and was not looking at them. Then he went on,

"I've found, as a rule, that he will do anything for you, give his last ounce, when sure he isn't being wasted. To work a ship in a gale, and dive from the gear to the pumps, and from the pumps to the gear, not sure she will last it out, is more than hard work. It tries the soul. It will start the bolt-heads of the heart. The exhausted men flounder, and curse you. They must curse someone. 'All right,' you say, 'then drown. Pump or drown,' and they pump till they drop. When you've run before wind and seas south of all things, south of all men, you know a bit beforehand of the last evening we ever see. The next sea astern coming down on you might be high land travelling fast, with snow atop of it. In the half-light the foam gleams like a ridge of snow. You think, that's the one will get us, here we go. But it only fills the deck. You drive on, no end yet, you just keep afloat, scud, billows, and ship all going one way in gloom and uproar round the earth's spindle flying loose.

"That's the life. I've had it before, but I noticed it more this time, I suppose because we were caught. One night the cabin lamp went out as the skylight was stove. That flood stopped my study of the chart, and nearly filled the cabin. We were pooped. Much more than the skylight had gone, but I didn't know it then. She just lay down in it, and kicked. She wouldn't answer the helm. Nothing could be seen, except when another burst of foam gave her a shape; and it was a shape! At last she came up to breathe, and paid off. The mate had persuaded her. He appeared beside me again, and we bawled advice at each other—the din itself flattens sense—and then he left me to do more. I never saw him again. Nobody saw him go.... You can't believe they've gone when they disappear like that. You can't help expecting that they will show in the gap, some-time."

The sailor didn't name the man. He supposed that if Mrs. Penfold knew of him she would speak now; but she sat silent looking down at the hearthrug. Captain Killick remembered the distress of David when light came, when it was certain Bonser had left them. No, when they go like that it is hard to believe it; and you can't write home about it; you can't put it down.

"God rest his soul," said the priest.

"Yes. Though I don't see how a soul could rest there, except as an albatross, as old sailors say. There's no rest in that latitude. We worked out of it at last, and stood to the north. I thought we were clear. Soon there would be warm weather to dry up the mildew and cure the sea-boils. I was dozing below one night, and uneasily. Without the mate I was at a loss, with nobody to lean against. I missed him, if only because I couldn't trust the man on watch in an emergency. I was drowsing, and it was nothing out of the way that that fine fellow we had lost was there with me, talking of something I ought to know, but didn't get. Then he was shaking me. That woke me. When I looked round, of course I had it to myself. Only the cabin fixings stood there as usual, though they looked odd in that moment. My tarpaulins moved slightly on the door hook. I must have been dreaming as the ship listed, but I went on deck. Very likely my nerves weren't at their best. I went topside, and did not wait.

"All was well. I took a look at the binnacle, and noted the helmsman's face in its glow. Old Hudson had the wheel, and he could nurse her like a baby. He had just taken over. It was the middle watch, too dark to see the main deck. There was nothing to worry about. The sea was subdued, and I don't know why I didn't like that, but I didn't, nor a cold mistiness. All was well, it was a quiet night, we were on our way home, but I wasn't happy about it.

"I chanced to look overside, and saw a glint which wasn't the wash from the bow, and shouted 'Hard up the helm!' She answered like a bird, and we scraped alongside a shelf of ice while I stood rigid, waiting for the crash. You could have jumped from our quarter on to it as we swung clear.

"Morning came not before I wanted it, though when the mist cleared we had a clear and brilliant day I didn't enjoy. I could see how much more lucky we had been in the night than I had known. We were surrounded by bergs. It puzzles me still how we missed those frightful peaks astern. We had sailed into another world, not knowing it was there. Your Dave, Mrs. Penfold, pointed once, and said to me, 'That one is like the cliffs of Dover.' In size and shape it was, but those white and bluish freaks and steeples seemed lit up inside. It was splendid, and it was fearful, for we were close aboard. Cascades poured down their gullies like smoke. There was not a sound from it all, it was as still as death, till a heavy swell set in from the north-west, and the way the rollers burst against those pretty walls told me I'd better get the ship to do her best.

"We were dodging them all that day, and the next. You can believe at times you are bewitched, and there is no undoing it. Once we sighted another ship, but she was no comfort. She was perched on a berg, well up its side, no more than a black model on too big a stand. The seas were thundering below her. I suppose she had run full tilt into it one night, and was held. The ice afterwards shifted its centre of balance, and up she went. I don't know. There she was . . . what was she, sir? I cannot say. I know that no more than what happened to her, and in which year. If it meets you there, nobody is looking on, and nobody will hear of it."

"No," said Aunt Ruth.

31

Smoke on the Horizon

THE chief engineer of the steam-ship *Monarch* raised his head from his pose of devotion before a gauge. "Gay," he shouted petulantly, "are you deaf? The whistle man, the whistle. Twice. Damn that whistle." He waved his hand at a white bulkhead.

Dave roused from the mesmeric flashing of the burnished and impetuous metal arms. He had been applying an oil-can to a pair of eccentrics affectionately, as if wishing them a long and happy life. He had heard no whistle. There was too much rumbling and vibration, though he was getting used to it. But Mr. Rumbold could hear the slightest thing that wasn't the harmonious chorus of the engines. If a blue-bottle was buzzing about in the engine room he would hear that, though the machinery was running like mad. Dave had been promised by the Chief that so priceless a gift of hearing would be his in time, if he was worthy; but to win this honour he had to think more of steam than of himself, or else he would remain for ever a miserable sailor. But Dave had been warned that it was still uncertain whether he was rather better than those makeshifts on deck, who imagined the ship did the right thing because of their intelligence. Pshaw!

The Chief began again to frown over the mystery of the vacuum. Dave darted over to the wall by the desk where the log-book lay open. Beside the desk, the mouth of a speaking-tube had poked out a red tongue to show the watch below that the navigator on the bridge had a word for them. He put his head to the wall, and listened, shaking a drop of sweat from his nose, and stoppering the other ear to shut out the immediate noise. He corked the tube with its whistle, and turned to Mr. Rumbold. "The captain wants you on deck, sir," he reported.

"What the devil has the deck to do with me?" cried the engineer. "What does he want?"

"He didn't say, sir."

"Didn't you ask?"

Dave made no reply. The thought of asking the captain of a ship his reason for making a disturbance was too much for speech.

The engineer waited a moment, peering down solemnly at Dave over the top of his spectacles, for he was so tall and bent that his chestnut beard hung free of a concave body. He had explained that this was due to a life-long devotion to lathes, over which he had always bowed, as a male should.

"Gay," he said, as if confiding a sad secret, "the deck must learn its place. It still fancies this is the high old time of Captain Trunnion and the three-deckers. But you've escaped. Here you are. The sweat's running into your eyes. It's hot work. Don't stare at me like that. Get it into your all-but virgin head that the deck above is below us. Below us. Don't you see? Below us. We are the people. In this ship the place of power is reversed. The power and the glory is there." He pointed gravely at the cylinders, and winked slowly.

"The men who steer think heaven keeps them going. They can't help it. Force of habit. I don't suppose they'll ever learn. I don't suppose they'd believe a tip from your friend Gabriel that boilers are better than prayers. Boilers are going to beat all the favouring gales and hearts of oak that get the cheers at Drury Lane. Sailors don't know. Their noddles are stuffed up with old canvas and traditional junk. Not a chink for daylight. Nobody knows the truth of it but a few of us, and I'm letting you into the fun. Don't grin at me, young man, as if I was daft. It's reason speaking. Science and reason make people grin only on deck. Not here. When you stand on the foot-plates, give heed to fairy tales, especially when they're quite impossible."

The engineer then went to the ladder that led to the skylight, and began leisurely to climb. Dave continued to stare at his chief, but not to grin, as he diminished towards the cold and the weather. He was a new sort of man to Dave, with views of machinery and God that were, in a way, more fascinating, more awful, than that world of ice through which Captain Killick once manœuvred the old ship in a southern latitude, and at present Dave felt those views to be as cold as that far apparition of desolate splendour. It seemed to him as if the truth, which he had once supposed was helpful in unalterable serenity, once you knew it, was making faces at him. He took up his oil-can and resumed his round, and presently forgot the Chief in the rush and glitter of the miraculous rotations.

The engineer, as he emerged into the wind and light, was dazzled and buffeted. The opposition of the outer wilderness affected him as uncouth nonsense while he mounted to the bridge. The weather was boisterous, with following seas, and she was rolling. Worse than that, since he could not see the purposeful movements of his machinery, the steamer appeared to have been brought to a standstill by the immensity of space. The *Monarch,* bound from Boston towards Bristol, on the return passage of her maiden voyage, was in mid-ocean, and Mr. Rumbold was more accustomed to problems in the workshop and to trial runs with experimental novelties than he was to the Atlantic.

Captain Crispin was by the wheel, dressed as for Sunday in the Park, and was astounded by the costume of his engineer. That was Mr. Rumbold's own design, in canvas, buff-coloured as far as grease allowed, closely buttoned everywhere to escape the clutches of revolving gear; and on a ship's bridge it was desecrating. To the sailors standing about it was hard to believe that this scarecrow, taking off its spectacles to wipe watering eyes, was the man who had persuaded the owners to build their new ship for a screw propeller instead of paddle-wheels. Captain Crispin had grown up in brigs, had commanded packet-ships, and but a year before had been persuaded, against his inclination, to take charge of a large paddle-steamer. He assumed now he knew all there was to know of steam-ships, and to him, as to his men, a screw propeller was but a frivolous impropriety. The *Monarch,* not trusting fully to her engines and her propeller, was taking advantage of a helpful wind with the rig of a barquentine. It was easy for her sailors to believe that the wind was doing most for them, just as they knew how to make the most of the wind. Nor did machines pertain to gentlemen, a fact apparent in the contrast between Captain Crispin and an engineer, as they stood together at the rail, looking ahead.

The captain pointed dramatically, though there was no need to point at all. An American clipper ship was ahead, bound east, under all canvas, even to sky-sails and studding sails, and she was, as the captain declared, a beauty. She delighted him, as a grand manifestation of the truth of his profession.

Mr. Rumbold frowned. Had this man brought him up there to show him that thing? It was an insult. But he said nothing.

"There she is, that's the *Highflyer,*" said the captain, and he spoke as if indicating a reigning lady. "She's the last word, and isn't she a dandy! Mister, have you ever seen anything better?"

The engineer wiped his eyes again, but remained silent. He wanted to laugh at the way he had been sold, but these men about wouldn't see the joke.

"She's sticking to those flying kites to keep us away," said the captain, "and we haven't gained a foot in hours. Now she's making off. She's going to beat us, propeller and all. I sent for you because I thought you'd like to see."

"Sir, like to see what?"

"What the smart Americans are doing to keep their passenger trade. She can carry a load this steam-ship can't, and she's faster. And there's lines for you. Look at her. Doesn't she fill the eye?"

"Fill my eye? She could be twice that size, though that's impossible with a wooden ship, and all the kites she could fly wouldn't save her from being what she is."

Captain Crispin turned on his engineer with a stern question in his expression.

"Old Noah," said the engineer, "and his ark. That's what she is. We'll run her off the seas."

There was a cry from a sailor, and the two men, confronting each other in a contest of ideals, turned at the shout to see the *Highflyer* again. A change was there. Her additional sails had dared too much, and the wind had seized them. She was in a difficulty. She was a confusion of wild canvas, broken spars, and cordage.

The engineer, after a brief enjoyment of the spectacle, pointed in the direction of the entertainment, to draw the captain's attention to a matter he ought not to miss. He then asked, "Is that all you wanted me to see, sir?"

Captain Crispin continued to view the ship ahead, and was steadfastly deaf to the question. After a respectful pause, Mr. Rumbold withdrew to his own place.

His place below was dim. The skylight did not help very much. Daylight down there was little more than a few iron lamps burning colza oil. The heat of the room was heavy with a saturation of volatile grease. But Dave was acclimatised. He was able to breathe down there now without the fear that his breathing would stop. He was concentrated on his work. He did not see the Chief descending. While conscious of the correct music of the engines, and with a fair apprehension of cause and effect, confident he could stop the rotations if necessary, he could also sink into a reverie. He was in one now. The regularity of the bright movements induced it.

He would soon be home again. His faith in that screw propeller, under Mr. Rumbold's tuition, was as strong as his hold on life. He accepted the screw as a drive as naturally as Aunt Ruth did the Bible. It worked, and he knew it. Whatever doubters might say, and they were many, it was right. Yet that very fact reminded him of the sharp difference he found in Mr. Rumbold. The Chief accorded in no particular with his fair and easy memory of old shipmates. Perhaps it was because the engineer was so alarmingly clever. It had never occurred to Dave that Bonser and Captain Killick were clever. They were the right men to have about, that was all. How puzzled Bonser would have been by all this! What could he have made of it? He wouldn't have got on with Mr. Rumbold; not in the least. It was no good the engineer talking the way he did about sailors; that would never do. He was ignorant about that, though you'd suppose he knew everything. He had never watched Bonser do all but make a ship talk. And more than that, Dave felt there was a gap in life, when he remembered Bonser, which could never be filled, never be made good.

Dave had seen his present captain but once, and then

distantly. This ship was like a town. You didn't know who lived at the other end of it, and didn't care. And Captain Crispin wasn't the same as Killick. Dave would never believe the seas anywhere had another man as sound as his old master. Nothing ever put Killick out. His face wouldn't change if the ship was foundering. He'd step out as if he was expecting it, and then would hold her up when everybody thought her last chance had gone. Even the morning after Bonser was lost, after that night when they thought she was finished, the captain only appeared to be sick of them all, and said nothing, except tell the cook to make some strong coffee, and nothing to eat, and call him in two hours, unless he was wanted sooner. And he never mentioned Bonser again, though Dave knew that Captain Killick was soft-hearted, when it suited him, and did no harm.

The shadow of Mr. Rumbold was beside him, and Dave came out of his dreaming to counter a sharper lurch of the ship. She was increasing her rolling, with these following seas. He looked up. The engineer was not critical of him, as usual, but was swaying about, and staring at the footplates as if they were new to him. Had he been drinking with the captain? For he staggered over to the tool-chest lashed to a bulkhead, sat down, and with his fingers in his hair and his face in his hands seemed shaken by deep sobs. Either that or he was laughing to himself. His beard, all Dave could see of his face, was responsive to his emotion. Perhaps the captain was pleased with her performance, and they had been celebrating with champagne. Dave was regarding his Chief with puzzled concern when Mr. Rumbold sat up, put his hands on his knees, and his smile had its usual touch of mockery.

"What's wrong, Gay? Do I look funny? If I do, why don't you laugh?—don't fob me off with that loving expression."

Dave smiled back, but not with assurance, still baffled as to the meaning of this. He was often baffled by Mr. Rumbold, especially when the engineer was serious, and went to the heart of a matter, for then Dave saw with the disappointment that comes of unwrapping a prize packet to find nothing in it, that this matter, so important in appearance, had no heart. All it had was a fated compulsion, which was invisible. It was beginning to dawn on Dave that the companionship of machines might alter a man. It was possible that no heart was necessary for an engineer, but only a brain, though that had to be a quick one. You had only to look at Mr. Rumbold's eyes. They could light up with fun when people were making fools of themselves. But they were cold and sword-coloured. You did not dare mention anything to him unless you knew what you were talking about, or else you would think you had only just begun to read, and your books were ridiculous.

Mr. Rumbold rose from the tool-box with a sigh. He walked slowly round peering into the job till he reached Dave again. He took hold of his junior's arm, though whether through affection or to steady himself was more than Dave knew.

"Not so bad. They are doing as well as a cheerful chap would look for on a first voyage. Give them your best, and they'll show pride. I made them, and they know their father." He stood reflecting, wiping his hands with a dirty rag.

He gave Dave a nudge. "Gay," he said, "do you know your luck? I've a fancy your head shows some signs of intelligence, and you are in at the beginning. This is more than a maiden voyage. It's the release of an idea. I've been thinking. All we want is a boiler to stand fifty pounds' pressure, and we'd make a ship fly. Wars and bloody revolutions would be abolished. That sort of boiler would bring about a peaceful revolution from here to China. It would hoist up the Antipodes from down under. It would put Tasmania next door. All of us neighbours. Don't you see? Try to see it. Faith is what you want, faith in the power of the brain, faith in me. . . ."

He chuckled. "Up top side they think I've a tile loose, more than one tile, rafters exposed; and what's worse, I'm no gentleman. I see through 'em . . . Pompous old ass, our captain. Crew of correct marines up there. Gaping at Noah and his outfit. Brought me up to see the Ark in the middle of the flood. Nothing better afloat. Some American timber-built craft with too much canvas. Famous ship. But what was under the feet of her admiring mob, what we are watching this minute, is going to clear all American canvas off the Atlantic. Every sail. No good telling Crispin, though. No good telling him his ship is writing a chapter of history. He'd make a mess of it. Would he let a dirty engineer upset everything he thinks comes of the grace of God? Pious old fool. We'll show 'em, Gay, and no talking, and take it they must. All that counts is the result, and that will be ours."

Dave had heard Killick remind Bonser of what was coming along for ships, and it resembled the comments of the Chief, but was not so hard and cruel. Bonser was glum while he listened, and then said he hoped he'd be dead and done with before those happy days.

Yet that time had come. They were in it. It was today. That surprising order to stop her was for the pilot. Great news! Lundy Island was abeam. So the voyage was nearly over, and they were only half a day behind Mr. Rumbold's largest hope. It was a record; yet the Chief had told him she would do better than this, when her works had overcome their infant shyness, and a little difference had been made to the pitch of the propeller.

Nearly home. The weather was clear and calm, she was going in on the flood, and the machinery was turning over as if it knew what he knew and was determined not to disappoint them. The thrusting rods and throws were moving like light, without effort. The engines were chanting triumph. You'd think they knew what they were about. You'd think they knew what the Chief wanted and were proud to get it; urgent, no pause, no doubt, on and on, everlasting. The ship was trembling in her energy, all expectant. She was driving to beat the band. He heard a stoker bawling a rollicking song in the boiler room, when its iron door banged open for a moment. The excitement had touched him off. It would make anyone shout Alleluia.

But there was something else. It was still and quiet and unseen, and he would never forget it. He used to think nothing was better right round the earth than his perch in the foretop of the *Star of Hope* when she had a trade wind; and perhaps there wasn't. The sky was full of buoyant islands, all rounded, bright as the sun. They were floating the same way as the ship, and he sat on the curve of a cloud below, adrift on the waters. The wide world was as happy as a child; it skipped along. All went with the ship, warm wind, splendid sky, and the march of the dark seas, and he was rocked on the summit of his own cloud, the fore-sail's bulge, sure it was all very good. Her sharp stem sliced into the clear blue. She lifted, and she plunged, and away went a spread of boiling foam. The foam rolled like snow hissing over blue glass. The rigging was a choir trying over a good one.

This engine-room was another story. Wasn't it as good? The Chief didn't say it was better, because he knew of nothing else. It would be wasting time for the Chief to go aloft to sit in the rigging on a fine day, trying to enjoy it. You couldn't even tell him about that, unless you wanted to hear the things he could say. Still, it was true; the engines had a lot to say for themselves. They didn't have to wait on the wind. Tell them to go, and they were off, whatever the weather. They would drive this ship through head-seas that would part the timbers of the old *Star*, and sink her. They could throw off the seas, and face the wind, and they were made by Mr. Rumbold; and didn't he let you know it! He was proud of them.

The Chief had a right. He could stand up before any of them, and claim that his engines were as lovely as the tallest spread of canvas. So they were. They did what he meant them to do, and did it easily. They were a grand show. They were waltzing home. They never tired. They were as fresh and fast at midnight as at sunrise. They sang as they danced along, to a tune of thunder and lightning. Their furious dance was terrific. You'd think nothing could stop it, that no human hand had power over it, that it would have to go on madly till the ship piled up on the rocks.

But they obeyed. That little wheel there, give it a turn, and the engines knew at once what you meant. You'd see the power of the great arms suddenly fail. You would check the flashes of lightning. The thundering would cease. Silence would fall in a moment, and the ship stop. Tell these engines what you want, and what you ask for they'll give. You can't say that of the winds. This ship was driven by men's thoughts, and their movement was magnificent. No wonder the Chief was proud.

Eight bells. Exmoor was abeam. Home was in plain sight. Here we come, Bristol, and won't you be surprised when you see our smoke.

32

The Sailor's Return

"I SUPPOSE," said Aunt Ruth at breakfast, "you are going to Blackwall today, as usual."

She stressed this visit as a common occurrence, because she did not know a sufficient reason for it. She tried to see, without moving, what Dave was drawing on a paper beside his plate, but couldn't make sense of it.

"Yes, as usual," said Dave, absently, without looking up.

"Well, then, hadn't you better eat something first? It was cooked for that."

He folded the paper and put it in his pocket, and with relief. He examined briskly what was before him, and turned to her with merry approval, as if life was jolly, and she was the best part of it.

She was not deceived by that. She knew it is the way of a man to suppose a woman can be put off with drollery, when she is curious, as if idiots had no right to be trusted. But she saw also he was childishly unaware that she was not amused. Of course, like his father, like all of them, he thought a woman's best place was outside his thoughts, unless she interrupted with a swoon. How kind they were then! But they would be just as kind to dumb animals.

She had got hardly anything worth hearing out of him since his return. After all that time at sea, and the countries he had visited, and the things he had seen, growing up while he was away, he came home as if he had nothing much to talk about. Once or twice he did mention Captain

Killick, and with a mild respect she was satisfied to hear, as something on account; but not once had he spoken of that night the captain had told them about, when the ship was nearly lost, and the poor mate was. It might have been nothing to him but an excitement which was all over. Still, very likely young men had no proper feelings, and that certainly saved them from the worst of the plentiful buffets they got, while tender. She didn't know. It was very noticeable, though, that the morning they confronted each other, at long last, his greeting was as awkward as if it was a part he had to act, but didn't know how to do it. That, in fact, was about all she recognised in him, his boyish way of holding back. He still kept things to himself.

For all that, as he stood side-face in the window light, ready to depart, still moody, it gratified her to note that Killick had told her some of the truth about him. The long while he was missing her anxiety had been for a simple lad. The last she remembered of him was the most she could make of him. It wasn't this tall fellow she had been praying for, unless perhaps her prayers had turned him into the figure she was admiring. He had the bearing already of one who would have his own way, if she knew the signs, and she thought she knew them. He must have been through much, though he had not spoken of it, to have been hardened and disciplined into that shape. That hand of his, and its long fingers, prudently closing his bag, looked unusually strong, and lady-like too, except for size and colour. Well, he'd never know, all the same, how day and night the face of an innocent child had been ever before her, and she couldn't help feeling now, since she saw it no more, as if something important had gone for ever. This man could do without her. Well, why not? It must come to that.

He was off. He opened the door while she stood

watching. He glanced back in abstraction, and gave her a perfunctory farewell nod, as if the sight of her still there was unexpected. She couldn't say why he did what came next. Who can say why men behave as they do? He stopped, smiled strangely, put his bag down, balanced his hat on it with exaggerated care, a little nonsensical by-play. Then he came to her as if he had just seen who she was. There was no doubt in the squeeze he gave. It was the first, and if he didn't mean it then life has no meaning. His silence was more convincing than anything he could have said. She was glad he said nothing, except when he was at the door again.

"There's work here," he said, patting his bag. "I'll tell you the terrible news about it when I'm home tonight. I've only this very morning tumbled on what I ought to do with it. Aunt, you'll get such a shock. Do you know, it's for a ship's engine, a beastly thing like that."

"Is it? Well, if it does no more harm than take you to Blackwall and home again, it's all to the good. Don't be late."

33

Blackwall Yard

O N a Blackwall omnibus rattling over the stones of
Limehouse towards the gates of the East India Dock,
Dave was delighted with new country; it was new to him.
He could see this place was settled ages ago along high-tide
mark. Ships had made it. Ships kept it going. Though no
water could be seen, it smelt of stale brine and tar. He
guessed it knew more of Bombay than of Windsor. He had
been that way often enough of late, and usually on a rainy
day, but he was elated this morning, so it appeared fresh
and unexplored. Before this morning it was only the road
to the shipyard, where his task was a stubborn puzzle that
would not come straight. Now he was free. He had finished
it. He could look round. It fitted him nicely, this corner
of London. It might have been aware of his happy release.
Today it was in the sun.

He had feared that last touch to the design, to round it
off, would never come. Only a trifle was wanted to complete
it, but come it would not. He was kept shut within himself
ever since he landed, searching for what could not be found
in an empty head. He would have given it up, except that
to admit failure is harder than to admit the impossible. You
couldn't look yourself in the face again.

Queer, he thought, the comfort there is watching an
idea, with the last part of it missing and hopeless, jump full
circle in a moment. It is ready to work. The wheels will go
round where nothing moved before. He didn't suppose the
sculptor of the old story felt more surprise when the image

of a girl he had hacked out of rock grew warm and rosy, moved and stepped down, and kissed him. Did the poet mean the same thing when he spoke of lucky words? The right answer comes, if it does come, out of nothing, and from nowhere; but before you get it you may beat your head as much as you like against one hard fact after another. You can't relate them. The facts remain separate. They do not belong. They won't help at all. While not seeking it, there the happy thought suddenly is, and all the facts are alive and flow together. A new shape has come. It is yours; and the dear old earth, which had been indifferent the whole time, is bright in the sun. It winks back at you. You've won a place in it and are welcome. Won it for the time being, mind. A problem solved only leads to another and a harder one. But it does lead. What more do you want?

It was not altogether surprising that the right notion had met him here; for what a place of ships it was! Ideas must be lurking at every corner, waiting to catch a man who can use them. Topmasts rose above all the walls and roofs. There were warehouses, rope-makers' walks, mast and block makers, sail-lofts, wagons heavy with merchandise going and coming, nautical-instrument makers, and ship-store dealers. The women strode about as if sure of their place, and every man he could see was a shipwright, a rigger, a docker, or a sailor, when he wasn't an owner. The passenger beside him had just given him a nudge and pointed to a man on the side-walk, as to a prince. Dave turned to look at Richard Green and his dog; that was the great name at the shipyard. Green, Duncan Dunbar, Money Wigram, John Allan. Down here they were more important than the names of Chevy Chase, and you were supposed to know it. In Poplar, unless you could talk of ships as you would of books or of whatever pleased you, then you were ignorant.

You weren't worth talking to. You ought to know the names and records of the paragons as well as you know your own and what you are good for. It was the same thing, here. Either you belong to the family, or you do not. But you had to be wary. If you had rounded Cape Horn, that was nothing to shout about. As well as he could make out, in any little house down here more might be known of Table Bay, Java Head, Jamaica, Tuticorin, Calcutta, and Rangoon, all such places, than of kings and archbishops. You could learn in these by-ways news of the leading marks in every sea, even of Hudson's Bay, and of being frozen-in there for the winter. A man in the yard told him a story of that only yesterday. The churches and schools grew up out of prosperous voyages. The Royal Navy and the East India Company were built into the foundation-stones of Blackwall. Dave on his omnibus was only a young late-comer, and his faith in steam was not much better than bold heresy, in Poplar; because long before his day Frobisher, Raleigh, Humphrey Gilbert, and Henry Hudson had been on the foreshore there, attending to their business, as now he went to his.

His place in the shipyard was called a drawing-office; but except for the long desk where the plans were neatly spread with the drawing instruments upon them, it was a dingy room, untidy with discarded models and patterns. It did not suggest creation, but a shocking muddle. But as Mr. Denny had one day pointed out, muddle is the place where creation begins. "Remember," he said, "that it's not on the river, but here and in our machine shop that the new merchant service is coming to life." Mr. Denny had deep respect for Rumbold, as though the Chief were a great man that could bring good things about where nobody else looked for good, and would not see it if they looked.

Dave was considering a little matter relating to this,

gazing out of the window that lighted the plan before him.
He was vaguely aware of a ship on the stocks in the yard,
and of the rhythm of mallets, muffled to him, and of the
distant figures of men moving in an active world apart
from the quiet of his office; though it gratified him to
remember that even the foremen out there would listen to
what he had to say with close if sceptical attention. He had
not been a long voyage for nothing. He had not been a
friend of Chips, the old carpenter, without hearing of a
thing or two. He would never be able to wield an adze,
but he knew what planking ought to be after an adze had
been properly over it.

The beat of mallets struck immediately louder. The door
was open, and he turned. Mr. Denny was there, very polite
to an old swell and an elegant miss, as they entered.

Dave bent closer to his subect. This was not for him. He
ignored the party with evident forgetfulness; the back he
turned to them was hardly less obvious than rude
indifference. Visitors were often in the shipyard, but were
seldom admitted to the secrecy of this room, where new
things began, unless they came from the Admiralty. It was
better to stick to the job and appear as far as possible
unconcerned, though it was awkward to go on as though
you were unaware you were not alone.

The visitors gossiped idly. They turned over a few
diagrams and sail plans. The party came slowly along and
stopped behind Dave, who heard then of the merits of
several owners and their ventures. These merits, to the mind
of a young sailor, were not without gaiety. The lady was
silent. Dave couldn't hear her move. She was no more than
a very faint reminder of gilliflowers, and quite attractive,
as far as that went, Dave thought. He wished she would
speak. He wanted to confirm the impression of his first
glance, which was hurried, that the voice of such a lady

would be better than most pleasant things. He was disappointed. It was to be expected, of course, that elegance would have no concern with the dust and lumber of his room. Even the conversation of the gentleman presently fell lame.

"What is this young man doing?" asked the gentleman, and appeared abruptly beside Dave.

The young man did not tell him. He left the answer to Mr. Denny, but he gave way a little that the visitor might freely view the drawing. He saw the face of a patrician, from over an old-fashioned white stock, scrutinising his work severely, but not with evident perception. Dave judged at once that if this visitor was an owner, then it would be of a whole fleet, and therefore stood respectfully motionless.

"I fear you won't care much for that, Mr. Darton," said Mr. Denny, and laughed. "It only outlines improvements for a marine boiler."

Darton? That important name, and familiar too, once on a time? Dave hoped that his neck did not look as hot as it felt, but he was careful that no other sign of the increase of his interest gave him away.

The famous owner made a noise through his nose, as if bothered by dust, and turned away. The young man had ceased to exist.

The party drifted further along the room, towards its exit, but paused by the model, placed there but this morning, of the shipyard's latest frigate-built craft.

"You asked about her. There she is. That's the *Eurydice*, sir," said Mr. Denny.

The attention and expert knowledge of Mr. Darton were now sharply attracted. "Yes, I wanted to see her before she was launched, but could not come."

He reviewed her characteristics, and argued them, with

eager discretion, but sighed. "She is what I respect, she's of the best, but too elaborate and expensive for any trade of mine."

"So I think she is for her own," said Mr. Denny. "And too slow, and too small. It's my opinion she is the last of her class we shall build."

The two gentlemen, for some minutes, were then involved in the mental stress that comes of attempts to reconcile the archaic and traditional with the unforeseen; that gave Dave an opportunity to venture another glance at these distinguished guests. He found the lady was not attentive to maritime progress. Her regard was for him. She held his own eyes easily and directly for but a second, though to Dave the encounter seemed long, revealing, and momentous; she lowered her eyes before he remembered that perhaps his curiosity was too firm.

There could be no doubt of it. She was Lucy Darton, and a finer figure than her father now, and as proud, he supposed; though there was nothing of her father's haughtiness in the look that met his own. How strange it was! The importance of the master of Branton and his heiress no longer mattered to him. He didn't care. Times had changed. But what a very pretty woman she was! He had not seen a girl like that for years, if ever he had seen one before.

Dave was bent upon his drawing, to all appearance, though it had become vague to him, as the latch clicked at the farther door. The party was over?

Yes, they had all gone. He was alone again. He fiddled with a rule. This would amuse Aunt Ruth tonight, when he told her all about it. All about it? Well, it would be giving nothing away to say that he believed Miss Darton recognised him, though nothing was said. He might go as far as to say that she had grown up. He had not resumed his task, but was still idling with the rule, when the catch of that door moved once more.

Miss Darton entered. She flowed along the room swiftly to him, without restraint or embarrassment, and marked him as steadily as once she did on Branton sands.

"You are David Gay, aren't you? But I'm sure you are."

"Yes."

She still regarded him meditatively, as if seeking confirmation of her judgement before accepting his answer. Her discernment was gratifying, and he smiled; but would she have presumed, had she not known he was only one of the workmen? He could put that by. She was a lady of spirit to have left her escort to do this. That helped to a kind of equality. Yet, had she really recognised him, or had Mr. Denny whispered his name?

Miss Darton did not return his smile. "Tell me, why did you run away? Were you afraid?"

"Afraid? No, I don't think so. Yes, I was afraid. I didn't want to cause trouble for my aunt. You remember her?"

"I do. Very well. She was brave. Nothing ever frightened her. Where is she now?"

Dave told her. Miss Darton did not appear to be listening closely to his news of the house in the Minories. She was watching, in patient abstraction, the scene beyond the window, it might be for a reason to depart, or for no reason. He found, while trying to win her attention, that he could speak only in ordinary words, though he wished to be genuine, as well as to say witty things, for he saw morning on the profile that was near to him. He felt also a sense of infinite sadness.

"You need not have run away," she said, still watching the world beyond them. "I told Papa long ago, when they blamed you, that it was not your fault you were with me.

That is all I came back to tell you. I thought you ought to know."

She turned to the drawing on his desk. "Are you a sea engineer now?"

"No. I'm only on my way to it."

"Really." She gave the drawing a closer inspection. "It is so deep and clever. I don't know what it means, and Papa never will."

She surprised him in the quick offer of her hand, and he hesitated to take it. It was fear that prompted him to accept it before it could be withdrawn. She turned away as Miss Darton should, without another look, and was gone. Dave stood for a while watching the shut door, as though it had a gift for opening on surprises, and there might be another if he were careful not to move.

34

David is Promoted

MILK pails clanked in the street below, and the milk-man called as musically as Hermes of a new and better day. Aunt Ruth woke, with an impression of trouble, she didn't know why. All in the room was comfortably trite, but there was a shadow she couldn't see. Very likely she had been dreaming. The sun was up. That pattern of gold on the ceiling was stretching out as she watched. The early sounds from the street below were leisurely and amiable in a world that was without regrets. But as to her, something had got between her and the sun. Ah, that was it; that was it, of course. Dave was departing. He was going again. Tomorrow!

She had hoped, as a thoughtless creature would, that his delight in his new work, which to her was odd, would at least keep him off the sea. Not a bit of it. It was because he was so good at it that he was going away; and not a promising voyage, either. The Black Sea was one she had seldom heard of. It had an unlucky name. It would be better if dried up.

He already had that new certificate, young though he was, to warrant that he could command a ship, but that was not enough for him. He didn't want to dodge about the coast in a brig, he said, and he couldn't expect to be appointed captain of one of the new big ships, for he didn't drink and swear hard enough, not yet. Give him time.

She had been glad to hear him say so. He was in love with engines, and was always at his drawings; and you'd wonder what scribbles and scrawls you couldn't name had to do with life afloat. It was a puzzle to her, but it seems it was that very thing made him the man they badly wanted this year.

Because of the war, she supposed. It was the fault of those Russians (she called them Rooshians). For her part, she couldn't see what harm the Russians had done, or wanted to do, and she hadn't spoken to a soul yet who could tell her, to make plain sense of fighting them over it. Some said they were cruel to Christians, though there was nothing new in that; and others that they meant to take Constantinople. Why we should want to save Turks from even imps out of hell she couldn't make out, for fire and brimstone was their meat; but there it was. It seemed to her that if you didn't know a reason for fighting you could mix one to your taste.

Well, that left the buttons on Dave's new uniform to be sewn on firmly. The very tailors were so dashing through the news of war, the poor fools, that they forgot to finish what they were doing. And what did tailors know of bloodshed, that they should feel like men of might? The only basting they could manage was with needle and cotton. A nice thing, to send boys to battle with their buttons coming off.

If great cannon must be fired, then she prayed God that those who knew good cause to let fly at the enemy understood powder and shot better than some cocky people did how to cross the street. The wind must be southerly. She could hear the stir at the Tower very plain. It would be much to her own good if she could rouse to the loftiness of those defiant bugles. But how is a woman to feel martial? The boys go out through the gate, and who knows how long after that you may have to stand there, gazing down the empty street? She listened to gusts of savage orders, and the tramp of armed men. The shrilling of those fifes and piccolos was so sharp it twinged her vitals.

A woman with the firmest faith in Providence might not show she was dithered, but all of a shake she would be. The only thing to do was to get busy. Dave was off tomorrow. Aunt Ruth went to her workroom at once after breakfast, to be alone. There is no chance to sort out thoughts in a sad state until nobody is looking on. Fasten the door against everybody's good wishes, and have it out with yourself.

She was gratified a little later, nevertheless, when the door slowly opened, and Dave's head came round it, to see if she were there. He came across, pushed away the work beside her, and settled down.

"I wondered what had become of you, and here you are, hiding yourself. What, and busy on my new and spanking best? What's wrong with a coat that hasn't made me feel proud yet? Aunt, you're just pretending. It only came two days ago."

"That's all. But you look at that. Two threads to hold metal to the thick cloth. How long would that last you?"

He sat silent for a time, idly surveying a room he wasn't used to, and she stitched away. "They're right lively at the Tower," he said, turning to the window. Drums were rolling.

"I hear them. They're mettlesome for it."

"It wouldn't do if they weren't."

"No."

He glanced sharply round to her, uncertain of her mood. "It'll soon be over," he said. "It will be over before I can be in it, I shouldn't wonder. I was told so yesterday by a gloomy post-captain. What a miserable sell that would be, wouldn't it?"

"The things one does hear, to be sure."

"Do you think it's more than a passing squall?"

"I wish I knew what was right and best to think."

"I say, you're not supposing it will last for years, are you? It can't do that, it can't."

"Well, whatever happens, here it is, and to be tackled."

"That's the right line to take, and follow it up. Let's see what comes."

"Of course. But a war is nearly all chance, so I've heard tell. That's what I don't like about it. Not that I know more of war than most of the clanjamphie. But what do they know? Only the tales they heard from father in the chimney corner about Old Boney, the tales I heard."

"Heavens, that's right, now you've brought Napoleon into it, that was the last champion flare-up we had. But this war can't run about everywhere like wild-fire, not as that one did."

"I should hope not. God grant it comes to nothing so bedevilling to ways and means. Even I know the amazement Boney put into the heart, and the hunger in the cupboard."

"Oh, he is a bogey we laid. He's dead and gone. Come, cheer up, Auntie. This time the French are with us, as well as the terrible Turks. Besides, haven't we got ourselves? And that's something worth a mention. Wait till our new ironclads get home a word or two. Why, if you'd been aboard my transport yesterday, you'd have danced a hornpipe at the spirit of it."

"A hornpipe," she said, "is a gallant way to come at what must be done, and I'm all for it."

Her handsome way of putting it almost dismissed contrariety. It was like her, of old, to come out with a bright remark for a wet day. She was jolly good, he knew, at taking what she did not like, without making a face at it, when that was all she could get. How he wished he was far at sea and busy, past the doldrums and the farewells! That new set of engines was one he had to nurse. He must go with it. If it failed, so did he. He might make a name for himself out there, something to bring back with him that nobody could deny, something to show them who he was. When he took stock of himself, however, in secret, he had to admit that he wasn't so much after winning a fine name, either. Not that. Above his pride in his appointment was his hope to see the fun of the fair. He had never seen great guns let go at an angry target, and not for worlds would he miss the chance.

Was he afraid, when he ran away? Miss Lucy wanted to know. A pleasant idea that, to have in her mind about him. But he'd find out what he was made of, and so should they. You don't know you are alive, you don't know what you are, unless death is a card in the pack, and you must play. That makes you sit up to the game. After all, he had stepped over the dead, when only a kid, and might have been one of them but for his luck. Anyhow, tomorrow was sailing day. His eye roved the room with more ease.

"I thought I knew it," he said. "That's the old original over there. That glass case on the wall, with the shells and seaweed. You used to tell me it was to bring good luck to the fishers. That's from the parlour at Branton."

"That's where it came from. It hung by the window. The sun caught it in the morning, and you remember it. You never heard this about it though. Your Uncle Penfold and I picked up those things on the shore the day after we were married, and there they are still, this very week. Such little things last, though of no importance, except to remind us of what did not last."

She went on with her sewing, but paused in it, after a

silence, fixed her needle in the cloth, and sat looking at it. Then she asked, "Did you see Captain Killick yesterday?"

"Yes. Wasn't he here? Why, he told us he was offered command of a transport, and wasn't sure he would take it. He said in fun he would rather tend a garden."

Aunt Ruth did not admit she recalled this fact. She was examining a button.

"I thought you heard him," Dave continued. "I wonder whether he will sail. Yes, he will, though he did say once he'd had more than his full whack of salt water. He is sure to go."

"No."

"He won't? He never said that. I never heard him say that. How do you know? Has he found anything against the ship?"

"Nothing, that I know of. He won't go, he says . . . well, you see, it's a matter of choice, and what do you think of it? Either he's away again, like you, or he marries your Aunt Ruth instead."

Dave moved as if to rise hastily, but changed his mind, and relapsed.

"That's how it is," she added. "Not another sailor for me."

"I say!" he murmured. "What news, and no warning signal!"

"Isn't it a surprise! It surprises me. You should have been first, I know, not me. Not Killick either, for that matter. But how long to wait for you, you without a sweetheart in sight, but only a war? . . . But there, I haven't said I'm going to. Killick may have to sail."

Dave sat forward, clasping his hands, and seemed to be pondering this, or the carpet. He spoke slowly as if to himself. "Here, that's not fair. The Black Sea instead?

That's a pretty thing to say. It's not a straight course. It's hauling on and off. It's not fair."

"Don't you ever seek fairness in such a business. It isn't there, and so you'll find."

"I don't know."

"No, you don't. But some day you will, and then don't be a fool, and try to be fair."

"Not fair? Aunt, that doesn't sound a bit like you."

"It's all or nothing. It's give, but don't look for much. And it doesn't call for a deal of thought, let me tell you. That's why I don't know whether Captain Killick shouldn't sail."

Dave shook his head. "It doesn't seem right to me. No. I guess I know what I'd do."

"What would you do?"

"Keep him off that voyage, if he is all against it."

"You would, would you?"

"I would so. There's plenty of men able to take out that ship, and willing, too, but not one of them like the captain."

"So that's it, is it? Then perhaps we'll do what we ought not to do, and give it more thought."

"Well, Aunt Ruth, you know what I think of him, don't you?"

"Yes, you've told me. And I should say myself he would pass muster as a shipmaster."

Dave turned to her to see whether her face said more than her words, but she was only smiling at him.

A smart clopping of high-stepping horses checked in the street below, and it sounded as if at their door. They went to the window. Dave whistled at the notability of the turn-out down there, standing outside their house.

"Who is it?" he asked.

"I know," she said, but not as if her knowledge pleased her.

A tall and gracious lady alighted, while a footman attended, and Dave whistled again, though it was subdued to a greater respect than was due merely to a pair of beautiful bays.

"Is she a duchess?" he whispered.

"Thereabouts," his aunt told him. "You've spoken of Mrs. Cree. Now you see Dinah's mother. That is Lady Geraldine. Her ladyship visits here at times. She is a friend of the poor, and we have a large stock. They're one of her hobbies, the poor, though if she heard the truth about them she'd faint, so we never let on, and she'll never know it."

"Don't you like her, then? Mrs. Cree and her husband were very good people."

"And her ladyship is as kind. I like her very well. One can't help it, she's nice as well as noble, and so simple. . . . For all that, why is she here today? This isn't the time for the sad and sorrowful cases. I know one thing, I don't want to be down there now; here I stay. This is your day."

But as Aunt Ruth judged, at the back of her mind, so it happened. A message was soon in the room; she was wanted. And if Mr. Gay were at home, would he kindly come down? A visitor wished to meet him.

Dave was somewhat alarmed. "Why me? She doesn't know me. What have I to do with it?" he begged, when the maid had gone.

His aunt laughed. "Now, Dave, what have you been doing? Out with it. You've done something unusual that you've never whispered to your aunt, though her ladyship knows it. My son, you are coming on. You'll rise among the quality, unless you are not more particular."

"Must I go down?"

His aunt inspected him. She could see he was not only shy and nervous, but might be contumacious in consequence.

"Go down?" she repeated. "You certainly must, and you will. I'll see to that. Let me look at you again. . . . Yes, you'll do. The sight of you won't disappoint her, if her ladyship is the usual sort of woman, and I'd say she is all that."

He was won over, and put at his ease, as soon as they entered the room below. Lady Geraldine just glanced over at him, and then came direct to his aunt in evident affection and greeted her warmly. Her ladyship was not exactly good-looking, but her attire was superb, and for a moment disconcerting, but he recognised through her oddity and suavity an assurance in civility's privilege, the firm but unconscious right of good manners and breeding. Yet it satisfied him that Aunt Ruth appeared unaffected by the occasion, and was as comfortable as she was with Miss Summers or anyone else. Her ladyship then turned to him, holding his hand, and with a silent interest that raised his colour, and that already was bright.

"So I meet the young sailor at last," she exclaimed, coming near to drama, and continuing to appreciate him. Dave had time to wish her regard could be turned by a more sufficient interest, but stood his ground.

"My Dinah wrote from New York and told me about you after that very, very dreadful voyage you both had. She said you went through it like a hero. But no, I dare not repeat her words, or candid Mrs. Penfold would say I flatter you. That would never do."

"I met Mrs. Cree long after that in Boston," explained Dave, hurriedly, not without the hope that this would remove attention from himself.

"Yes, you did. I heard of that too. That was after your ship was back from San Francisco, and you had left her. Mr. Cree met you there, and Dinah, my dear homesick child, was so glad to see you again, and to talk of Branton

and London. I had the loveliest of long letters from her
after your visit, and it made me very happy. When I
discovered you had returned, what could I do but come to
see you?"

"And Mrs. Cree? I trust she is well. Is she still in
Boston?"

"Yes, and I want you to tell me of that city, of Dinah in
her new home. Everything you can remember. There was
half a promise in her last letter that she may come back to
us. Mr. Cree is terribly anxious. This dreadfully disturbing
news from the Balkans and Turkey! Dinah says he foresaw
a war with Russia, and he feels they ought to be in England.
I think you may expect to see them in London presently."

"Then they will have to be quick. I sail for the Black
Sea tomorrow."

Her ladyship raised her hands. Tomorrow? She was
astonished. She could not believe it. So young, yet off to
savage war, to cruel war! Not waiting to be led, but leading.
At the head of the line! She turned to Mrs. Penfold. "How
proud you must be!"

There is nothing to make a young man more sheepish
than to speak of him before others as a lion, and Dave was
shaky for flight, but there was no way out. He dared not
so much as look round at Aunt Ruth. He guessed what her
face would show. He must stand firm, and wait with true
courage for the next thing.

"Tomorrow. That means you must come back with me;
you really must. Now, no denial. I will not hear it. We
have a little farewell gathering today for an officer of the
Guards, and you must join it. No, no refusal, sir. Not to me.
I cannot let you go without hearing what I am so anxious
to learn. My house would never forgive me if I returned
to it without you."

When Dave would have sought the firm support of his

relative, his last hope, a word from a woman who knew what nonsense it was to neglect preparation for a ship's immediate departure—or, at the worst, her approval of a foolish excursion sure to disappoint her—she was not there.

35

Ancestral Voices

THAT drive to Berkeley Square in state, while a
celebrated lady earnestly conversed in the intervals
of street uproar, and he tried to say the right thing in the
best way amid the moving sections of London's panorama,
left him too dazed to care much what happened when
they arrived; or afterwards to recall, when questioned, the
order of events.

He recovered some poise when taken aside by his lordship, a signal favour, for strangely his host proved to be as
isolated in mind from a modish affair as he was himself.
He was led into a study, or perhaps it was a library, a little
cupboard was opened, and bottles were indicated with
friendly intent; he could have fancied he was being
indulged as a rare guest, though that was a ridiculous
notion.

"Not for common use, this. Only my own, when alone.
No? What? But aren't you a sailor? Sailors never say no.
Just a wee one, so high"—measuring a glass—"for you'll
need it when you join the company. I always do, and not
only before, but afterwards. Come along. You won't care a
damn when you've had it, you'll hoist your colours."

This time Dave held to plain intelligence. He would not
allow wine to add to his disturbance. His serious but nervous
resolution amused his lordship, who said he had never
before met a man of the sea who refused to maintain a
tradition so old and tried. No admiral would do it. His
lordship appeared insensible to the entertainment in his

house, and not because he preferred his bookshelves, but rather because he affected the plebeian tastes of a simpleton; but he put Dave on the alert with his shrewd quest of information of Dinah, America, and Cree. He knew what to ask for. He knew more of ships than was necessary. Before Dave left that room he suspected that his host was not a peer for nothing, but could be very contriving under a careless and artless demeanour. He was the sort of man to hold fast, when nobody expected it, if things came adrift.

"Then we'd better go. Let us add to the hubbub," said his lordship. "There will be trouble if I keep you. Come along and hear the stories you won't find in the newspapers. I expect you are sure you know why you are going to the Black Sea. I'm afraid you'll find you don't. You'll hear so many extras of the things you think you know that you'll go away believing that nobody is ever right. Now's your chance to get at the truth of it. Only don't let it upset you, young man. The truth will change tomorrow. This way, Mr. Gay. We'll go through this door and enter unseen."

They did not enter unseen. Lady Geraldine was aware of that door, might even have been watching it; and Dave, for a few minutes, was taken in charge, and was brought confidentially to the notice of some selected people because of virtues, in himself and in them, which he knew must be accepted as well over towards kindly poppycock. Her comely bearing was a lesson to him. She would always have her own way, everywhere, yet you would be sure to think you were gaining an advantage. She whispered to him that, when he wanted to go, if he could not see her, he must warn a servant to send for her carriage. She had given instructions, because his time was very precious, and the Tower was so distant. She was a great lady. Instead of stooping to one below her rank, she wanted him to believe that it was he who was important.

He was then abandoned; or else it came about that he was left free to converse at his choice. There was a room full of choice, by the sound of it; for under a lofty ceiling —Dave was affected by the height of that ceiling after the low beams to which he was used; it diminished him to an insignificant item in an illustrious and animated assembly— yet though there seemed plenty of choice, for groups were in earnest converse all around him, he was unremarked and excluded. Everybody was engaged and intent, was in the height of challenge or examination. He believed he was the only listener to the continuous sough of many voices.

There could be no doubt, too, that the soughing was of war. Sometimes a laugh broke above the level of the rushing sound. He felt lost in the foreboding of a fantasy, for this stately apartment and its gathering of distinguished strangers hardly belonged to the world of fact. What a magnificent chandelier! He speculated on what would happen if that cloud of crystals exploded in a shower over their heads. That would break the tension. There, centrally, that tall and handsome fellow in scarlet was the honoured Guards captain, Sir Digby Lovecott, rising above the company like a beacon that had drawn the ladies to it.

There were many uniforms. He saw with admiring envy that soldiers could be gorgeous and ornamental in variety. Everybody admired them. His own uniform would be dowdy and of no account among these cuts and colours. Nobody here would know what it stood for. This was the glad day for soldiers, and he could see he had better be off at once. From what he did overhear, from what he did catch out of the rumours pouring about, fragments of recognisable speech cast up in the flow of sound, all these many voices came of but one emotion pent. The drift and current of it had but one abundant and unfailing source, and that happened to be his own present occupation too, as well as his destination. It was Russia. It was war.

Yet till now he had not given it much thought. He knew very little about it. He had read nothing but scraps. There had been no time. Simply, in an overwhelming burst, there for him it was. The immense moment had come up behind him while he was busy, and struck, and he was carried off in the rush; and the very next day he must depart, helping to drive a troopship out to Russia. That officer of the Guards would be a passenger, and all in the room knew it; and Dave was afforded a trifle of satisfaction with the knowledge that, though he alone there was aware of it, the speed with which that ship reached Russia depended largely on what he could do.

Indignation in a near voice caught his ear, and he forgot for a moment to make for the door. "Need we discuss it any more? We are wasting a pleasant day. Reasonable apologies for the Cabinet won't help us, though I don't trust Lord Aberdeen. There is only one thing to do. Our argument now is broadsides, and make them hot and often."

"Yes, to be sure," assented a gentle person. "After all, though, I think I remember the pother began over whether the Greek Church or the Roman Catholic Church should hold the keys of the holy places in Jerusalem. I am wondering how broadsides can decide that."

A girl laughed.

"You ought not to laugh, Matilda," said an older woman. "The French Emperor is right. He must not allow the Tzar to rescue from the Turks—yes, yes, I know the Turks are dreadful savages, though our allies—but it would be wrong to allow the Tzar to save his sort of Christians, while ours were left outside the sacred places without right or privilege.

I don't care at all whether they are Protestant or Catholic, or even your own precious Nonconformists, they have as much right in Jerusalem as Russian Christians. More."

"The Christian part of it, though useful, is all my eye," commented a man, reminiscently. "Let us make the best use of that, and let it go. What surprises me is that this brand-new Napoleon should be so willing to side with us. The truth is, I suppose, he thinks he ought to sound the drums for a grand circus. The French are a skittish people, and it is about time their fickle attention was fixed by staging a show. Napoleon doesn't want the Second Empire to go the way of the Orleans monarchy, you may be sure."

"Even if you are right about the French—and I think you are"—was an answer from the unseen, "it's all a great pity. I always understood the Tzar desired our goodwill for a final settlement with Turkey. That could have been done without the assistance or the interference of our old enemies the French. Haven't we had enough of the Turks in Europe? We know they have gone on like bandits in Greece and all over the Balkan countries, and we shouldn't wonder that the Russians don't enjoy it. Why didn't we come to terms with the Tzar?"

"Ah! At last we arrive," said the first voice. "Why not agree with him! Why not come to terms with our own undoing! Now let us imagine the Russians in Constantinople, and their fleet in the Mediterranean, to say nothing of their land approach to India. Look at it, my dear sir, look at it! It has a meaning, hasn't it? We could agree with the Tzar, with pleasure. But where is he going to stop, with our neck in a noose? You can't trust political settlements, when you never can tell what the other fellow is aiming at as he signs the treaty, and shakes hands."

Dave withdrew his attention. He must be off. He was wasting time. If this talk was not utter nonsense, it had the sound of it, like a chorus of tinware. That was the warning his lordship had given him. That wise word came back to him. Nothing was to be gained here, nothing to report at home for common sense to pick up thankfully, to add to wisdom. He measured the distance to the far door, and began abstractedly a meandering passage through the guests. He was still some distance from it when Mr. Darton and his daughter appeared there, and the room was changed.

Dave stood. The sense of time failed him. Time stopped when he did. The news of war, the distracting and flashy events of the day, the hazards of a voyage to come, all went. His mind in an instant was still, vacant, expectant, and receptive. Lucy had seen him instantly in so lively a throng, as if he were there alone.

Or was it chance? Yes, it was that. Chance. For it made her flush; he was mistaken; it was but a sad accident. She went straight, with her father, not another glance, to the resplendent Sir Digby Lovecott, who already had as much attention as was good for a man. The worst of it was that Dave could see, for he did not move, what a proper complement they were, the proud and smiling soldier bending to her, and she as vivacious and self-possessed as a woman at home to high and low, and admired by all.

He turned away. There was no hurry now, but he gave his back to a scene that had little to do with him, and continued for the door; back to the life that was his, which was outside.

A voice at his elbow overtook him before he had gone, and brought him round.

"Why!" exclaimed Miss Darton in rebuke, a little breathless, and still flushed. "Not a farewell? But Lady Geraldine told me you sail tomorrow in the *Serapis*. You've made me run after you. How dare you!"

He could find no ready answer. He could not be sure

whether he was smiling foolishly or frowning in resignation; his expression felt, and rigidly, like a little of each.

"Why," she went on, "we shan't see you again, till it is all over, and yet you turned away without waiting. You've changed my mind. I'm not sure now that I shall be at Gravesend to see the ship depart, though I've told Digby I would be there. You may go now."

He fancied a slight supplementary pressure of her hand, as if to tell him that her promise to Sir Digby might be kept, should she reconsider it.

36

Departure for the Crimea

THE tide was turning. The wall-sided *Serapis* was in
mid-stream, the White Ensign lazily coiling aft,
the Union flag at the jack-staff, a slow drift of smother
from her funnel. Her upper deck, with troops, was like an
elevated and isolated garden of geraniums. It was a glorious
afternoon at Gravesend—the clouds, sky, sunlight, and
fields, the illusion of peace without end, the immemorial
serenity of England. A tug stood by, its hawser slack to the
bows of the troopship. A bo'sun's pipe screamed aboard the
ship, and the sound of her incoming cable checked the babble
of the crowds ashore. They were silent now, watching.
Even the barking of a dog could be heard.

Aunt Ruth was on the pier, Captain Killick with her.
She had noticed Miles Darton was there, with a party of
gentlefolk; that young lady with him she was sure was
Lucy; but she forgot them both.

She watched that ship steadfastly. There was nothing
else to see. What was it waiting for? How long to wait?
All eyes were on the ship. Now and then a meaningless call
came across the water. The tide was rocking the
boats by the pier. A flight of pigeons clapped wings
overhead.

Something was about to happen. An order was cried
aboard. Then Killick took her arm. Her other arm, too, was
taken. She was so preoccupied at first that she must look
again to be sure that it was Miss Darton beside her.

How kind of the girl, thought Aunt Ruth, but did not

speak. She had to dab her eyes, to clear them. The ship was blurred.

"We cannot see David there, Mrs. Penfold," said Lucy.

A turmoil of water broke white at the ship's stern as she spoke.

"But he is there, look at that, he is there," said Captain Killick.

The turmoil ceased, as though quelled by their too curious regard. It broke out again with fiercer energy, and continued.

"She's off," said the captain. "Way—o," he cried. "There she goes!" He raised his hat.

Lucy was waving her handkerchief, her eyes moist with excitement. The shores were roaring at the ship, and the troops were cheering the shores. A band struck up aboard. The *Serapis* receded downstream to the tune of "The Girl I left behind Me."